SCREAMING IN THE SHADOWS

GRAHAM SIM

STRANGE ANGEL PUBLICATIONS

DEDICATION

To my parents, for everything.

CHAPTER ONE

Detective Constable Rook sat in the guts of Scotland Yard, waiting to be fired. He had been in this room often, but he'd always been on the other side of the table. The side where the interviewer sat, not the poor sod being interrogated. He knew every crack on the room's ceiling, every stain on its walls, and every odour that poured out of its dull red carpet.

The taste of last night's whisky coated Rook's teeth like rancid sugar. Anger bubbled inside him, forcing its way up his throat in acidic waves. He squirmed as he tried to fit his long thin frame into the chair in a way that didn't bring a painful twist to his spine.

The day he was suspended rose in his mind. Once the story had broken, his suspension had been inevitable, yet that hadn't stopped it from hurting like a snapped rib when it happened. He remembered Detective Sergeant

Paulson's proud belly trembling with laughter when he'd said, 'Rook, threatening members of the public isn't good policing – even when they deserve it. But failing to notice you were being filmed and ending up a minor tabloid sensation is taking the piss.'

That was two weeks ago. Now here he was, at 8 a.m., in a room where the only noise was the distant hum of activity somewhere else in the station, dreading his second meeting with the police psychiatrist. A psychiatrist who had spent most of the first interview asking Rook weird questions.

Rook wished he could say he'd spent his suspension getting fit or learning a new skill. Instead, he'd retreated to the debris of his flat, ignoring the occasional messages from those few friends and family members he hadn't driven away.

Why the higher-ups on the force wanted him to see a psychiatrist again mystified Rook. Whatever the reason, it wasn't likely to be good. They had enough to fire him without it. And he was going to be fired, if not today, then soon. But still he'd come in, dressed in a dark suit and faded winter coat, with nothing but a buzz-saw hangover to cushion the blow of being kicked off the force before his thirty-third birthday.

A few long minutes later, the bulky figure of Dr Marlowe entered. He carried his weight in his belly, his stomach entering the room a good couple of seconds before the rest of his body. He wore the same green tweed suit he'd worn the last time he interviewed Rook. It came with a waistcoat that was held together with three golden buttons, each straining against Marlowe's stomach. It was the type of suit England's upper class wore to shoot pheasants on cold winter days.

Marlowe squeezed himself into the seat across from Rook, took out a weighty report from his black leather bag, and placed it on the table with unnecessary care.

'I assume you're waiting for the results of my evaluation?' he said, his bulbous eyes shining as beads of sweat formed on his bright red brow.

'I was expecting to learn what is happening to my career,' Rook said.

'I'm not going to sugar-coat it for you, Detective Rook.' Marlowe's tongue escaped his lips. 'You have not come out of this looking good. In fact, this report does not help your future career in the police force at all.'

'Because I shouted at a guy, called him some names, told him to fuck off? How's that even worth a suspension?' Rook replied, his fingers tightening around his glass of water.

'It wouldn't be worth a suspension,' Marlowe said, 'if that was all you'd said. But you told this gentleman to "get his tattooed face and chav arse out of London or you would introduce him to some serious police brutality". So, you had a go at his appearance, his class, and threatened police brutality all in one sentence. If you'd included racism, I could have shouted BINGO.' Marlowe smirked, drinking in each flinch of discomfort he elicited from Rook.

'That he'd been repeatedly threatening and bullying a homeless guy doesn't help me?' Rook asked.

'Sadly not, Detective Rook. Sadly not. The gentleman's good lady did not deem it necessary to film that bit of your interaction. And if it's not filmed, it didn't happen.'

'That would explain firing me. Not why I'd be having another meeting with a psychiatrist.'

'Point of fact, I'm not a psychiatrist,' Marlowe said. 'And having you fired wouldn't have suited my purposes. Of course, your career is over – with limited hope of return. Officially your suspension has been made indefinite and without pay. In practice, you are simply fired.'

Rook felt his lungs collapse as Marlowe spoke. The last flicker of hope that he would keep his career snuffed out with all the charm of a back-alley mugging. He wasn't sure he even liked the job anymore, so why did he feel like the remaining piece of string holding his life together had been cut?

'If only that were enough,' Marlowe said. 'But I require your reputation to be discredited beyond rehabilitation.'

'Why can't you get rid of me?' Rook responded, the words clawing their way out of his throat.

'Because, Detective Rook, I have a specific job in mind for you. And you need to fit some specific criteria to fill that role.' He started listing his reasons on his pudgy fingers. 'One: you must be good at keeping a secret. Two: you have no one to tell the secret to. Three: no one should believe you even if you told them.' He took a breath and lowered his hand. 'From our meeting and other... investigations... I've learnt that you're secretive by nature. You're a loner who barely makes the effort to keep in touch with his family, never mind friends. And now, thanks to this' – he tapped the report on the desk – 'should you try to tell people of this secret, we'll trot this beauty out to cast doubt on all you say.'

'What does your report say?' Rook said, clenching his teeth hard enough to hurt his jaw. He searched Marlowe's face for a sign this was a joke. All he found was a look of superiority.

'Oh.' Marlowe flicked through the pages of the report without even glancing at the words. 'That you like to view yourself as the hero of your life, that you have delusions of grandeur, that your loner tendencies have left you disconnected from the modern world and, of course, there are the anger issues.'

'Is any of that true?' Rook jerked his head to better look Marlowe in the eye.

'Well, we can both agree that the anger issues are real. As for the rest of it? Some is, some isn't. Don't know, don't care.' Marlowe wet his fat lips with his tongue. 'The point is, it's all wrapped up in this very official document.' He held up the report as if he was proudly showing off his work. 'Look, it's got citations and everything. Journalists love those. Makes them feel smart to read documents with citations. Not that they ever check them.'

'What the fuck is the point of that?!' Rook said, raising his voice and leaning across the table, so close to Marlowe's face he could smell the sweat on the psychiatrist's brow.

'You need to learn to keep that anger in check, soon-to-be Ex-Detective Rook,' Marlowe said, the quiver of a smile appearing. 'Anyway, don't you want to know the secret?'

Rook sank down in his seat. 'Go ahead then, tell.'

'I can't impart that information at this precise moment. Or at this location,' Marlowe said, emphasising his point by darting his eyes around the room like he was worried about spies hiding in its corners.

'So, you've got me fired, written a report to humiliate me, and won't tell me why? Is this a joke? Because I'm in no mood for humour and we've already established I have a temper.'

'If it will keep this conversation civil, I will tell you what I can. I' – Marlowe placed his open palm on his chest – 'work with a small number of others for a rather covert section of this country's government. Our work pertains to monitoring, policing, and keeping in check a secret group within our population.'

Rook groped for a response. All he came up with was, 'What?' He wasn't proud of it.

'I'm aware you will have many questions. But, as I can't answer them in such an insecure location, I suggest you don't bother asking any. All you need to know is that we have use for someone with your investigative skills. Not that you're in any way special.' He gave a chuckle. 'But you are convenient. Very convenient. There was a murder last night that requires your immediate attention, alongside some rather troubling burglaries. Although, I must say, if it weren't for the murder forcing our hand, we may not have offered you the job at all. I was rather hoping we could handle the burglaries in-house, without the need for your skills,' he said, putting air quotes around "skills."

'I'd still be a detective?' Rook said.

'You will even get to keep your ID, although it would be better if you didn't wave it about in front of actual police officers.'

Rook sat back in his chair, ran his hands through his hair, and stared at Marlowe. Marlowe stared back at Rook, letting the silence fill the air.

'If this is some joke,' Rook said, 'some wacky gag you and Paulson have cooked up for a laugh... Know there will be nothing funny about my reaction, and I will get across that table before anyone comes through that door to help you.'

'No joke, Detective. I'm not that funny.'

'Okay, assuming you're telling the truth. What's stopping me from telling you to fuck off?'

'Nothing at all, Mr Rook, nothing at all. But you'd need to find a new career. Whereas if you accept, you still get to be a detective of sorts and you'll stay on your current salary. Do you really want to turn this offer down?' Marlowe said.

Rook looked at the cracked ceiling. 'And if I play along?'

'All you need to do is go outside, where my colleague Nicole Martingale will tell you the gory details and take you to your first crime scene. There, you will see the truth.'

CHAPTER TWO

R ook shielded his eyes from the harsh winter sun as he stepped out into the car park. It had filled up while he'd been meeting with Marlowe, and he didn't notice Nicole bounce towards him until she was almost in front of him. A short Black lady with a rounded figure, her form fit so neatly into a civil-service grey suit that it made Rook wish his suit was better pressed, his shirt better ironed, and his long coat smelled less of cigarettes.

'Detective Constable Christian Rook?' she said, looking up at his face from about a foot below him. Her hair was tied back, and she wore a smile brighter than this bleak February morning deserved.

'Well, I'm not sure about the detective part anymore. And everyone calls me Rook.'

'Oh, you're still a detective. But in a unique capacity. I'm Nicole Martingale. I believe Doctor Marlowe has told you about me?' she said as if she wasn't one-hundred-percent sure Marlowe would have remembered.

'He told me you'd tell me what the hell is going on. And he also said something about a murder I need to investigate.'

'That's right, Rook. I'll tell you all I can on the way.'

'I haven't officially accepted the job yet.'

'Then you have until we arrive to decide. Now tell me, did you drive yourself this morning?' She peered around the car park as if she could divine which car was his.

'Taxi,' Rook said. He considered telling her he'd been too hungover to drive but decided not to. It wouldn't give a great first impression.

'That's good. We would have had to take my car anyway,' Nicole said. With that, she strode away towards a black Mercedes, Rook following behind.

'Now, can you tell me what this is all about?' Rook said, making himself comfortable in the passenger seat.

'Yes, sorry, Marlowe couldn't do it. We needed a clean location.'

Rook glanced around the car's interior. It was spotless; in fact, it was pristine. There wasn't a speck of dust to be seen or a single scratch or blemish on the leather or dashboard. Even the air smelled fresh, although no air freshener had been allowed to dangle from the rear-view.

'I meant *clean* as in we know it's not bugged,' Nicole said as she watched him inspect her car.

'Of course.' Rook quickly closed his winter coat across himself and tried not to feel like an idiot.

'What I'm about to say cannot be known by the outside world. I doubt there are more than ten humans in the country who know what I'm about to tell you.' She emphasised the importance of what she was saying with a hard stare. 'Are you aware that Homo sapiens weren't the only early human-like species to walk the earth?'

'Assume I got a C in science, and that was a fluke.'

'You've heard of Neanderthals and Homo floresiensis, right?' Rook felt his face turn into a picture of non-comprehension. 'Well, they weren't the only humanoid species that had to get out of the way of early man. Other species shared the earth with us too. As I understand it, we outbred, outnumbered, or killed most of them. Those remaining stayed out of our way. Over time, they became myths and then stories we told each other. But some of those species survived.'

'There are Neanderthals still around?'

'No, Neanderthals are extinct. But trolls, ghouls, vampires, and orcs live in the world right now. Many of them are in London, in fact. They bear little resemblance to the creatures you'll see on TV or read about in fantasy novels. Although they do look different from us, when you learn what to look for. They also have certain abilities.'

'This is a joke, right? Or have I gone mad?'

'You're not mad, and this isn't a joke,' Nicole said, letting out a nervous giggle at odds with her otherwise professional demeanour. 'I'm afraid I'll have to tell you more on the go. We have a crime scene to get to.'

'Who's dead? Nosferatu; Dracula; Spike; that shiny guy from *Twilight*?' Rook said.

'It is a vampire. But you must get any preconceptions out of your head,' Nicole said. 'Vampires can pass for human, if you don't look too closely at their teeth. They don't do any of that magical stuff they do in movies, like mind control or turning into bats. They can even go out in sunlight, although they do burn easier than humans because they evolved as night-time hunters. But with some strong sunscreen they manage.'

'Okay, say I believe these creatures exist. Are they a danger to us? Are they wreaking havoc in the night?'

'Humans were right to fear them at one time: when vampires hunted us at night and we'd stay out of the way out of trolls, ghouls, and orcs. But that was long ago. Now they hide from us. You still need to know about their capabilities, of course. Trolls are stronger than any bodybuilder. Orcs are tough as nails and take a hell of a lot of stopping. Vampires can move faster than you can see and will rip your throat out in a heartbeat. But, in the main, they only want to stay hidden. Like the rest of nature, they've learnt nothing that gets in the way of humanity survives.'

'What about ghouls?'

'Ghouls have a pallid grey complexion that can give them away. Most of the time they are stick-thin with long legs that let them run for days. They can smell blood from miles away and they can bite clean through your arm. I believe they evolved as scavengers, like humanoid vultures, and their eating habits haven't changed.'

'What does that mean?'

'Ghouls don't just like their steaks bloody, they like them with the skin on and a side of bone.'

'So if a ghoul is cooking, don't accept the food. Good to know, I suppose. How come trolls are living in London? Aren't they basically monsters? Like in films.'

'They aren't monsters, Rook. I'm not sure monsters exist. Trolls are big, though – big and tough. They have white-blond hair and even paler skin. Like Vikings on steroids. We think they came from the Arctic Circle, hunting wild animals on frozen tundra, and they could put up a good fight against a polar bear.'

'Well, they sound dangerous.'

'Actually, most trolls are very community-minded. Much of their culture is based on helping the tribe survive.'

Rook tried to let this information sink in, but it wouldn't, leaving him to swim along with the weird until something made sense. Outside the car, jostling crowds were hurrying to work, some weary, some happy, some sad.

None, Rook realised, would be having as strange a day as him. He glanced at Nicole, her eyes on the road and her hands smoothly moving the wheel. He couldn't believe what she was saying, but every sense said she was telling the truth. So, either she was a fantastic liar, was mad herself, or Rook really was falling down the rabbit hole.

'Okay, I'm not saying I believe you about all of this. But something is going on and I want to know what. And I better get paid.'

'You will get paid. Don't worry about that. And don't worry about not believing me. Soon you will have all the evidence you need.' She paused to check her wing mirror. 'I should tell you about Jacob.'

'Jacob?'

'Jacob is your partner, after a fashion.'

'What's that supposed to mean?'

'He will help you get any information you need.' Her hands squeezed hard on the wheel.

'Is he a vampire?'

'Jacob is an orc.'

'I thought orcs were from *The Lord of the Rings*?' Rook said.

'No,' Nicole said. 'Not originally, in any case. Tolkien came across some references to orcs in his research and used the idea for his work. Orcs evolved on the Eurasian Steppes as endurance hunters.' She glanced at Rook's blank expression. 'That means they would hunt in groups, chasing animals for days until their prey was too exhausted to go any farther. Then they'd go in for the kill. It means they have greater stamina than us, greater tolerance for pain, and even heal a lot faster than we do. Oh' – she bit her lip – 'they're also green.'

'Are you telling me green orcs are running around and no one has twigged? Not one YouTube video is out there?'

'The green isn't as noticeable as you might assume.' She glanced across at Rook. 'Trust me, you'll understand when you see Jacob. And as for YouTube, who'd believe it, anyway?'

'Okay... Anything else? Are there werewolves prowling the London nights, howling at the moon?'

Nicole laughed. 'Nothing so dramatic as that. But there's a lot to learn, and it's best to wait until you're back in the office for a full rundown rather than try to do one in my car.'

'Fair point,' Rook conceded, happy to change the subject back to the crime he was about to investigate. 'What can you tell me about the victim?'

'Caleb? Not a lot. He was young, he was a vampire, and now he's dead, I'm sad to say. That's pretty much it. If you have more questions, I'd save them for Jacob. We're almost there. That reminds me. Look in the glove compartment.'

Rook did so and found some crime-scene gloves in a sealed packet. 'Well,' he said, 'guess you came prepared.'

'I'm always prepared, Detective Rook. Are *you*?'

'I honestly don't know.'

'You can turn around now. Go back to your life. Forget all about any of this,' Nicole said, her voice gentle, like a doctor telling a dying patient it was okay to let go.

Nicole is right, Rook thought. He could leave whatever this is. Return to his dirty flat and his empty life. Find a new job. Whatever the hell that would be. But what would be the point? At least this way he'd remain a detective. As much as he'd fallen out of love with the police force, he'd never considered being anything else.

'I'll play along,' he said.

'The key is, forget they're vampires and orcs or whatever. These are people, Rook. Lost and scared people, but still people.'

Soon they arrived at a street in Wandsworth where each garden was manicured and every door perfectly painted. Well, except for the one they pulled up to. In front of this house, the weeds were bigger than some trees and the grass was so tall Rook thought they might need a machete. The white paint around the windows had turned smoker-teeth yellow and cracks in its walls spoke of a long life without love or care.

'This is your stop,' Nicole said. 'And that grumpy-looking guy standing in front of the house is Jacob. He'll be giving you a lift to the office afterwards. I've got an appointment to keep.'

Nicole drove off as soon as Rook closed the door, leaving him in the freezing cold, looking at the first orc he'd ever knowingly seen.

Jacob pulled down the hood of his grey sweatshirt, revealing a bald head with a face like a stone archway in an ancient castle. His green eyes were so deep in his skull that they were almost in shadow. He was wearing faded blue jeans, and a heavy, brown, sheepskin-lined coat that was probably fashionable in the 1970s and may now be fashionable again for all Rook knew.

As Nicole had said, he did have green skin. It wasn't the vivid green Rook had pictured, it was more of a subtle green tinge. Like he suffered from a rare form of jaundice. Rook could believe he'd never have given this orc a second look if he'd passed by him on the street.

'You had a long enough look at your first orc?' Jacob said, standing with his shoulders square and feet planted.

'S... Sorry,' Rook stuttered.

'Good. Then let's see a dead vampire.'

CHAPTER THREE

Rook's first vampire was a bloody corpse lying face upwards in the middle of a dirty, blood-soaked room. The curtains were open, the morning light illuminating each spray of blood that had landed on the discarded jeans, T-shirts, and DIY ashtrays littering the floor. Blood had even reached the dirty mattress pressed into the corner. Rook coughed as the pervading fug of stale air, old cigarettes, and marijuana forced its way down his throat.

The vampire had been stabbed across his chest, neck, face, torso, and wherever else there had been flesh. Blood covered his white skin and jet-black hair. Rook would have closed the corpse's eyes, but one of them was hanging out of his skull, the killer making up in violence what they lacked in precision.

'Who was he?' Rook said.

'Caleb Parker. He came here from Manchester last September,' Jacob said.

'He'd only been in town for five months and he ended up like this? Doesn't seem fair. You know anything else?'

'I'd seen him around. But he'd given me no reason to get to know him further.'

Rook straightened out his coat and forced himself forwards to investigate the vampire in more detail. The corpse beneath him couldn't have been much further from a vile creature of lore. It looked like any other young kid. Crouching down, he inspected the vampire's fingers and toes. They were bulky, with knuckles that jutted out like rugged mountains.

'It helps them climb trees,' Jacob said, resting his back on a decrepit desk that was squatting against a wall. Unfazed by the carnage surrounding him, his hands were jammed firmly in the pockets of his coat. 'Vampires came from the forests of Europe, back when Europe was all forest. They hunted at night – it's why they have such good night-vision and hearing. Their hands and feet let them move through the trees faster than their prey, without making a sound. Then they would ambush their prey from above, ripping their throats out with their teeth. I don't know where you humans got the idea they are immortal. A vampire will be lucky to last seventy years. They aren't that strong either. Those light bones that make them so fast are easy to break.'

Rook put on the gloves Nicole had given him and lifted Caleb's top lip as delicately as he could. The teeth were not the over-the-top fangs from movies and TV. The front teeth were indistinguishable from human teeth. Perhaps a brighter, cleaner white than normal but otherwise the same. Behind the vampire's canines was where things got weird. Each tooth was long, thin, and sharp. Made for cutting and ripping rather than grinding. A shudder ran from the top of Rook's spine to the soles of his feet. There was something alien about looking into a mouth that was simultaneously similar to a human's and completely different.

'You scared of teeth?' Jacob said, his lips curling into a mocking grin.

'Funny,' Rook said, praying Jacob didn't notice his shaking hands. 'Give me a second to adjust, will you? I woke up this morning blissfully unaware that vampires and orcs existed. Now I'm looking at a dead vampire while an orc makes jokes at my expense. Will you help me investigate the scene at least?'

'That would be your job,' Jacob said, inspecting the back of his calloused hands.

'Okay,' Rook said, half under his breath. 'Can you tell me anything else about vampires?'

'Such as?'

'I don't know. Do they drink blood?'

'Only as much as any other predator.'

'Is anyone else going to look over the crime scene?' Rook said, taking in the mess and gore on display.

'Other than us? To do what?'

'Collect physical evidence. Take fingerprints. Stuff like that.'

'No one keeps the other species' identities on record,' Jacob said. 'Even if you could take our DNA, there isn't any database you could compare it to or lab you could send it to.'

'And I guess that means no one is coming to collect crime scene evidence. Just you and me.' Rook said, sighing as he looked around the room.

'You haven't joined some wide-ranging secret organisation with multiple offices, Rook. You are one of the few humans who knows of our existence. We wouldn't stay secret if we told the entire police force about us, would we?'

'I guess you wouldn't,' Rook said, and meant it.

'Is this a problem?'

'I'll have to learn to live with it. Did Caleb live with anyone else?'

'I don't believe he did,' Jacob said with a lazy shrug of his broad shoulders.

'I don't suppose you have any idea how he came to live in such a pleasant area? Even if the house is a dump. You normally don't get squats this spacious in this fancy an

area. When you do, there's more than one person living in
them,' Rook said.

'I don't know. Housing doesn't work for us as it does for
you. We can't find a place through an estate agent. That
requires more paperwork and forms of ID than we have.
Nicole has a list of places we can use. Normally from people who've died without a will or family to try and claim
their property. We also have our own networks. Sometimes
someone makes a deal with a homeowner without troubling the banks or lawyers. If Nicole didn't get him this
place, then Caleb must have known someone.'

Rook took his notebook from his coat pocket and
scrawled a reminder to look into that later. He went
through the room, taking a picture of every square foot
with his phone – whether it had anything in it or not –
prior to searching that area and that area alone. He covered the entire flat in this way while Jacob looked on. His
breathing calmed as he went through the familiar methodical process. Only then did he look around the rest of the
house before returning to the crime scene.

'How did you learn of the murder?' Rook asked Jacob
as he rooted around in a mercifully unbloodied pile of
clothes to see if he could find anything of interest.

'I was called. If something like this happens to one of us,
I'm one of the people you can call.'

'Who called you?'

'Rebecca. She's the orc with the big hair in those pictures.'

Jacob was referring to the many pictures stuck on the wall. All full of smiling young people in various stages of inebriation. Rook removed a few of them, making sure he had one of every person represented on the wall.

'Her?' Rook asked, pointing to a young woman who was in multiple photos. Jacob nodded. 'How did she find him?'

'She said Caleb had called her at around two in the morning. She found him like this.'

'Do the other species normally socialise?' Rook said, looking at the pictures.

'Socialise?'

'In the sense that orcs and vampires would drink together and such?'

'In the past, there has been some friction between our different species, but these days we just all hate humans.'

'Good to see barriers being broken down, I suppose,' Rook said, checking to see if Jacob's face showed a trace of humour. It didn't. 'Did she give any more information?'

'Caleb had been at James's all night. She'd been elsewhere. He called her, she came over, and found him like this. She was distraught when I found her. I sent her home.'

'Who's James?' Rook asked.

'A troll who runs an underground bar for the other species.'

'So, we can start our investigation in the pub? First good news I've had in a while,' Rook said.

'Got any leads from the room?' Jacob asked.

'From all this? Of course not.' Rook raised his eyebrows and gave Jacob a wry smile. 'What do you think I am? Some TV detective who could tell you who was here because one of the cigarettes is a different brand? I can guess he knew his attacker, as there was no sign of a break-in. The savage nature of the attack suggests a personal motive, but some people are just psycho. Other than that, there is little to go on.'

'What will you do now?'

'First, I'll go door to door down the street. See if anyone saw anything. We may get lucky.'

'Want me to come?'

Rook looked the orc up and down. 'No offence, but I'm not sure you have the friendly demeanour necessary to conduct gentle interviews with the British public. I'll catch you up later. If you could set up an interview with Rebecca, it would be useful. And we should go to James's pub, where we can piece together a timeline.'

Jacob didn't bat an eyelid at Rook's rebuttal; he just looked on as the detective continued his search. Rook examined the vampire's corpse but found only an empty wallet and no phone. The latter presumably taken by the murderer, although Rook doubted robbery was the motive. He moved to the table Jacob was resting against but found nothing in the yellowing newspapers and old magazines that covered its surface. It was only when Rook moved the mattress that he spotted something. Someone had cut a discreet hole in the side of the mattress that faced the wall. In that hole, Rook discovered a delicate wooden box with scratches on the outside.

'Well, I didn't expect to find that,' Rook said after the box revealed its shiny contents.

'What is it?' Jacob said.

'It appears to be an Omega.'

'A what?'

'A watch... A very fancy watch that costs a lot of money. Like a Rolex,' Rook said, examining his find. Its silver strap gleamed and its face was a deep royal blue with the word *Seamaster* engraved on it in neat writing. Rook did not know much about watches, but he knew this one was expensive. 'Not what you'd expect to find in this vampire's squat?'

Jacob shook his bald head, but his expression did not change.

'That's going to be a useful clue or an annoying dead end. But it suggests our friend Caleb had some shady hobbies. It's hard to believe he came by this honestly.'

'Could it have been a gift?' Jacob asked.

'It could have, but this could be worth £10,000. People who live in squats like this don't often have friends or family handing out watches like this. Whatever the answer, we need to find it,' Rook said, feeling the weight of the Omega in his hand. 'The question is, if it's not a gift or an heirloom, then why not sell it?'

'He could be saving it,' Jacob said.

'Saving it?' Rook said.

'We can get bank accounts, but it's difficult, and we know not to attract attention by depositing large amounts of cash. Savings accounts are trickier still. If we have something valuable that can be exchanged quickly for cash, then we hold on to it until we need to sell.'

'Like gold jewellery or a very expensive watch,' Rook said.

Jacob nodded.

The sound of the front door opening stopped their conversation in its tracks. Rook looked at Jacob, who moved into the corner of the room without making a sound. His new position hid him from whoever was coming up the stairs.

Whoever it was, they weren't concerned with stealth. Their shoes clattered on each step as they whistled a mangled tune. The door flung open and in walked a man who looked like a ferret in a bad suit. He was a few years older than Rook, in his early forties or late thirties. His dark hair was slicked back so it looked like it was painted onto his head. In his left hand, he carried a black sports bag that thudded when he let it drop to the floor.

'Well then,' the man said, a sharp glint in his eye and an insolent smile on his face. 'I guess you are the new pig in these parts.'

Rook took a moment to glare at the man who had so brazenly interrupted. 'That's right. I'm Detective Constable Rook. And who the fuck might you be?'

'He's Carver,' Jacob said, stepping out from his hiding place, his mouth twisting with distaste as he said the man's name. 'He does errands for Marlowe.'

Carver jumped as soon as Jacob spoke, a reaction that gave Rook genuine satisfaction.

'I help Dr Marlowe solve his problems.' Carver gave a smile full of yellow, jagged teeth and no mirth. 'Like today, I'm solving the problem of how to get rid of a dead vampire with no one on this lovely, middle-class street being any the wiser.' He examined the broken body in front of him like a removals man would look at an irregularly shaped cabinet. 'It would be a lot easier for me if they turned to dust, wouldn't it? Guess one of you lot really didn't like him, eh?' he said, looking at Jacob.

Jacob stared at Carver from underneath his deep brow but said nothing.

'It's good for me that vampire bones are fragile,' Carver said. 'Best to cut him up with this and pack up the bits, I think.' He reached into his bag and pulled out an axe.

Chapter Four

For the centre of a conspiracy to hide orcs, vampires, ghouls, and trolls, the office was a let-down. Hidden behind the faded green door of a first-floor flat above an accountant's office somewhere in the London Borough of Balham, it was one of those pokey three-room flats that only existed because of the city's rising house prices and landlords' greed.

Rook could see everything the flat offered from the door. What was once the kitchen-lounge area was now home to two desks, with a computer monitor sitting on each. Smudge marks covered the desk nearest the kitchen, the type left behind when someone had recently tried to remove stubborn coffee stains. Nicole sat at the other desk, which was clear of all clutter, smudges, or stains. Underneath her desk, however, was a space heater and some fluffy white slippers.

The kitchen consisted of a lonely-looking hob and a single black kettle around which various mugs clustered alongside a single whisky tumbler. Next to the kitchen was the bathroom, or at least that's where it often was in flats like this. Behind the makeshift office was an open door to what was once a bedroom but was now a storage space for office junk. The whole place smelled of cleaning wipes and quiet sadness.

'Welcome to our centre of operations. Cutting-edge, don't you think?' Nicole said, spreading her arms out from behind her computer.

'It's quieter than my old office at least,' Rook said. 'Are you going to say some more about what those operations are?'

'Once you've told me about what you found this morning.' Nicole picked up a pink coffee mug and handed it to Rook. 'And made some coffee. You are the new guy, after all.'

Rook gave Nicole the details of the case as he made two coffees (black for him, milk and two generously sized sugars for her).

'An Omega? That's interesting,' she said when he got to the part about the watch.

'How so?'

'Cases get flagged whenever they mention certain keywords or features. Then you investigate them. We don't want the public to know that the other species exist. Sometimes that means catching the criminal before the regular police.'

'And you've got a case that involves an Omega watch?'

'Alongside other very pricey watches, we do. There should be a file on it on your computer.'

She passed Rook a Post-it Note with a password on it, and soon he was finding his way through his predecessor's files. The 'Purcell Case' sat next to three files concerning burglaries. Whereas the others were all burglaries of jewellery shops, this one had occurred at a residential property in a very posh part of Chelsea.

Mr Purcell had reported the theft of fifteen watches to the police, including an Omega Seamaster like the one Rook had pulled out of Caleb's mattress. The officers who caught the case wrote it off as insurance fraud and followed up with minimal effort, only making cursory inquiries. Then whoever had been Rook's predecessor had taken over the case. Judging by the absence of useful notes, they had pursued this case with the energy of a fat housecat on a warm day.

'There doesn't seem to be much in the way of case notes on here,' Rook said.

'I'm not surprised. Your predecessor, Terry, wasn't the most motivated by the end. Unless he ran into the victim while he was out drinking, I doubt he gave it a second thought.' She caught Rook's look. 'I think he found the job lonely.'

Rook shrugged. 'I take it the whisky tumbler sat among the coffee mugs is his?'

Nicole answered with a sad grimace.

'What happened to him?' Rook said, his tone neutral. It was always tricky finding out about the people who used to have your job. They could be useless but still liked.

'He quit.'

'What about Jacob?'

'What about him?' Nicole said.

'Wouldn't he be able to investigate?'

'That's not what Jacob does,' Nicole said.

'I noticed he wasn't too interested in investigating the crime scene.' Rook leaned back in his chair. 'What does he do?'

'Jacob can help you with the other species,' Nicole said quickly. Rook was going to ask how, but she continued, 'Did Caleb's neighbours hear anything?'

Rook shook his head and drank his coffee, which was a touch too bitter for him. 'Most were surprised anyone even lived there. Do you have any idea how he got his place?'

'None.'

'Jacob told me you're the person to call if a young vampire needs a place. He never got in touch?'

Nicole shook her head. 'The first I heard of him was when he was murdered. Any other leads?'

'No. Still figuring out a timeline leading up to Caleb's death. Although, I have an interview with this Rebecca

Ramsey.' Rook put his coffee on the table and gave a laugh that contained all the mirth of a cracked skull. Nicole looked over the top of her screen at him, her perfectly manicured eyebrows arched.

'I'm sorry. This morning I woke up hungover and expecting to be fired. Now I'm working for a secret part of the government. I've got pictures of a dead vampire on my phone and I'm talking about timelines like I've got a clue how to get started with any of this.'

'I know working with the other species can be a shock, but you will get used to it. Once you get past the weirdness of it all, they're only people who need help like everybody else.'

'But how do you live the rest of your life knowing this big secret?'

Nicole pursed her lips and gave the question a moment's thought. 'The key is compartmentalisation.'

'Compartmentalisation?'

'Leave everything in this office. You've got to train yourself to forget that you work here when you're around friends and family. With practice, you'll forget you're living a lie.'

'Sounds fun,' Rook said without feeling.

'It gets easier. And we are useful. No one else is looking out for the other species. Actually, this could be good for you.'

'Good for me? How?'

'I've seen your CV. You were promoted fast but then stalled. People who do that tend to either be talented but lacking the people skills to go further, or they've burnt out.'

'Why not both?'

'No reason,' Nicole said with a chuckle. 'But remember, I'm the one who conducted the background research on you. You were flying high until about three years ago. Since... what happened to your mother... your work gradually declined, negative reports of your attitude increased, and, judging by your social media profiles, your social life has crashed. I may be wrong, but it looks like you might have lost your sense of purpose. Maybe you can find it again here? After all, you get to help people and don't have nearly the amount of red tape to deal with. Does that appeal?'

'Guess we'll find out,' Rook muttered, feeling like a moth stuck with a pin.

Nicole dispelled the heavy silence with another smile, asking, 'Fancy a biscuit?'

'Sure.'

'Chocolate bourbon or custard cream?'

'Tough question. I'll go chocolate.'

Nicole walked over to the kitchen and opened a cupboard. She had to almost stand on her tiptoes to reach the biscuits, despite there being no food on the lower shelves.

'Why not put those packets on a lower shelf? Or on the counter next to the kettle?'

Nicole averted her eyes in mock guilt.

'If they're a bit out of reach, it makes it that much harder to grab myself a biscuit. Meaning I'm less likely to grab one or three. We can't all be rakes like you,' she said, tapping her waist.

Rook couldn't think how to respond in a way that was funny and complimentary but not weird. Luckily, two polite knocks on the door saved him.

'That will be Steele,' Nicole said, putting the biscuits back and opening the door, which revealed a man who epitomised the term *aristocratic bearing*.

Steele was possibly as tall as Rook, although his bolt-up-right stance may have added an inch or two. He wore a dark greatcoat over a slate grey suit, with a white shirt and deep blue tie. Even under his coat, it was clear he would make a matchstick look fat. He was completely bald and even his eyebrows were faint, as if only what was absolutely necessary was permitted on his face. His cheekbones stuck out of his featureless face like they were trying to make a point. He stood over Rook, regarding the detective with the focus and warmth of a computer programme.

'Well,' he said, holding out a thin hand. 'You must be Detective Rook. Pleased to make your acquaintance.'

'And you are?' Rook reached forwards to shake his hand.

'My name is James Steele. I'm from the Home Office, and one of my duties is to run this discreet department. I'm sure you have a lot of questions, and I'm here to give you some answers. At least, as many as I have time for today.'

'I thought Marlowe was in charge?' Rook said, watching Steele's reaction.

'Ha-ha,' Steele said dryly. 'He likes to give that impression, doesn't he? But no, that would be me, I'm afraid.'

'So, you ordered Marlowe to ruin my reputation?' Rook said, bristling with a sudden and open hostility. He glanced across at Nicole, who was making every effort not to make eye contact with either Steele or him.

'Come now, Mr Rook,' Steele said, in a tone that suggested Rook should cease with his foolishness and accept the realities of his position. 'Your career was already over and you had inflicted quite a lot of damage on your reputation by yourself. Marlowe simply made it so that we could offer you the role. You could have said no.' Steele let out a neat cough. 'Let's make sure we are clear on the important aspects of our operation, shall we? Our purpose is, above all else, to keep the other species' existence a secret. If the public found out that their government had been hiding these creatures, there would be an uproar. A violent uproar. You are required to clean up any messes that are made, ensuring that all the other species stay quiet and secret. Do you understand?'

'Seems simple enough,' Rook said, his eyes itching with anger.

'Good,' Steele said, either oblivious to, or uncaring of, Rook's rage. 'Nicole looks after the logistics and practicalities required to maintain the status quo and you're to use your skills to ensure any criminal element stays in line and any problems that require your experience are dealt with expediently. You and I should require limited contact with each other. We are only conversing now so that you and I know each other, should there be the need to speak in the future.'

'So, what you're saying is, "Nice to meet you, do your job, and let's never speak again"?' Rook looked into Steele's faded grey eyes.

A thin smile spread across Steele's face, like it was being cut out with a scalpel. 'I'm glad you grasp the situation. Although, before I go, I must stress how important it is that the recent troubles are cleared up without further disturbances.'

'You mean the murder?' Rook said.

'Of course, Detective, the murder is important. But don't let the three burglaries of jewellers or the alleged theft of some quite expensive watches in Chelsea slip your mind. Assuming the latter wasn't insurance fraud, as Terry concluded.'

Rook raised his eyebrows.

'This murder,' Steele said with exaggerated patience, 'while deeply unfortunate, will only be of concern if it risks exposure of our work. If it is an inter-community issue, then it should be resolved, but I won't lose sleep over it. Vampires pulling off impossible burglaries, if continued unabated, could be troubling.'

'Are you saying to prioritise the watches theft over the murder? Why do you even think these burglaries involved the other species?'

'We believe these burglaries may involve the other species because of certain details that perplex the police but may be explainable by those of us aware of the other species and their abilities. As for which is a priority, I'll leave it for you to use your judgement to decide which is most likely to shatter our veil of secrecy. That is all. And since that is all, I'm afraid I must leave you.'

'You wouldn't like a coffee?' Nicole said, rising from her seat.

'No, thank you, Nicole. I best be on my way,' Steele said, sweeping out of the office.

'Is this all the government oversight of the other species there is? Us two in a flat in Balham, Marlowe, and some aristocratic official who doesn't want to be disturbed?' Rook said.

'Well, they have their own sort of quasi-government too. It's run by someone called Rowena, who you will meet soon, I'm sure. They handle as much of their affairs as they can internally, and we help where they need to intersect with our world, and run interference when there is a danger of discovery,' Nicole said.

'And when you say "we", you pretty much mean you, don't you?'

'I suppose I do,' she said, giving a short laugh. 'From what I've been told it's always been a small department. We know it existed after the Second World War, but we can't say when it started with any accuracy. That's the bad part about keeping as few records as possible. And the idea has been to employ as few people as possible. I'm sure you can guess why.' She looked at Rook, and he realised she did actually expect him to guess.

It didn't take him long to think of the reason. 'Because people just can't keep secrets. I've seen it on the force. Someone sets up some clandestine task force. They only want a few people in it, but once you get admin involved and those people on the force have a few drinks down the pub, then everyone knows. So, I can see why real secrecy requires keeping as few people in the loop as possible.'

'That's right,' Nicole said with a hint of a proud school-teacher whose pupil had got the correct answer. 'Actually, I replaced two people. But they were perhaps a bit more "old school" and struggled to adapt to the digital age. Now that everything is online, the other species need more help operating in our world without revealing their presence. As I'm a logistics expert who also has a good degree in computer science, they thought I could replace both of them and help modernise operations.'

'Well, aren't you the genius,' Rook teased. Nicole responded with a mock-smug smile.

'By the way, I understand the police like to create "crime boards" to help them visualise the case. Or at least that's what they do on the telly. So I've put some whiteboards in the storeroom, should you want them.'

The whiteboards were indeed in the storeroom, along with some markers. Rook set them up side by side and wrote the outline of the case as it was now, which he had to admit wasn't too useful. But at least it made him feel somewhat like he was in a normal investigation.

'What did Terry say about the burglaries?' Rook said, sitting back in his chair.

'That he found nothing. Is there nothing else in the files?'

'Only that they happened.' Rook stared at the screen.

'I'm sorry,' Nicole said. 'I did say he wasn't thorough.'

Rook looked towards the whisky tumbler nestled in among the various mugs on the counter. He could almost feel its reassuring weight in his hand.

'In that case,' Rook said, shaking the thoughts of a descent into alcoholism from his mind, 'it's time I paid a visit to Mr Purcell. I want to see how a vampire stole his watches.'

CHAPTER FIVE

'What the bloody hell do you want?' Purcell said when he opened the door, his voice as northern as Yorkshire pudding and a lost mining heritage. He was a middle-aged man with a red-wine complexion and heavy physique held together by a smart blue shirt. He wore his sleeves rolled up, exposing thick forearms.

'We're here to talk about the recent break-in, Mr Purcell,' Rook said, flashing his ID and feeling a twinge of guilt as he did. Even though he was allowed to use his badge in this new role, he already felt a long way from being real police.

Purcell ran his bloodshot eyes over Rook and Nicole. 'I thought you lot had decided I'd done it for the insurance. I've dropped the damn case. Wasn't worth the hassle.'

'We believe it was a genuine burglary, Mr Purcell,' Nicole said in the polite but emotionless tone of a career civil servant. 'And we'd like to make sure we've considered everything. Now, if you could show me and Detective Rook where the watches were stolen from, we would appreciate it.'

'Fine,' Purcell said. 'I'll take you to the study.'

They followed Purcell to an attic room with a skylight. It had been turned into a workspace with a two-screen computer set-up, a plush orthopaedic chair, and some pictures of Purcell with someone Rook assumed was his much younger wife. The room was clean and free from clutter. The air smelled fresh and felt cold, suggesting the skylight had been recently open.

'It would be easier if we had the place to ourselves,' Nicole said politely, but leaving no room for discussion.

'You expect me to leave you two here by yourselves?' Purcell said, his chest puffing up like a porcupine.

'Please, Mr Purcell, we just require a few minutes to look over the scene and it will be faster if we can work uninterrupted.'

For a moment Purcell looked like he was about to disagree further, but he wilted under the force of Nicole's persistent smile, muttered, 'Fine,' and plodded down the stairs with heavy steps.

'So,' Rook said, 'what am I looking at?'

'You're the police,' Nicole said, standing in the doorway. 'You tell me.'

'The police report said Purcell came up here one morning to find the skylight open. There were no other signs of forced entry into the house. Purcell claims he kept his collection of antique watches on his desk, and someone stole all fifteen of them. Worth about £50,000 altogether. Now there's one massive problem with all of this.' Rook walked around the office as if some new clue would reveal itself.

'And what's that?' Nicole said, her hands on her hips.

'It's fucking stupid, that's what. For a start, there's no way someone would get in via the skylight. They would have had to carry a bloody big ladder right up to the house with no one seeing, and that couldn't happen. They also must have known that the watches were here, in this precise room, and were only targeting them. Otherwise, they would have gone farther into the house to look for other stuff to steal.' Rook took a breath and looked around the room. 'Meaning that this was either a very targeted burglary or they were the world's luckiest chimney sweep, wandering along the roofs of London and coming across an open window and a stash of antique watches.'

Rook opened the skylight to see if there was anything unusual about it, but saw nothing but roof and sky. 'So, he must have come from below. But the report says no one tripped the alarm on the ground-floor. And there's no way to get through any other window. The only natural conclusion to draw is that Purcell has tried to pull off the world's laziest insurance fraud. Except that this morning I met an orc and started investigating the murder of a vampire. So, I guess you're going to tell me that Caleb flew up here...'

Rook took another breath after his monologue. A knowing half-smile spread across Nicole's face.

'There's no such thing as magic. And the only things that fly have wings,' she said.

'There's really no magic? I'm disappointed.'

'Were you hoping a magical hat was going to put you in Gryffindor?'

'No,' Rook said. 'Anyway, I'm Hufflepuff through and through.'

'Ravenclaw for life.' Nicole held out her fist in a mock salute.

'Anyway, coming back to the impossible crime. You knew it was a vampire before I found that watch in Caleb's place?'

'A vampire could climb up the side of one of these buildings and dance across the rooftops without being heard or seen. While the police who submitted the report assumed it was an insurance job – and Terry was happy to agree – I thought it more likely to be a vampire.'

'Well, we can now be fairly sure that the vampire was Caleb,' said Rook.

'Unless someone planted the watch?' Nicole said.

'Someone's been watching their detective shows,' Rook teased. 'We can't rule it out, I suppose, but it's more likely he is the thief. The watch could have been payment for services rendered or he just kept one for himself. The question is, if he was responsible, how did a vampire just down from Manchester know the watches were here? I think it's time to talk to Purcell.'

***

They found Purcell sitting in a spacious kitchen, decorated in green and white tiles and the type of pans that cost as much as Rook's entire wardrobe. He was drinking coffee from a dainty white cup that looked miniature in his meaty hand. The smell of strong coffee filled the room.

'Mind if I have a little chat with you about the break-in?' Rook said.

The heavy-set man snorted. 'Why? The first coppers who came said it was an insurance job. Like I'd need the cash.'

'I've seen the notes, Mr Purcell. Not sure those guys were having their best day.'

Purcell grunted but offered Rook and Nicole coffees, which they declined, and motioned for them to sit at the kitchen table.

'Damn right. Kept implying I was in on it. Like I didn't know it should be bloody impossible to get in by the sky-light. Course I know it can't be done. Still, that was better than the last guy they sent around. The others were trying to hide their smiles. He was barely even trying to hide his hangover.'

That would be Terry, Rook presumed. It sounded like all Rook had to do was stay sober and he'd be better than Terry. Something he would have felt more confident about doing if the previous night's whisky wasn't still lingering on his taste buds.

'Well,' Rook said as he took out his notebook and a biro that probably had about three lines of ink left in it, 'let's hope I do better.'

Purcell twisted his mouth into an expression that suggested he didn't expect to be impressed by Rook's efforts.

'Let's not worry too much about *how* they stole your watches. Let's think about *who knew* the watches were in this room. After all, it's not like this could have been a crime of opportunity, could it?'

'No,' said Purcell, 'not many people knew they were there.'

'Well, let's figure out who could have known. Do you ever have meetings with clients or business associates here?'

'Only by video call. Doubt that counts.'

'No,' Rook said, chewing on his lip. 'I'm sure they wouldn't have been able to see the watches, assuming that is the way the computer screen is always angled. Who else knew they were there?'

'Hardly anyone. It's not like I take people up to show them my watches. The only time they see them is on my wrist.'

'This is a tidy place,' Rook said, looking around the spacious kitchen. 'Do you have a cleaner?'

'Never seen the point of hiring someone just to do the odd bit of vacuuming, and it's not like we've got kids making a mess,' Purcell said, shaking his head.

'Your wife knows they were there,' Rook said, searching the man's face for any reaction.

'Why would that matter?' Purcell said, puffing out his chest and spreading out his shoulders, like a primate responding to a challenge. Nicole shuffled in her seat, this line of questioning clearly making her uncomfortable.

'I've got to be thorough, Mr Purcell,' Rook said, faced with the bristling Purcell.

'You've seen pictures of my wife, Mr. Rook?'

'Yes,' Rook said, involuntarily elongating the word as he tried to figure out what Purcell was getting at.

'She's younger than me, isn't she? And pretty?'

Rook's palms began to itch with the knowledge he was being led into a trap, so he stayed quiet and let the man speak.

'So, you've seen this picture of a pretty young woman and figured she's got her claws into this rich northern ogre.'

'That's not—'

'Listen, Sherlock, my wife's got her own money. Made it herself too. We met through business.'

'Okay, okay,' Rook said, backtracking as fast as his tongue would allow. 'It's not your wife. But I've got to keep asking questions until we get something useful. What about this? You tell me the last time someone you didn't know was in your house. For any reason.'

'Well, I had some builders in to do the new bathroom about six months ago. Although for the amount they charged, I doubt they'd need the money either,' Purcell said.

'Do you remember anything particular about them?'

'Not really, they were builders. They were big, drank cups of tea, and snuck out for cigs a lot. Other than that, I didn't see them too much.' Purcell drank the last of his coffee, delicately placing the cup down on its coaster.

'Could you tell me how you found them or who they were? Do you have their phone number?'

'A friend recommended them. And my wife has the phone number. She dealt with the builders.'

'That's great. Would you mind passing the details on to me when you've found them?' Rook gave Purcell his number and let himself out.

'Did that help?' Nicole said as they got back into her car.

'Maybe,' Rook said, yawning. 'That he had builders in wasn't in the initial report. It's possible there's a link between them and Caleb. But I'd still need to prove it. And there are other ways someone could have known about the watches and known Caleb. Ways we can't see now.'

'And that could be connected to Caleb's murder?'

Rook gave a shrug. 'If Caleb didn't work for the builders, then one of them could have tipped him off. Meaning Caleb had an accomplice. This accomplice may not be too happy about Caleb holding a watch back for himself. Could the builders have been vampires, trolls, or whatever?'

'Sure, quite a few of the other species have jobs and anything cash in hand is best. You've got a new lead. That's impressive for half an hour's work.'

'It's a start,' he said, holding back a smile. For the first time in a while he felt some sense of energy in his bones. Some purpose to focus his mind. It beat hanging around his flat, wondering what he was going to do with his life beyond getting drunk.

'Where to now?'

'Guess we go back to the office. You can fill me in on anything else I need to know about all this "other species" stuff. Then I'm off to find some answers at a troll's pub.'

CHAPTER SIX

J acob's house was hidden away in Streatham. It was an old-fashioned red-brick two-up two-down with a well-looked-after front garden. The grass ran perpendicular to the path, with not a blade daring to move out of place. A long basket hung in front of the window. Right now, it was empty except for frozen dirt, but Rook imagined that in summer it would bloom with flowers.

Two concrete council estates flanked the house, all grey concrete and brutal lines. They were the type of estates that always had their washing hanging out to dry and where a sense of community was locked in a daily battle with desperate poverty.

How Jacob's house had stayed standing as two council estates had sprung up around it was a mystery. Developers would have been dying to gobble it up and turn it into something more 'space-efficient' like a block of flats. It was like a tiny fraction of an older London had remained unchanged despite the city planner's best efforts, its existence sticking a middle finger up to the world around it.

Jacob opened the door, gave Rook a nod, and walked back into his house. Rook followed, entering a room filled with the odour of stale air unique to quiet houses, as if there hadn't been enough talking to get the air circulating. The room itself held a well-worn red sofa facing the television, while a wooden dining table hid in the far corner next to the stairs.

The room, already short of space, was crowded and Rook felt uncomfortably oversized as he entered. Lying on the floor, with his face staring at a TV that was playing some Disney movie, was one of the biggest men Rook had ever seen. He hadn't looked up when Rook entered, and all Rook could see of him was his size and the dark-blue tracksuit stretched over his bulk.

Sitting on the sofa was a lady dressed in a well-cut navy suit and a long red coat that perfectly matched two ruby earrings that hung from her ears. She shared the same slight green tinge to her skin as Jacob. Her greying brown hair was cut into a loose bob that highlighted diamond-sharp cheekbones. Rook guessed she was middle-aged, but the faint crow's feet spiderwebbing away from her eyes suggested she may be older.

'Aren't you going to welcome your guest, Michael?' she said, regarding Rook like an auction house appraiser inspecting an unusual vase.

Michael rose to his feet slowly, like he had to do it in stages. Rook wasn't used to having to look up at people, but he had to look a long way up to see this guy's face. Michael was almost half a head taller than him and twice as broad across the shoulders, each arm thicker than Rook's entire torso. His skin was marble white, his shaggy hair the whitest of blonds. Even standing in front of Rook, and being the size he was, Michael couldn't bring his pale-blue eyes to meet Rook's. Instead, he kept them focussed on the carpet.

'Nice to meet you,' the giant said, the words having to work hard to overcome his shyness. 'My name is Michael.'

'Hi... I'm Rook,' he mumbled as he looked up at the man's wide face.

Michael didn't respond. Instead, he squirmed as if trying to shrink himself into invisibility. Luckily, the lady on the sofa stood up to end the awkwardness.

'Well done, Michael,' she said. Michael winced at the praise. Then she faced Rook and said, 'I'm Rowena McCloud.'

It was clear the name should mean something to Rook, but for a few panicked seconds he couldn't for the life of him remember what. Thankfully, his memory kicked into gear before the moment got even more awkward.

'Of course, Ms McCloud, Nicole has told me about you. You work with Steele and Nicole, managing the affairs of all the other species,' Rook said, praying he had remembered correctly.

'You can call me Rowena,' she said in a tone suggesting that had Rook called her Rowena, she would have insisted on being called Ms McCloud. 'Mr Steele and Nicole are not colleagues of mine. Closer to counterparts. They manage what we need from your world. I take care of our internal affairs. Or, at least, I'm in charge of the few of us who do.'

Rook was still at a loss for how to respond. After all, it's not every day you meet the prime minister of all the vampires, trolls, ghouls, and orcs of the UK. He found himself about to say, 'Good for you,' but managed to get out, 'Pleased to meet you, ma'am.'

'You too, Mr Rook,' she said. 'I'm sure we'll talk in more detail soon, but I'm afraid I must leave. Jacob told me you would be coming this evening, so I thought I would stop by to meet you in person. Thank you for having me, Jacob. I appreciate you keeping me informed.'

With that, she walked purposefully out of the house, her red coat flowing behind her. Once she'd left, Rook asked Jacob, 'You often entertain your PM?'

'She is not our prime minister. We don't get elections or parliaments. She's in charge. That's all,' Jacob said.

Rook took a seat on the sofa, even though Jacob hadn't offered. 'So, what's the plan?'

Jacob drummed his fingers on the table. 'We're waiting for Carolina. She will look after Michael while we're out.'

'And then what?'

'Then we're going to James's. He's in there every night.'

'So we can find out who Caleb was with and have a pint.'

Jacob nodded.

Within minutes, a petite, short-haired blonde young lady knocked on the door, then entered the house with nervous steps. Her body was lost in an over-sized, long-sleeved jacket. She scanned the room with big green-kitten eyes. Rook looked as closely as he could without making her feel uncomfortable, but, to his surprise, she appeared human.

'Hello, Michael, what are you watching?' she said, sitting herself down next to the giant with only a quick hello wave towards Rook and Jacob. Her accent sounded Eastern European, but Rook couldn't be any more specific than that. Michael glanced up when she spoke, his face breaking into an awkward smile.

'Do I need to know anything about this pub?' Rook said once they were outside under darkening skies and bright streetlights. The temperature had dropped a few degrees and he rubbed his hands together to generate a modicum of heat.

'Such as?' Jacob said.

'I don't know. I've never been to a pub for the other species. Is it safe for humans?'

'Safe enough,' Jacob said. 'If you're with me.'

CHAPTER SEVEN

J ames's pub was beneath a three-storey disused building that stood out like a corpse at a summer fair. It was the only derelict building on an otherwise busy high street. Its cracked windows were full of flyers for concerts, shows, and the occasional missing person or pet.

To get to the bar, they descended some stone steps that smelled of urine and decomposing rat, at the bottom of which stood a dirty blue door. The door opened, revealing a skeleton-thin man with a rodent-like face and skin a few shades greyer than that of a house-bound octogenarian. The colour was noticeable when you looked but wouldn't have drawn much attention in a crowd. Just how, if you saw an orc, you would assume their strange complexion was due to a skin condition. He was wearing a red tracksuit as crumpled as his face and trainers that were a couple of wears away from falling apart. From what he'd been told,

Rook guessed he was a ghoul. A ghoul who wasn't pleased to see either of them.

'Who's this, Jacob?' the ghoul said, sneering at Rook.

'New police,' Jacob said. The ghoul grimaced and moved out of the way, although not so far enough away to spare Rook the stench of his foetid breath as he passed by him.

Rook almost fell over as soon as he got through the door. Instead of walking straight into a room, he found himself on top of more stairs leading down to a cavernous space. He assumed it was the old storage cellar for the building above.

The bar sprawled out beneath him. The furniture was a hotchpotch of mismatched chairs and tables pushed together, with no regard for the principles of decor. Someone with misplaced confidence in their DIY skills had knocked up a makeshift bar against a wall. A fridge behind was loaded with low-cost beer. Weak strip lighting offered some illumination, but the walls farthest away remained in shadow.

The only other patrons were an old ghoul in a dirty green anorak and a group of young guys in denims and T-shirts, all with bone-white skin and coal-black hair. Their murmurings stopped when they saw Rook and Jacob descend the stairs. Rook guessed they were vampires.

'How'd this place become a bar?' Rook said, gesturing to the space around him.

'I believe Nicole found this space,' Jacob said, only elaborating further due to Rook raising his eyebrows. 'Just as she looks out for flats and houses, she also lets us know if any big spaces aren't being used. Sometimes we find places like this ourselves, but it's easier if she is involved. She can tell us when humans are about to move in and we need to move on.'

With that, they walked to the bar, behind which sat a big bald troll whose features didn't manage to fill his face and whose hairline had retreated from the top of his head, leaving tufts of white around the edges. His red jumper was thinning at the elbows and clung tight to his body, although it could have served as a tent for a family.

'Evening, Jacob,' he said, his voice weary and his tired eyes resting on Rook.

'Two Peroni, please, James.' Jacob said in greeting.

James picked the beers from the fridge behind him, opened them, and placed them on the bar. Even with the remains of his hangover still sitting in his stomach, Rook was dying to have a drink. After the day he'd had, he deserved one. But he resisted the urge to take a gulp as Jacob was clearly about to start talking to the troll.

Jacob waved a hand towards Rook and asked, 'You know who this is?'

'Figure he must be the new police.' James ran his hand through what remained of his hair and yawned.

'Then you can guess why we're here,' Jacob said.

'Couldn't say I do.'

'We're here because of what happened to Caleb. Don't say you haven't heard about the murder, James,' Jacob said, holding up a finger to admonish the bar owner for even thinking of lying.

'Yeah, I've heard. The poor bugger.' James's shoulders sank and a weary sigh escaped his lips. 'I don't know anything, though.'

Rook decided it was time for him to interject. He was the police officer here, after all. 'This was the last place we know he was before he went home for the night. And we need you to tell us what you saw.'

'Don't think anything happened last night,' James said, picking up a glass and polishing it with a nearby dishcloth.

'You would have been here last night. And we know he was too,' Jacob said, as he carefully but firmly placed his bottle down on the table, looking directly at James as he did.

James returned Jacob's stare but said nothing.

'Who was he with, James?' Jacob said.

'Few of his friends. Couldn't say who,' the troll said, relenting under Jacob's stare.

'You could say,' Rook said, taking a quick drink of his beer, 'and you should.'

James lowered his heavy head and took some deep breaths, like a bull about to charge.

'We need to establish what happened to Caleb before his murder. That's all,' Rook said in his calmest voice.

'I don't know all of them, and it was busy. I think he was with that Nathan kid and a couple of others. If you want to know more, ask Abby, my waitress. She knows Caleb.'

'Was she working last night?' Rook asked.

'She was,' James said.

'She working tonight?' Jacob said.

'Couldn't face it,' James said, shaking his head.

Rook and Jacob found a table next to the group of young vampires. Three of them were ignoring Jacob and Rook, chattering among themselves. The fourth was glaring at Rook through long, straight hair that failed to hide a scar running from his cheekbone to his chin. Every angle of his heroin-addict-thin body pointed at Rook.

'So,' Rook said, ignoring the vampire's attention and pulling out the photos he'd taken from Caleb's flat. 'We know two people he was with last night for a start: Nathan and Abby. Can you point them out?'

Jacob put a finger on a male vampire gurning in the background of one photo and a female vampire, who couldn't have been more than twenty, smiling in another. She was kissing Caleb on the cheek as he looked at the camera, grinning like only the young, drunk, and happy can.

'Can you set up a meeting with this Abby and Nathan?' Rook asked.

'I can,' Jacob said.

'That's good. Hopefully we'll turn something up. Then we'll have somewhere to start.'

'What about the watches?'

Rook took a long drink. 'I'd hoped we might uncover something by calling the builder who worked on Purcell's bathroom. But I called them this afternoon, and he wasn't happy to help the police with their enquires.'

'Why not?'

'My guess? He uses cash-in-hand help and doesn't keep his accounts in a way the taxman would appreciate. All he would say is he couldn't remember who worked on the Purcell job and couldn't access his accounts right now. It's not like I can get a warrant, that's a dead end.' Rook took a drink and stretched out. 'Anyway, the murder is the priority, and that means speaking to those who saw him last and establishing a timeline. We'll see what his friends know about how that watch ended up in Caleb's flat.'

'Sounds like you have a plan,' Jacob said, sniffing and then taking a swig of his beer.

'At least the start of one,' Rook said, trying to sound more confident than he felt. 'Anyway, how come James was so reluctant to talk to us? He got something to hide?'

'We other species live in hiding. It makes us secretive. Especially when talking to humans.'

'Would he have talked to me if you weren't here?'

'You wouldn't have gotten into the bar if I wasn't here.'

'Well, thanks, I guess,' Rook said. The conversation then dried up, something that seemed to happen a lot with Jacob.

'Is Michael your housemate?' Rook said in an attempt to talk about something other than the case.

'My son,' Jacob said, looking over his beer at Rook. 'His parents died when he was young. I've looked after him since then.'

'Do many trolls...' Rook realised he didn't know how to finish his sentence without sounding like an idiot.

'Have special educational needs?' Jacob said, putting Rook out of his misery. 'About the same percentage as humans, I assume. They're just even more ignored.'

'Does Carolina know that you two aren't human?'

'No, and she's too polite to ask why we appear strange. Most people are. I have her watch Michael because I worry about him being alone. He's not a danger to anyone, but he doesn't have as much company as he should. Carolina is sweet. He loves her being around. Probably prefers it to spending time with me,' Jacob said, a thin smile breaking through his stern features.

'How come you have a human look after Michael? Could you get—'

'One of my own kind? No one wanted the job.'

Rook sensed there was more to that story than Jacob wanted to tell. But the drunk ghoul sitting at the bar interrupted, slurring, 'Why did you have to bring one of those here, Jacob?'

When Jacob didn't acknowledge his comment, the ghoul harangued, 'What, too high and mighty to even talk to me? Don't want to look bad in front of the human?'

Rook had dealt with enough drunks in his time as an actual police officer to know that he wasn't any good at it. But since Jacob didn't seem interested in stepping in, Rook stepped up.

'Can I help you?' he said.

'Yeah,' the ghoul said, 'you could stop smelling of shit and fear.'

'Excuse me?' Rook said, baring his teeth in a failed attempt at a grin.

'You. Fucking. Stink. Do you have any idea how hard it is to be a ghoul in this city? My nose can smell blood from a mile away. Better than a shark in water. And I live in London, near humans like you. No wonder I drink.'

'You drink because you're an alcoholic, Ryan,' Jacob said. 'Now be quiet. I didn't come here to talk to you.'

The ghoul was about to speak, but Jacob put his bottle down with such force that it banged on the wooden table and beer splashed out of the top, causing Ryan to turn around so fast he had to grab the table to stop himself from falling out of his chair.

Rook was about to smile when he noticed the vampire with the scar still looking at him. This time, Rook held his stare. The vampire opened his mouth as wide as it would go, showing off the rows of pointed teeth going all the way to the back of his mouth.

'Nicole mentioned how powerful a ghoul's sense of smell is. But is it really that hard for them, being in a city like this?' Rook asked Jacob, turning away from the vampire.

'Most adapt. They've had to. We all have. We have to hide our abilities or humans will realise we are different. And if you do, our extinction will be inevitable. After all, your species rarely allows the dangerous and the different to live in peace.'

Rook looked at the ghoul sitting by the bar. He noticed that, instead of bar snacks, the plate next to Ryan held two weighty bones, the type you might give to a dog. Ryan picked one up, gave it a sniff, put it in his mouth, and bit down until it crunched. He then took it out of his mouth. The ghoul had bitten through a bone like it was an apple. Rook tried to suppress a shudder at the inhumanity of the act, made more unnerving having come from a creature so like a human. While Rook didn't want to agree with Jacob's assessment of humanity's likely reaction to the existence of the other species, right now he couldn't bring himself to argue the point.

They spent the rest of the evening in stilted conversation as Rook had a pint or two more than he should have. The bar filled up around them with more huge trolls, tall and slim ghouls with grey faces, the occasional orc, and a few vampires who would pass as human if you didn't look at their teeth or their long fingers. Not one person didn't look at Rook and whisper something to whoever they were with.

A few too many drinks more and Rook was following the sure-footed Jacob back up the stairs out of the pub. 'Why'd you bring me here, Jacob? It wasn't to make conversation, and you could have gotten that information from James by yourself. He didn't want to talk to me.'

'In your job, you're going to have to question people and I can't always be there. Now they are more likely to talk to you.'

'How so?'

'Because if they don't talk to you, they know I will talk to them.'

CHAPTER EIGHT

Rook left Jacob and found his own way to the Tube station. The bar had been dim and quiet, but outside he had to protect his eyes from the harsh streetlights as he fought against the sharp wind cutting into his alcoholic haze. His route took him through one of the many scraps of green space dotted around London. Lights lined the only path across, leaving the rest in darkness.

The shouts and other drunken noises from the streets around the park pierced the calm, the sound obscene and clanging compared to the murmurings of James's pub. Despite the dirty looks and the general unease everyone had had around Jacob, Rook had enjoyed drinking there. It was quiet and he hadn't had to queue to get another beer. Which was everything he looked for in a pub. It almost beat drinking alone.

In terms of actual distance, the brightly-lit streets weren't far away. But the pitch-black of the surrounding park made them seem like a distant land. Rook felt like a lone traveller stumbling through an unknown land. Exposed and alone.

A scream lacerated the night, jerking Rook out of his booze-induced haze. But the scream was soon followed by laughter. It was just another sound of alcohol-fuelled revelry. Chuckling, he fished one of his last cigarettes out of his pocket, smoothed it out with unsteady fingers, and after a few shaky attempts got it lit.

Rook was focussing on his first drag when his head hit the pavement. Something had landed on him from above with force. The impact jammed the cigarette into his mouth, filling it with the raw taste of tobacco and ash.

His attacker had their knee across Rook's back, one hand pushing his head into the rough concrete path, the other tugging on his shirt collar. Rook only had a split second to wonder why they were exposing his neck before teeth were tearing at his skin.

Rook's arms flailed. Although not a good fighter, he had long limbs and a vicious streak. Thrusting himself upwards, he swung a hard elbow at his attacker's head. A crack told Rook he'd found his mark, and the weight on his back vanished. Shouting something unintelligible, Rook sprang to face his attacker. But he was screaming into an empty park.

Spitting the remains of his cigarette out of his mouth, his eyes probed every corner of the park. But there was nothing to see but darkness, the only sound his harsh laboured panting.

Rook wiped the sudden sweat that had appeared on his face and waited for his heart rate to decrease. He tried to focus on any details that might prove useful later. The attacker had been silent, moved with extreme speed, and had jumped on Rook from the top of a streetlamp, where they had hidden in the darkness. They were also light enough that Rook could lift himself off the pavement with them on his back. *Jesus,* Rook realised as he dabbed the bleeding wound on the back of his neck, *I've been bitten by a bloody vampire.*

CHAPTER NINE

'You aren't going to turn into a vampire,' Nicole said, sniggering into her oversized mug of morning coffee. 'I've told you, there's nothing magical about the other species. Vampires don't turn you into vampires, they can't fly, they can't turn into bats, and they don't glisten or whatever nonsense that *Twilight* movie had them do. They can give you one hell of a bite, and whoever did it could have ripped out your jugular if they'd wanted. But you won't develop a need to drink human blood.'

'And it's not why I feel so vile this morning?' Rook said, picking at the bandage that covered his bite.

'More likely to be the drinking and the kebab,' Nicole said, rolling her chair away from her desk so she could get a better look at her hungover colleague.

'That kebab was pretty good, to be fair. Saw me through my wait at the hospital,' Rook said. He could still taste the garlic sauce in the back of his throat.

Nicole blinked. 'You got yourself a snack *and then* you went to accident and emergency?'

'Sure, there's always a wait at the hospital, and I was hungry.'

'Weren't you bleeding? What did the guy serving you say?'

'Didn't bat an eyelid.' Rook scratched the bandage again. 'Pretty sure he's seen worse.'

'Did anyone at the hospital say anything? About the bite?' A more serious tone slipped into her voice and a furrow appeared between her eyebrows.

'Not much, just another night in South London. They figured I'd gotten into a drunken fight with a psycho and gave me some jabs and a bandage. Then sent me on my way.'

'Could you tell who attacked you?'

'I was getting some pretty dirty looks from a vampire in the bar. So, he's my first suspect. But other than that, no. To be honest, I'm not sure I've got enough time to investigate it. Isn't that bizarre? Three days ago, I was sitting at home wondering what was going to happen with my career. Now, being bitten by a vampire isn't in my top two priorities.' He looked up at the ceiling, his arms outstretched, as if hoping guidance would fall from above

'I know,' Nicole said. 'This becomes normal fast in this job. One day I was working out the logistics of installing flood barriers in Cumbria. The next I was sourcing equipment for a secret health centre for the other species. I prefer this.'

'You do?'

'Of course. We're helping people here, Rook, people who no one else cares about. Yes, we do it in secret, in a flat in Balham instead of an office in Whitehall. But it's good to be helping, isn't it?' She gave a perky smile that would have been irritating on a less sincere face. Even in his hungover state, Rook couldn't find her ultra-cheery disposition irritating.

'Maybe,' Rook said. He looked around the makeshift office. It wasn't much, with its old kettle, the sad smell of disinfectant, and a jumble of noises coming from the street. But Rook still had to agree, he was enjoying it. Yes, he missed the technical support he would have received when still on the force; the crime lab and the workforce. But he wouldn't miss the red tape, the bureaucracy, or the helpless feeling when there wasn't the will or the resources to investigate a crime. Or the way his intestines would twist when a hardened criminal went free while some dumb kid was sent down because life had given up on them a long time ago. Even being bitten by a vampire was a refreshing ⁻e in its own way.

'You think the attack on you is related to Caleb's murder?' Nicole said.

'It could be. But my money is on some drunk prick who thought it would be fun to give the new copper a bite mark.'

Nicole laughed. It sounded out of place as it bounced around the flat-cum-office.

Rook's phone buzzed, and he swore. He couldn't face another message from his father. He still hadn't figured out what to tell him about his new role. Despite the distance that had built up in their relationship, Rook didn't enjoy lying to him. But he didn't know what to say that would dull the disappointment his father felt about Rook's career.

Rook took his phone out of his pocket as if it were a venomous snake in a bad mood. It wasn't his father, after all. It was his brother, Will, who was also telling him to get in touch. People must be worried if Will was getting in touch, so he sent out a blanket WhatsApp saying all was well and he'd be in contact soon. A message he hoped would hold them off from meeting for a few more days at least. A week if he was lucky.

'I've got something to help you with your investigation,' Nicole said.

'What's that?'

'CCTV footage of both entrances to Caleb's street for the twenty-four hours prior to and after his murder.'

'Well, that is helpful. Send it over.'

She did, and Rook was quick to open the file, praying it would reveal someone they knew wandering down the street with a knife and coming out a few minutes later covered in blood. While people may love a mystery, the police do not, and Rook was no different.

The video showed Caleb staggering down the street at 11:50, his arm wrapped around a girl, with another guy stumbling nearby. Judging by the pictures from Caleb's flat, the girl was Abby and the guy Nathan.

Half an hour later, Nathan walked back down the street. Followed by Abby at 1:55 a.m. While it was hard to be sure, given the poor quality of the CCTV, neither of them appeared to be covered in blood. At 3:30, Rebecca came down the street, walking with the misplaced confidence of the high or drunk. No one else came in or out.

'Hmm,' Rook said, stroking his chin.

'See anything?' Nicole asked, trying to hide the eagerness in her voice.

'Well, it confirms what James said last night. And gives a good timeline and a window of opportunity. It gives me a headache, though.'

'A headache?'

'Both sides of this street are terrace housing with no access from the front of the street to the gardens behind. Meaning that the houses act as enormous walls. No one else other than the people we know of came in or out of the street after Abby left until Rebecca arrived. They could have entered through the back door, but the key was still in the lock.'

'So?' Nicole said, leaning forwards, hands clasped around her coffee.

'Caleb left the pub with Abby and Nathan. But we know he was alive after they left his house because he called Rebecca later. She then went to Caleb's, finding him gutted. So, she called Jacob. I'll see what they say first; they don't look like good suspects from this.'

'Then what about Rebecca?' Nicole asked.

'It's possible,' Rook said, scrunching up his face. 'But why call Jacob after the crime? Why not leave? And Jacob didn't mention her being covered in blood.'

Rook got up and updated the timeline on his crime boards under Nicole's watchful eye.

'Are you going to tell Jacob about what happened?' she asked, her voice quiet.

'Happened?' Rook said.

'Your bite?' She pointed to her neck.

'Sure, why wouldn't I?'

'Of course you will.' She started typing at her keyboard. Somewhere outside, a mournful sound of a distant siren wailed.

'Nicole,' Rook said, 'what aren't you telling me?'

'What do you think happens after you've arrested one of the other species?' she said, shifting in her chair like it was lined with pins.

'I imagine there will be some sort of trial?' Rook said.

'How do you think that would work? Do you think we'll take an orc to the Royal Courts and put them in front of a judge and jury?'

'Okay,' Rook conceded, holding up his hands. 'Perhaps not a proper trial. But something low-level. You must be able to rustle up some type of judge-like figure or something?'

'Sometimes higher-ups like Rowena make a final decision in difficult cases, that's true. But then what do you think happens?' Nicole said.

'Depends on the crime, I guess. A fine? Prison?'

'Sometimes a fine is appropriate, paid to the victims. Sometimes we ask people to leave cities or areas. A type of exile, if you will. But that isn't enough in all cases, and we can't send them to prison. Prisons are too official; they would be too hard to staff and maintain. And even a residential house refitted to be escape-proof could attract a level of scrutiny we can't allow and a level of staffing we can't afford. And they couldn't go to a human prison – that would put one of the other species in close proximity with too many humans.'

'Okay, I see what you mean. What do you have instead of prisons?'

'We have Jacob,' she said, her mouth down-turned in an apologetic frown.

'Jacob?'

'If someone commits crimes, like murder' – she took a deep breath – 'they're executed. And Jacob is the executioner.'

'You're saying my partner kills people?' Rook's body felt like it had just been heated by twenty degrees in twenty seconds. He tried to quell his anger but knew it was a losing battle.

'I know it's not what you want to hear—'

'Not what I want to hear?' Rook interrupted. 'You're telling me that when I arrest someone, Jacob kills them. Without a proper trial. What happens if I get it wrong, Nicole? And when were you planning to tell me? After I'd arrested someone? When Jacob was ready to swing the axe?'

'I'd have told you, I promise. I only wanted you to bed in first. You won't stop working here, will you? What you do is important.'

Rook looked down at his desk where the pictures taken from Caleb's were spread out. The photo looking up at him now was the only one he'd taken that hadn't been of Caleb and his friends. It was of Caleb with a beaming older couple whom Rook assumed were his parents. It had been an awkward picture of the mother, whose mouth was slightly agape like she was in the middle of speaking.

The father, however, was looking straight at the camera, a proud smile beneath brown soulful eyes and thick black eyebrows. It was strange to think that vampires were born just like humans, and not made by being bitten. But here they were, Caleb's family immortalised in pictures.

'I'm sorry, Rook,' Nicole said, her voice almost lost in an office that had lapsed into a fragile silence. 'I should have told you earlier.'

'Yes, you should have. But then I might not have taken the job, and then you would have no one to solve Caleb's murder. So you did what you must, not what you are proud of,' Rook whispered, still gazing at the picture of Caleb's parents. Parents who would now know of their son's brutal murder. At least Rook wouldn't have to break the news himself. He had done that before, had felt the pain of parents' cries echo in his skull, had seen them in court when the killer had been found. And he'd taken their calls when the case had gone cold, the killer not likely to be found. They would all come to him with desperate faces and cracked voices. Rook knew what it was like to lose a loved one and be denied closure. It was a pain you carried forever, making every step harder and every breath more laboured.

'I'll find this killer,' he said and went back to work.

CHAPTER TEN

R ook stood on an empty side street that stank of overflowing bins and discarded cigarettes, waiting for Jacob. It was one of those strange London alleys that were only metres from a busy high street (Fleet Street, in this case), yet were almost completely unused. Even the noise of nearby workers and tourists was muted. The street was lined by the backsides of buildings, dirty backdoors, and colourful but crude graffiti. London was full of streets like this. Streets that no longer served a purpose, forgotten and ignored by the growing and bustling city that surrounded them.

Rook had been fretting for twenty minutes and Jacob had still not arrived. The office had felt uncomfortable after Nicole's revelation, and Rook had needed some fresh air that he could corrupt with cigarette smoke.

Jacob emerged from Fleet Street with the collar of his sheepskin-lined jacket up, as if to shield his face from prying eyes. His purposeful stride carried him through the melted frost that covered the cracked pavement. Rook tried to say what he'd been thinking about ever since he'd left the office, but the words stuck in his throat like barbed wire.

'So,' Rook started, deciding this wasn't the place to discuss Jacob's duties as executioner, 'there's an other species health centre on this street?'

'There is,' Jacob said, walking up to a white door streaked with dirt and pressing a buzzer slick with dirty fingerprints. 'The other species cannot go to hospitals. For orcs, this is not a problem. We heal from most illnesses and injuries with ease. But for others, any illness that cannot be cured with over-the-counter medicines could prove dangerous. We have our own healers, of course, who understand the basics, but we can't set up hospitals or provide training. That requires too much infrastructure. We couldn't even get prescription drugs unless someone managed to steal them. Now Nicole has set this up with Marlowe. He trained a few nurses so they could handle straightforward cases and we have access to proper medicines.'

'What happens if it isn't a straightforward case?' Rook said.

'They get referred to Marlowe.'

'I thought he was a psychiatrist?'

Jacob shook his head. 'I don't think so. I understand he's a virologist. But he's the best we've got.'

Great, Rook thought, *a real psychiatrist didn't even write my fake psychiatrist's report.*

'And other species' physiologies are close enough to humans that he can help?' Rook said.

'It appears so.' Jacob pressed the doorbell again with more force.

Something clicked behind the door, and it opened. They stepped into a room filled with cheap wooden chairs and the smell of sickness peculiar to hospitals and health centres. At one time, the yellow of the walls was probably vibrant and bright, but now it was the wilted colour of dying daffodils.

A gaunt ghoul in an oversized black puffer jacket and blue beanie took one look at Rook and Jacob and shuffled out through a door at the back of the room, passing an orc Rook recognised as Rebecca. She was sitting behind a computer so old it hummed as it worked, a look of deep boredom and studied disinterest across her pretty face.

She was, without doubt, an orc, but her green tinge was fainter than Jacob's, her thick black hair a deliberate mess. Her thin body was all angles in a retro T-shirt advertising some band he didn't recognise and jeans that clung to wiry legs. She sat in an uncomfortable-looking office chair, a smile that was ever-so-close to being a snarl cut across her face.

'I've told you all I know, Jacob,' she said as they walked towards her.

'Hello. Rebecca Ramsey, isn't it?' Rook said, ignoring her comment and taking out his notebook. 'I'm Detective Rook. It's nice to meet you.'

'It won't be nice for you if I don't want it to be,' she said. Her eyes were the colour of the olives you got at fancy restaurants. Right now they were burning into Rook, and every angle of her body pointed at him as if in challenge.

'Okay,' he said. 'We're here to talk about Caleb.'

'I've told Jacob all I know,' Rebecca said, dismissively waving a hand at Jacob.

'I'm sorry,' Rook said. 'It's a lot to ask, but we've got to retrace Caleb's steps as best we can. And you're the last person he spoke to. So, I need to go over everything again. It's an important part of our process and will help us find his killer.'

'Fine. If it will get you two out of here.'

'Thank you,' Rook said. 'So why did you go over at half three that morning?'

'Caleb texted me and I was the right sort of drunk to make a mistake. When I got there, he was on the floor,' Rebecca said, her voice beginning to shake as she relived the memory.

'I am sorry you saw that, Rebecca. I'm surprised you're back at work today. Couldn't someone have covered?'

'They could. Yesterday they did. Now I'm back.'

'Not everyone would rock up to work so soon after seeing that.'

'How old do you think I am?' she said, wiping away a tear that had dared appear in the corner of her eye.

Rook gave a short laugh and ran his fingers through his hair. 'I'm not playing that game. And I'm not sure how it's relevant.'

'Go on, guess.'

Rook remembered something about orcs ageing at a slower rate but didn't think this was the time to test out his knowledge. Instead, he coughed and said, 'Okay, early twenties?'

'I'm forty-five. And I could live another 120 years. We orcs need to develop thick skin if we're going to live that long. We will have outlived a lot of vampires by the time we die. I liked Caleb and seeing him like that will haunt me. And today will not be a good day. But I'm older and less fragile than you think. And to be honest, sitting in my flat would be more depressing.'

'You're forty-five?' Rook asked.

'That's the information you're focussing on, Detective?' she said, arching her eyebrows.

'I've had to take in a lot over the past couple of days. It's getting hard to separate out all the weird.' He looked at Jacob. 'How old are you?'

'Seventy,' Jacob said.

Rook took a long look at Jacob. He was bald and the lines around his craggy face suggested it had endured more of life than it had enjoyed, but Rook wouldn't have placed him much over forty. 'I won't lie, you look good for it, Jacob,' he said, turning back to Rebecca. 'What had Caleb been doing before he messaged you?'

'He'd been at James's. Guess he hadn't had as much fun as he'd have liked, or he wouldn't have called me.'

'Do you have any idea who could have done this? Or why?'

'Couldn't say.'

'What about the watch?'

'What watch?' she said, her voice flat but Rook noticed the clenching of her jaw.

'We found a very expensive watch in Caleb's house. Don't suppose you could tell me how he ended up with such a fancy watch? Didn't seem to fit in with the rest of his stuff.'

'Maybe it was a gift,' she said, her tone daring Rook to call her a liar.

'You can't give us any more information than this?' Rook said, raising his eyebrows in exasperation at Rebecca's refusal to be more forthcoming.

Rebecca looked up; set her jaw. 'Guess I can't.'

'Rebecca,' Jacob said, in a tone that Rook would have called reassuring, if it weren't coming from the mouth of a killer, 'why did you call me if you didn't want anyone punished for this?'

'Who says I don't want anyone punished?' she said, looking directly at Jacob for the first time.

'Is there anything you can tell us? No jilted lovers in his past? No one who had any issues with him?' Rook asked, his arms outstretched, notebook in one hand, pen in the other, as if begging Rebecca to give him something, anything, he could use.

'Not much more to say. I sometimes slept with him. I went over that night to have sex. Found him... found him like that. Called Jacob.'

'And you can't think of a single person who may have wanted to hurt Caleb?' Rook said.

'No one I know.' She settled herself back into the slouched position she'd been in when Rook and Jacob had entered the health centre.

'Well, if you think of anything and decide to be helpful, let me know,' Rook said, signalling the end of the interview to Jacob.

Outside, their feet hit the pavement, the smell of the bins crept into their noses, and the cold air blew through their bodies.

'That was not a fruitful conversation,' Jacob said, pulling his hood over his head.

'We learnt something,' Rook said, lighting up a cigarette he knew he'd regret.

'What?'

'Rebecca knew about the watch. And maybe had an idea about who would want to hurt Caleb. But she didn't want to tell us.'

'Any idea why?'

Rook looked at Jacob's heavy brow and wondered how many people he had executed. 'I couldn't say.'

CHAPTER ELEVEN

The drive to Marlowe's took Rook and Jacob out of London's sprawling mass and past the silent commuter towns stuck in its orbit. The air was colder outside of the city and the fields they passed were gripped by frost.

Nicole had called shortly after their interview with Rebecca to let them know Marlowe had examined the body, and they'd gone straight away. Jacob had insisted on driving, which meant taking the piss-yellow tin can with wheels he called a car. It was a vehicle designed for a time when being over six-foot was rare. And Rook was struggling to fold his body in a way that was comfortable, or at least not outright torturous.

'Why are people so afraid of you, Jacob?' Rook said, scratching the bandage that covered the vampire bite.

'I didn't know they were.' Jacob glanced across at him.

'Okay.' The sinews in Rook's shoulders tensed. 'Why didn't Rebecca want to talk to you?'

'I couldn't say.'

'Well, I can take a guess. It's because you're the friendly neighbourhood executioner.'

'Oh, that,' Jacob said, as if Rook were talking about the weather or some other triviality.

'Yeah "that,"' Rook said, his teeth grinding.

'It's necessary to keep the other species secret and safe.'

'How does executing people keep you all secret and safe?'

'I see you've not been told everything.'

'Then why don't you fill me in?' Rook said, doing his best not to ball his fists in frustration.

'It's not only murderers or rapists.'

'Who else makes the list?'

'Anyone who risks exposing our existence to humans.'

'So, for the sake of argument' – Rook fidgeted, attempting to make himself comfortable in a car seat that was trying to dislocate every bone in his back – 'say a vampire attacked a human. Gave them a bite. What would you do?'

'I'd execute them.'

'Is that right?' Rook said, his voice working hard to give nothing away.

'Of course. If a vampire had shown himself willing to reveal himself to a human and injure them, then I could not let that pass.'

'Good to know, I guess. What about Caleb?'

'What about Caleb?'

'Say you found out he'd done the Purcell job. What would you do?'

Jacob sucked in his lips, making a rough smacking sound. 'If I found out, I would try to talk to him first. Get him to leave London. But if I got an order from higher up, then I would do what was asked.'

'Higher up?'

'Rowena or Steele, both.'

Jacob's car now felt like a coffin to Rook, and every scrap of his skin itched. 'So, I find criminals and you kill them?'

Jacob nodded.

'What if I don't want them killed?'

'Then don't find them.'

'I don't get it,' Rook said. 'Would it be that bad if humans did know about you all? Sure, it would be weird for a while, but people would get over it. We'd co-exist. Soon enough there would be orcs all over TikTok or whatever.'

'At first that might be true. But then you would turn on us. Then we'd go the way of the Neanderthals.' Jacob kept his eyes on the road and his voice unhurried.

'I think that's a bit dramatic,' Rook retorted.

'How many genocides are happening right now? And that's humans killing humans. How do you think people will feel when they realise a troll could rip off the arms of a rugby player? That a ghoul's bite can crush bone? That a vampire could hunt them in the dark, capable of killing them with one bite to the throat? People will be afraid. They may not say at first, but someone will whip them up. Then, when that happens, our end is certain. It's better to cling on to life in the shadows than die in the light.'

Rook wondered how many genocides were ongoing in the world at that moment. Once he got to three, he conceded that Jacob may have a point.

'Is that why you had to get Carolina to babysit Michael? None of the other species wanted to help their resident executioner?'

'I assume so. People may know that what I do is necessary. Doesn't mean they like that I exist.'

Rook went back to looking out the window. They had gone off the motorway now and were passing field after field, each empty and drained of life by winter's grip. Soon, a vast vineyard, full of bare and twisted vines, stretched out beneath them. 'That's Marlowe's office,' Jacob said, nodding towards the buildings. The "office" was, in fact, three compact, grey circular buildings laid out in a triangle. It looked like a spaceship had landed in the English countryside.

The three buildings puzzled Rook. They were clearly purpose-built, but he couldn't guess what that purpose was. All were made from the same concrete. The foremost, as Jacob drove towards it on the dirt road, was the main office. Marble steps led up to big glass double doors that showed the waiting area within. As Rook got out of the car, he noticed that the other two buildings appeared to have no external entrances. The only way into them was through narrow corridors that came off the main building.

The doors to the main building opened once they got to the top of the stairs. They entered to see Carver sitting behind a computer, his feet resting lazily on the desk, his face buried in his phone. Cold winter's light streamed through the doors, bleaching Carver's pale complexion and highlighting his blue eyes.

'Hello, Detective,' Carver said, his mouth contorted in a sneer. 'The doctor told me you'd be coming round. Said I should welcome you. So, welcome.' He gave a mocking wave.

'Is he ready for us?' Rook said.

'He's busy; you'll have to wait.' Carver flicked his hand towards two plush leather sofas behind them.

Rook and Jacob took their seats and waited in silence. Rook fiddled with his phone while Jacob's fingers drummed a heavy tune on the sofa's thick armrest.

A few minutes of uncomfortable silence later, Carver told Rook he could go in.

'If you're going to make someone wait for no reason, you should at least pretend to get a call,' Rook said as he stood up and put his phone back in his pocket.

'What's that?' Carver said, without looking up from his phone.

'He didn't even call to tell me to come in. You were making me wait to show you can. You could have at least pretended to get a message.'

'Guess I *could* have,' Carver said, with a crooked smile.

They entered Marlowe's office to find him sitting behind an unnecessarily big, dark wooden desk like a toad in a pond, silhouetted by the light coming from the two rectangular windows behind him. On either side of the windows were two wooden doors – presumably to the buildings Rook had seen from the outside. A brass sign hung on each door, one reading *Lab One*, and the other *Lab Two*.

'Hello, Rook, Jacob,' Marlowe said, standing up. 'I understand you want to see this dead vampire that Carver brought to me. Although, I can't see why.'

'We were hoping you could tell us something interesting about how he died,' Rook said.

'Other than being repeatedly stabbed?'

'A little more than that would be useful, yes.'

'Well, I'm about as much a pathologist as I am a psychiatrist.' He winked at Rook. 'But I can tell you what I've found. It's in Lab Two.'

After they'd walked through a narrow corridor, Marlowe led Rook and Jacob into a sparse lab lit by strip lighting. A shiny metal counter ran down one wall, on which a steel cabinet sat, presumably holding whatever tools Marlow required. Caleb's dismembered body lay on the metal table like a grotesque jigsaw. Despite the otherwise clean environment, the smell of the corpse had settled in the air.

'Was that necessary?' Rook said.

Marlowe blinked at Rook in reply.

'To have Carver cut him up like that?' Rook said. 'You couldn't have put him in a body bag like a normal corpse?'

'You bring body bags out of a house, people will notice. And we can't have people noticing. That's our number-one rule, isn't it, Jacob?' Marlowe said with a broad, jovial smile. Jacob didn't respond.

Rook chewed on his inner cheek. 'His parents will see him like that.'

'No, they won't,' Marlowe said. 'We don't transfer bodies of vampires across the country. Far too high of a risk. We burn the body and send the ashes to the parents.'

'Jesus,' Rook said, exhaling. He wouldn't like to tell a parent their child's body was going to be burnt before they could say goodbye.

'It was only ten minutes ago I realised I'd got the legs the wrong way around. That would have been embarrassing,' Marlowe said as he moved closer to the body.

'You going to tell me what you've found, or are we going to stand around making bad jokes?' Rook clenched his fists and failed to hide the edge in his voice.

'The jokes would be more fun.' Marlowe gave a theatrical sigh and a wink as he stood above the vampire's mutilated corpse. 'But if you want to get down to business,

I will. Haven't found a lot, I'm afraid. He was stabbed around twenty times, but the attack was so frenzied it is difficult to be precise. The knife was not unique; a straightforward blade that you could find in any good kitchen store. That it was a knife is interesting, I suppose.'

'How so?' Rook rested himself against the wall, trying to keep as much space between himself and the corpse as possible.

Jacob, who was standing with one hand on the metal counter that ran down the side of the room, responded, 'A troll could crush a vampire's head as easily as you could squeeze a peeled orange. An orc or even a ghoul could overpower one too. Cornering a vampire is the hard part, but once you've got them in a confined space, they're easy to kill. For a troll or an orc at least.'

'Speaking from experience, I'm sure. So, you think it was a vampire because they brought a knife?' Rook asked.

'Or a human,' Jacob said.

'It's thin.' Rook pursed his lips as he weighed the evidence in his mind. 'Maybe it makes a troll less likely, but, even then, they might have preferred to use a knife. It takes either a phenomenal rage or a serious psychopath to beat someone to death with your hands. Even if you can. What else can you tell me?'

'It's hard to be sure,' Marlow said, 'given the number of wounds, but it looks like the first cut was fatal. A deep slash across the neck. The rest were frenzied but less likely to be fatal.'

'Interesting. You check his blood?'

'Alcohol, marijuana.' Marlowe shrugged.

'Not unexpected,' Rook said, looking down at the body. 'Of all the other species, vampires are the most disappointing.'

'How so?' Marlowe said.

'I hadn't thought much about trolls, orcs, or ghouls. But vampires? Vampires are meant to be so damn impressive.'

'Did you expect them to be like the vampires on *Twilight* or *Buffy*? Or maybe you're a Lugosi fan?' Marlowe said with a teasing giggle.

'Very funny. I just figured they'd be more... something... somehow.'

Marlowe looked at Rook with frog-like eyes and shook his head in apparent disappointment.

'There's no magic, Rook. But that doesn't mean they aren't impressive. Ever seen a vampire move as fast as they can? They make a racehorse look like me after a few glasses of finely aged red wine. I don't know how they do that. Their bones are lighter than ours, but that doesn't account for everything. Trolls make Neanderthals look like schoolgirls. Some of them could throw an NFL player through a wall without breaking a sweat. Ghouls can smell blood better than a shark and have a bite as strong as a crocodile. And orcs... You ever shown him how well you heal, Jacob?'

'It's not a party trick,' Jacob said. The words came out like a warning growl.

'Oh, didn't know it was such a sore point.' Marlowe flashed a conspiratorial smile at Rook, a smile Rook did not return and doubted that Jacob appreciated. 'Don't know why. It's impressive. Orcs regenerate. They can't survive everything, and it isn't painless. But they don't get sick as we do, and they can heal from wounds that would have you fighting for your life in A&E.'

'Glad we impress you,' Jacob said, his jaw clenched.

'I know they seem sad,' Marlowe said, waving a hand in Jacob's direction, uncaring of the orc's anger. 'Pressed into the tiny corner of our world like forgotten refugees. But that's only because there are so many of us and so few of them. We didn't out-think the other species. Or out-fight them. We just outbred them.'

CHAPTER TWELVE

They left Caleb's corpse with Marlowe and drove back into the city, the atmosphere in the car as cold as the air outside. The only sounds were the roar of other car engines and the occasional blaring horn.

They pressed on through the mess of London's traffic until they made it to Leather Lane, where a vampire called Nathan worked in a magic shop. Leather Lane was home to a permanent outdoor market, where stalls selling cheap clothes and street food huddled next to each other. The smell of the food filling the cold air made Rook's stomach growl, doing nothing to improve his mood.

'Any info on Nathan?' Rook said as they pushed through the chattering crowds.

'Nothing useful. He may have been involved in some petty crimes in the past, but nothing that has merited my attention,' Jacob said, his face shadowed by his hood.

'No history between him and Caleb?'

'No. But I've never paid Nathan much attention.'

'How many people do you actually have info on?'

'Only those I need to kill.'

'Fair enough,' Rook said under his breath.

Rook spotted Nathan without Jacob pointing him out. He was a scrawny vampire, standing outside a beaten-down magic shop, dressed in a faux-punk shirt and skinny jeans and sucking on the fag end of a cigarette. His skin was even paler than the other vampires Rook had seen, a look that wasn't helped by his peroxide-blond hair. His brown eyes looked like dirty puddles in a snow-covered field.

'Hello, Nathan,' Jacob said as they got closer. 'I assume you realised we'd want to talk to you.'

Nathan swore when he saw them approach, taking a last long drag on his cigarette, throwing it to the ground, and stamping on it.

'Figured I'd get a visit from the police and whatever the hell you are, Jacob,' he said, flicking away the discarded cigarette end with his shoe.

'Hello, Nathan,' Rook said, fishing the notebook out of his pocket. 'I take it you know who I am.'

'Obviously.'

'You like magic?' Rook gestured to the shop behind them. It was called 'Prestos', but the white *O* of the sign had almost disappeared. Some boxes of magic tricks clut-

tered up the window, alongside other magician parapher-
nalia. A thin layer of dust coated every item.

'I work here, that's it.'

'A vampire working in a magic shop,' Rook said as his
gaze drifted across the shop's dirty facade. 'Hard to believe
this is my life now.'

Rook realised that both Nathan and Jacob were looking
at him like he was an idiot.

'Sorry, still adjusting to all of this,' Rook said. 'You were
one of the last people to see Caleb alive. You want to take
us through what happened?'

'Not much to say,' the vampire said, taking another
cigarette out of its packet, holding it in his long vampire's
fingers, and lighting it up with a cheap yellow lighter.

'I suggest you do better than that, Nathan,' Jacob said.

'Fine,' Nathan said. 'A few of us were drinking at
James's. Went back to Caleb's with him and Abby. Not
long after, I left and went back to mine.'

'Abby was the last to see him alive?' Rook said.

'I guess so. She wouldn't have done anything to him,
though.'

'Why do you say that?'

Nathan's mouth curled into a tight grimace. 'They were
together.'

'As in boyfriend and girlfriend?'

'Something like that, I guess.' Nathan expelled a thick glob of phlegm, landing it a couple of inches from Rook's shoe. He then looked up at Rook, a leer stuck on his face.

'Why did you leave?' Rook held his anger in check. He wanted Nathan to talk – he didn't care if he was a prick. He also noticed Jacob moving closer to Nathan as the interview went on.

'It was late. I wanted to go home.'

'Did Abby leave with you?' Rook knew the answer, of course, but wanted to know if Nathan would tell him the truth.

Nathan shook his head but didn't elaborate.

'And where is your place?' Rook said.

'A flat in Balham, about fifteen mins away.'

'A flat all to yourself?' Jacob said, sniffing.

'Yeah,' Nathan said, his shoulders giving a jerky shrug.

'Did Caleb appear worried about anything to you?' Rook said.

'He appeared drunk.'

'But you weren't aware of any reason for him to be afraid for his life?'

'He was drunk with Abby. Why would he be afraid?' Nathan took a big drag on his cigarette and blew the smoke into Rook's face. 'Any more questions? Or can I get back to the shop?'

'I'm sorry' – Rook held Nathan's gaze while Jacob moved between the vampire and the door to the shop – 'but I'd like to ask you a few more questions.'

'Don't care,' Nathan said, turning to go back into the shop. But Jacob's hand clasped around his shoulder before he'd taken his first step. Nathan's cigarette fell from his hands and his jaw clenched with the failed effort of suppressing a yelp.

'I'm afraid break's not over, Nathan,' Jacob said, spinning the vampire around to look at Rook. The arrogant bravado flowed out of Nathan under Jacob's grip like blood from a wound.

'How come you went back to Caleb's?' Rook stepped within a couple of inches of Nathan's face, filling up the vampire's view so he couldn't look away. He wasn't above admitting that the flash of fear across the vampire's face was some payback for the phlegm at his feet and the smoke blown in his face.

'Guess I was drunk too. Thought it might be fun.'

'Did you not feel awkward?'

'Why?'

'Well, you knew they were likely going back to have sex. Didn't you feel like a bit of a tag-along?'

'Like I said, I was drunk.' Each word came out of his mouth like a rotting tooth being yanked out.

'What about the burglaries?' Jacob said as he crushed Nathan's shoulder with his grip.

'I don't know about any burglaries.' He winced.

'Really?' Rook said. 'You didn't know about the watches Caleb stole? Or what happened to those jewellers?'

'I know nothing about it, okay?' His voice trembled with desperation. Whether he was desperate to get away from Jacob or to avoid answering questions, Rook couldn't tell.

'Now, Nathan.' Jacob said, his mouth inches Nathan's ear. 'I will be upset if you lie to me.'

The vampire looked away from Jacob, biting his lip so hard Rook thought he may draw blood. 'He sometimes got work from Sol. That's how he'd got that place to himself. Sol found it for him.'

'Sol?' Rook said.

'A troll.' Jacob released Nathan from his grip. 'He runs the parts of our world you would find illegal.'

'Like a troll Mafia?'

Jacob nodded.

'Well, I guess we will have to speak to him,' Rook said, scrawling in his notebook.

'Good for you,' Nathan said, grimacing as he massaged where Jacob had gripped him. 'Now, can I go? And can you try not mentioning my name when you speak to Sol? I like my limbs attached.'

CHAPTER THIRTEEN

The second interview on Rook's list was with Abby, who lived in a block of flats near Elephant & Castle Tube station. The grubby buildings loomed over the surrounding area like the memory of your first break-up. He guessed they'd been built in the 1960s and was sure it would have terrified the architect to learn they were still standing sixty years later. There must have been a couple of hundred people living in those flats, yet he only saw one or two as he and Jacob made their way up the stairs.

Rook had swallowed a sandwich for a late lunch on the way over, but he was still on edge. He'd been asking questions, but all he had to show for it was more questions and few answers. He was hoping that by following the process, filling in the gaps on Caleb's last night, and checking alibis, something would come up. Which brought them to Abby, the last to see Caleb alive.

Rook expected to hear the blare of music or the shouts of an argument, but there was nothing but the sound of his and Jacob's shoes hitting the concrete floor as they walked down the white-walled corridor.

'You can make arrangements to see Sol?' Rook asked.

Jacob grunted assent.

'What about Abby? Do you know any more about her than you did Nathan?' Rook was hopeful but not optimistic.

'She works at James's pub. She serves me drinks there. Seems nice enough,' Jacob replied, his voice quiet in the empty corridor.

'You're not an inquisitive soul, are you, Jacob?' Rook asked.

Jacob made another sort of guttural sound. It might have been a laugh or his way of ending the conversation. Rook couldn't guess.

Abby's door opened to reveal a young female troll. She was as tall as Rook, with straight bright-white hair that fell to an inch below her jawline, framing the quizzical look she was giving him. Her blue eyes were so pale they were close to white. Like the other trolls Rook had seen, her skin was white as polished bone.

'Hey, who are you guys?' she said in an ethereal voice that was likely linked to the fug of weed emanating from inside the flat.

'Police,' Rook said, taking guilty pleasure from the sudden narrowing of her wide pupils. 'We need to talk to Abby.'

'She's... She's... Not in,' the girl said, her voice wavering.

Jacob cocked his head to one side. 'Is that right?'

The troll's face was suddenly electrified in panic as she neither wanted to lie nor tell the truth.

'We don't care about the weed,' Rook said, rubbing his forehead in frustration. 'In fact, the only police in London who care about weed are the ones who smoke it.'

'Okay. She might be inside,' the troll said, her bottom lip disappearing into her mouth as she waited for Rook's reaction.

'Might be inside?' Rook said. 'Are you telling me you're not sure if she's in your flat? Let us in.'

'Err, okay.' She moved to the side and let them through.

It was a poky flat, and much of its space was taken up by clothes that had been strewn around the room. It wasn't as dirty as Caleb's flat (or Rook's), but there were few spaces that weren't occupied by various tops, vests, or skirts. As they entered, a young female ghoul leapt off the sofa and bounced into a bedroom with the troll who'd answered the door, the door shutting behind them a heartbeat later.

Abby was balled up in the corner of the worn grey sofa, her slight body hidden among the cushions. She was wearing light-blue jeans and a black T-shirt that contrasted with hair dyed a faded pink. She had a soft face with rounded cheekbones that emphasised the sad brown eyes which were staring at her feet. Her long vampire fingers clutched at the sofa as if worried she would fall off.

There was nowhere obvious for Jacob and Rook to sit. So they stood between Abby and the TV. Rook felt obscene towering over this young, slightly-stoned, slightly-scared girl.

'Hi,' she said in a weak voice.

'Do you know who I am? What I do?' Rook said.

'You're police. James told me about you. You want to know about Caleb,' she said in an accent that was pure South London.

'That's right, Abby. We think you saw him alive last.'

'I guess,' she said, the glistening of tears appearing in her eyes.

'Apart from whoever killed him,' Jacob interjected without intonation.

'That's right, yeah.'

'Of course,' Rook said. 'Can you tell us what happened that night?'

Abby swallowed. 'We were getting drunk at James's. Then we went back to Caleb's.'

'We?'

'Caleb, Nathan, and me.'

'Why did you go back to Caleb's?'

'Keep drinking, maybe have a smoke,' she said with a sniff.

'Did the three of you often go back to his?'

'Sometimes.'

'How about just you and Caleb?'

'Sometimes,' Abby said, looking up at Rook with a face trembling on the edge of despair.

'Why did Nathan come with you then?' Rook asked, wishing he could leave Abby with her grief instead of persisting with his questions.

'He doesn't live too far from Caleb's. Sometimes he'd walk back with us. Must have wanted to smoke some weed.'

'Wasn't that a bit awkward?' Rook asked.

'Guess that's why he left,' she said, picking at imaginary fluff on the arm of the sofa.

'When did you leave?'

'Don't know, not long after Nathan left. Maybe around two.'

'Why did you leave?'

She didn't respond, but tears began to fall like the first raindrops of an incoming rainstorm.

'I need to know everything, Abby,' Rook persisted.

'We had a fight,' she said, in a voice so quiet he had to strain to hear it. Her shoulders hunched and her head buried in her hands, like she was trying to turn herself into a ball.

'What did you fight about?' Rook forced his voice into as soothing a tone as he could manage.

'Rebecca,' she said, her mouth curling with distaste.

'You often fight about Caleb's other relationships?' Rook asked.

'Yeah.'

'Did he have any other relationships, aside from Rebecca?'

'Don't know.'

'You understand that makes you a suspect, Abby? Him cheating on you. You being there the night he died.'

'We'd have to have been going out for him to be cheating on me. Wouldn't we?' Her face transformed into a sudden picture of rage.

'So why were you fighting?'

'Because I was sick of it. Sick of us getting drunk and fucking because I was the closest girl he half fancied. Then I wouldn't hear from him again until he wanted to drink, fuck, or get high. I bet he was texting Rebecca as soon as I was out of the door,' Abby said, her voice shaking with the memory of her anger.

'Where did you go at two in the morning?' Rook said.

'I walked back here.'

'Anyone see you?'

'Tricia and Linda were up when I came back,' she said, nodding her head towards the door her flatmates had disappeared behind.

'Your flatmates are your alibi? It must have been past three in the morning by the time you got back here from Balham.'

'I got some cigs from that twenty-four-hour off-licence on Balham High Street,' Abby said, lip trembling. The anger caused by remembering Caleb and Rebecca left her body, leaving only grief.

'I know the one,' Rook said, taking out his notebook. What she'd said had lined up with what he'd seen in the CCTV footage. It wasn't a complete alibi, but if the off-licence CCTV could confirm it, he could cross her off his list of suspects. He hoped it wasn't Abby; he wasn't sure he could bear setting Jacob on her.

'Who do you think did this, Abby?'

Her mouth twitched, but all she said was, 'Don't know.'

'Was it to do with the watches he had stolen?'

'Don't think so.'

'So, you found out about the watches?'

'I know he didn't buy them.'

'No, he stole them. From a very fancy house in Mayfair, Chelsea. Could you tell me who he did the job with? I can't imagine he found out about the opportunity by himself.'

Abby gave a barely discernible shake of her head and whispered, 'Don't know.'

Rook noticed Jacob clench his fists, something he'd realised which meant the orc was trying to hide his impatience. Sure enough, Jacob bluntly said, 'Was it Sol?'

'He did some jobs for Sol, so yeah, maybe.'

'Did Sol know Caleb had kept one watch for himself?'

'You think that Caleb was killed over some watches?'

'We are following all leads,' Rook said.

'And it's the human's watch that interests you. Of course it is,' she spat with a sudden venom.

'What should we be focussing on, Abby?' Rook said.

'I don't know...' she stammered, apparently shocked by her own outburst and afraid of what more she might say.

'It would be a good time to tell us what you do know,' Jacob said, speaking as if he were trying to soothe a startled cat.

She looked up at Jacob, her brown eyes big and shimmering with the defiance of the desperate. 'You going to make me, Jacob? Is that why you're here?'

Rook was impressed. She looked like a vole trying to stare down a hawk. Jacob's brow furrowed and his head snapped back as if someone had slapped him.

'No one is going to make you do or say anything,' Rook said. 'We're just looking for Caleb's killer.'

Her mouth twisted into a smile. 'Is that right? Well, I've got nothing more to tell you. Talk to someone else.'

'Okay,' Rook conceded. There was a time to push someone, but this wasn't it. 'How about Caleb's love life? Was there anyone else? Other than you and Rebecca.'

'Of course. Probably lots. But I doubt any of them were stupid enough to care about him,' she said, her shoulders shaking as tears fell.

With that, the interview ended, leaving Rook and Jacob to leave and descend back down the stairs and into the noise of the London streets.

'So,' Jacob said as Rook lit up a cigarette. 'You think she did it? She wasn't happy with him, and she was the last person to see him alive.'

'And she was certainly angry with him.' Rook took a deep drag on his cigarette. 'And there isn't anyone else with a motive. Unless it's to do with that watch. But, if that's the case, why not take the watch? And why do it after two in the morning?' He flicked some ash on the pavement and watched the passers-by go about their day. Jacob had pulled his hood over his head, protecting himself from any intrusive gazes. Taking another drag of his cigarette, Rook said, 'There was also something she held back from us. In fact, there is something everyone has been holding back from us.'

'Such as?'

'I don't know. Abby almost told us something there, but she didn't. And Rebecca was the same.'

'What do you plan to do?' Jacob said.

'Right now? See a man about a horse.' Or a troll about a vampire, as it were.

CHAPTER FOURTEEN

Rook sat on a low wall behind two green bins big enough to obscure him from passers-by, enduring the smell of rotting food to have a better chance at ambushing the vampire that may have bitten him. The bins were beneath a block of utilitarian grey flats that filled the sky above him. As he waited, he listened to the sounds of arguments on the cusp of violence pouring out into the air above him.

He'd got the address of the vampire who'd been staring at him from a reluctant James. The big troll hadn't wanted to tell him, but he'd relented once Rook mentioned how, after a quick conversation with Nicole, James might have to find a new venue for his pub. Rook prayed that Nicole never found out about him using her position as a threat.

He had been waiting long enough that the sky had changed from a cold clear blue to pitch-black by the time his prey came into view. The vampire walked down the path in washed-out retro denim, listening to music on oversized headphones, oblivious to everything around him. Despite the guy's lank shoulder-length hair, Rook could make out the long scar on one cheek and a fading bruise on the other. The latter, Rook hoped, a memento of their scuffle the other night.

As he stepped past Rook's hiding spot, Rook snatched out a hand and grabbed him by the shoulder. The vampire attempted to flee, but Rook held firm, surprised by how light he felt. The detective knocked the headphones off the vampire's head and said, 'I'm only here to talk, Karl. No need to get feisty. Shit, I'll even buy you a beer if it will calm you down.'

'Sure you're not here for round two?' Karl said, his body tense under Rook's grip.

'If I were here to hurt you, I wouldn't have announced myself.'

'Well then, since I could do with a drink anyway, let's go to The George.' Karl's body relaxed and a crooked grin appeared.

The George was a dilapidated pub close to where Karl lived. It looked like the decor had last been updated in the 1980s. Blue beer mats sat next to ringed beer stains on the dark, wooden, round tables. The chairs were a mix of flimsy wooden seats and stools topped with red fabric faded from being sat on by countless heavy backsides. Judging by how the soles of Rook's black shoes stuck to the carpet, it had probably not been washed with anything other than beer for decades.

The sole occupant was a fat bald guy behind the bar, who looked at them with beady black eyes as his belly threatened to spill out of his check shirt. He took Rook's order and poured their drinks with minimal interaction. Rook carried the pints to the table Karl had found in the corner. It had been a risk leaving Karl by himself, but, from what he understood about their speed, had Karl wanted to leave, Rook would have struggled to stop him. In any case, Rook knew where he lived.

'Don't suppose there's any point pretending it wasn't me who attacked you?' Karl said.

'Caught you on CCTV leaving the park,' Rook lied.

'I must have been drunker than I thought.' Karl took his pint and slumped back deeper into his uncomfortable chair.

'I'm new to this whole other species deal,' Rook said, waving his arm around to show he meant all of his new situation. 'But I understand that vampires biting humans is a big no-no. And it carries a brutal sentence.'

'Guess it does,' Karl said. 'You want to know why I attacked you?'

'To be honest, I just thought you were a dick,' Rook said, wrinkling his nose.

'Yeah, well, I'd had a few. Figured you needed taking down a peg or two. And now you maybe don't think we are just some pathetic sideshow.' Karl's mouth formed a pointed grin.

'So you bit me?' Rook asked. 'You could have said something. Or were you waiting until Jacob left?'

'Maybe,' Karl replied. 'You think you'd become a vampire?'

'No,' Rook said, the word coming out quicker than he'd intended.

'Yeah, right.' Karl's smirk caused his scar to crumple.

'Anyway, let's put that in the past. And focus on how you can help me now.'

'And how's that?' His smirk froze in place.

'Well, for a start, you can tell me everything about Caleb.'

Karl looked around the deserted bar, quiet except for music so low they could barely make it out.

'Didn't know him that well.' Karl's eyes darted to his pint.

'I've asked around, and that's not what I've heard.' Rook said, folding his arms across his chest.

'Maybe I knew him a bit, doesn't mean I know anything,' Karl mumbled, his elongated fingers clasped around his pint glass.

'Sure you do. I know bits and pieces already. I know a little about his stealing and his colourful love life. But, despite that, I can't help but feel like people are reluctant to talk to me. Maybe because I'm human, or maybe because I'm police. I don't care why. But I need to know everything. And I think you're the one who is going to tell me.'

'Why do you think that?'

Rook let out an exaggerated sigh. 'Before we go any further, Karl, I'd like you to take a moment to think about who isn't here.'

'What do you mean?'

'What I mean is, we're having a friendly pint in a pub right now. We're not in a dark room with Jacob. Right now, I'm treating what happened between us as a dumb fight after a few drinks. Something we might laugh about in years to come. So I'm keeping the fact that you attacked a human police officer, and bit him, to myself.'

Rook let the silence surround them, watching as it squeezed the confidence from Karl's throat.

'But—' Karl said, swallowing and scratching at his scar.

'But,' Rook cut in, 'you don't play nice from now on, and give me the information I need, then I'll make that fact known to people who will not see the funny side.'

'You want me to be a snitch because I bit you? Are you that much of a dick?'

'The term is Confidential Informant. But otherwise, yes.'

'You're going to threaten me with death by Jacob because I gave you a nip with these.' He opened his mouth and tapped on the sharp vampire teeth at the back.

'Oh, I am. Because I want to find out who killed Caleb. But this offer expires as soon as I finish my drink,' Rook said. He leant forwards and drained his pint almost to the end in one big dramatic gulp, then he placed the almost empty glass down in front of the vampire.

'Fine,' Karl muttered.

'Great,' Rook replied, with false joviality. 'Of course, saying "fine" is easy. But I need to know I can trust you. So, you can tell me something useful right now. Or I will need to chat to Jacob about our little fight the other night.'

'How do I know what's useful to you?'

'Fair question, Karl. I'll give you a hand. I know he slept around. I only know two names right now, but I'm guessing there are more.'

'I don't know anything about his love life. Figured he got less than he said, but maybe not.'

'Okay, say I believe you. Maybe you can give me some information on his less-than-legal activities. I can connect him to at least one burglary, but I don't know who he worked with. And that would be useful.'

Karl glanced around the empty bar as if searching for something Rook couldn't see. 'I can't tell you about any burglaries. Caleb kept that stuff to himself.'

'Did he?' Rook said, leaning over the table to look into Karl's eyes. 'But that doesn't help me, does it? And you need to help me, don't you, Karl?'

It didn't make Rook feel good to see Karl's skinny arse shift uncomfortably in his seat. But it meant Rook's plan was working.

'You really don't know?' Karl said.

'Don't know what?'

'About the disappearances.' Karl's voice was low and quiet.

'What disappearances?' Rook took his notebook from his jacket pocket.

'Caleb was the first to figure something was going on. His mate Benjamin had gone missing. Caleb had known him from their time in Manchester and had tried to look him up when he'd got to London. He got in touch with Terry, then when Terry was useless, he reached out to some people in our government,' Karl said.

'What did they say?'

'Caleb was told that Benjamin had moved back to Manchester. So, that being where Caleb was from, Caleb rang around his old friends. There wasn't any sign of him.'

'Manchester is a big place,' Rook said, scratching at his chin.

'It is, but there aren't many of us other species anywhere. And Benjamin wasn't the only one who disappeared.'

'Who else disappeared, Karl?' Rook's voice was quiet but his tone insistent.

'There was Edgar Silas, Riothamus's brother.'

'Riothamus?' Rook asked.

Karl's long fingers tensed around his pint glass. 'A troll – he works construction. His brother went missing about seven months ago. Then there was... Jeremiah...'

'Jeremiah?'

'Jeremiah Fochs, an orc,' Karl said. 'I knew him growing up.'

'You were close?'

'We'd drifted apart as we grew up, but we were still mates, you know,' Karl said.

'When did he go missing?'

'Five months ago. Or at least that's when I noticed he was missing.' Karl's big Adam's apple bobbed in his throat as he swallowed.

'What happened?'

'I'd sent him a few texts about coming round for a drink and he didn't reply.'

'And this was unusual?'

'Yeah, he was always antisocial, but he wouldn't ghost me. Not like that. I thought he must still be ill or something, so I went round to his, but he wasn't there.'

'I thought orcs didn't get ill?'

'It's rare, but they get ill. They're just great at fighting it off. He'd had something he couldn't shake a few weeks.

For him, it was an annoying cough. If you or I'd had it, it would have been Covid on steroids. Anyway, he'd been to the health centre about it. Got some pills and I thought he'd got over it.' Karl stared into the depths of his pint, lost in a memory, sadness, or guilt. The weight of his friend's disappearance hung from his shoulders and grief clouded his eyes. 'But then he stopped answering his texts and wasn't at his place.'

'Where did he live?'

'Flat in Tooting,' Karl said, still looking at his beer.

'Anyone living there now?' Rook made a note in his notebook.

'He had a flatmate, but she didn't know what happened to him. Or his stuff.'

'Was it not in the flat when you went around?'

Karl shook his head. 'Someone had emptied it out. Not like he had much.'

'So, you couldn't find him there. Where else did you check?'

'Asked around the few friends I knew he had. They hadn't seen him, but that wasn't that unusual. As I said, he's a bit of a loner. Checked his work, he hadn't come in.'

'Where did he work?'

'The Raven – he worked in the kitchen. He helped with the food sometimes, mainly tidying and cleaning up after.'

'Cash-in-hand work?' Rook looked up from his notebook.

'That's right. It surprised them when he didn't show, but it's not like he's the first person in a job like that to quit without a word.'

'True. So, you've asked everyone you could ask but still not found him. What did you do next?'

Karl took a long drink of his pint, almost draining it, looked straight into Rook's face, and said, 'I came to the other guy.'

'Terry?'

'Yeah, smelt like he'd been drinking whisky for about a week straight.'

'You smell that with your vampire super-smelling or something?' Rook asked.

'It's ghouls that have the great sense of smell.' Karl gave a bitter snort. 'But you didn't need to be a ghoul to smell he'd been drinking.'

'Okay, what did Terry do?'

'Said he'd investigate. A week later, said Jeremiah had moved to Brighton.'

'You believe that?'

'At the time I did. But he never got back in touch. And then I hear about the others, all with similar stories, all in the past twelve months. We all thought something was up.'

Rook leant back in his chair and scratched his head with his pen. 'That doesn't explain why everyone is keeping it a secret from me.'

'Doesn't it?' Karl replied.

Rook raised his eyebrows.

'We'd been to Terry. We'd been to Rowena. They'd told us they hadn't disappeared. A few of us started investigating ourselves...'

'And then someone killed Caleb,' Rook finished, realisation dawning.

'That's right,' Karl said, picking up a beer mat and ripping it apart unthinkingly, his nervous hands on autopilot. 'We started asking questions and then someone murdered Caleb. It was quite the coincidence.'

'Maybe,' Rook conceded. 'But then, why am I here? Why have I been asked to look into this if people want it covered up?'

'Well, that's the question we've all been asking ourselves. Perhaps whoever is behind this thinks you'll fail to find anything, but people will believe they've tried? Or' – Karl stared at Rook, his brown eyes wild and his eyebrows raised – 'you are here to find out who else knew about the disappearances? To see who else you need to have Jacob keep quiet.'

Rook drained the last dregs of his beer and stood up, towering above Karl. 'I'm here to be police. That means finding a killer and what's happening to these people who have disappeared. And no, Jacob didn't kill Caleb or kidnap anyone,' he said, praying it was true.

CHAPTER FIFTEEN

'No!' Nicole said, eyes narrow and voice sharp.

'You sure about that?' Rook asked, leaning back in his office chair.

'Of course I'm sure there's no conspiracy. Why would we have brought you in if there was?' Nicole's face was pinched and combative.

'I wasn't brought in to investigate these disappearances, though, was I? You hired me to investigate a murder and a few burglaries. Specifically, the burglary at Mr Purcell's. Which is the only thing Steele cares about, it seems.'

'That's not fair,' Nicole said. 'He cares about the murder too. But he wanted you to understand how important the burglary could be.' She stood up and went to the cupboard that hid the biscuits, plucking out a whole packet of chocolate bourbons and putting them down next to her coffee. Only after devouring one and brushing the crumbs off her suit did she feel ready to continue. 'We don't even know that there were any disappearances.'

'Three people missing, Nicole.' Rook reached over the desks to get a biscuit himself. 'It might be a coincidence, but it could be a conspiracy.' He looked around the room again and wondered if this could be the centre of a conspiracy. A dust-filled office in a flat above an accountant's didn't seem like the place where people made such dark decisions. But he could be wrong. Maybe Steele gave the order from the kitchen area of the office, next to the mugs and shitty kettle. Whatever was going on, he hoped Nicole wasn't in on it. Looking at her now, hiding her face behind her coffee and eating chocolate biscuits, it was hard to believe she was lying. But only fools thought they could spot a lie. Truth was, anyone could lie to anyone.

'So, I take it you don't know anything about them?' Rook said.

'Of course not.'

'Terry was told about one at least.'

'Well, he didn't tell me,' Nicole said in a tone that failed to mask the offence she had taken at Rook's questioning. 'Anyway, you've seen his files. I doubt he even investigated it. He probably forgot all about it as soon as he tasted his next drink.' She flicked her head towards the kitchen, where Terry's whisky tumbler was still nestled among the coffee mugs. Rook had considered getting rid of it, or at least taking it home, but he suspected that a day would come when he'd need a drink stronger than coffee.

A deliberate knocking on the door released them from their awkward conversation. Rook opened it to reveal Jacob waiting outside in his brown sheepskin-lined jacket, hoody, blue jeans, and heavy boots.

'Hello, Jacob,' Nicole said, forcing a smile.

'Good morning, Nicole.' Jacob offered a curt nod. 'Why did you want me to come in?' he asked Rook.

Rook sat back down in his seat, moved it a couple of inches away from Jacob, and said, 'I got told something interesting last night.' Jacob shrugged, so Rook continued, 'I was told that three of the other species have disappeared in a little over a year. A troll, a vampire, and an orc.'

'What are they called?' Jacob said.

'You don't know?'

'Oh, of course he doesn't know, Rook. There isn't anything to know,' Nicole jumped in.

'Why would I know who they are, Rook?' Jacob said, turning his deep-set eyes on Rook with the urgency of a glacier.

'Well,' Rook said, 'the person I spoke to said it was a conspiracy. That Caleb was getting too close to what was causing these disappearances. So, he said that you killed Caleb. And now we're out there trying to figure out who else knows so that you can silence them too. Is that what's happening here?'

'No,' Jacob whispered, his knuckles whitening as his fists clenched. 'That isn't what I do, Rook.'

'I thought that was exactly what you do.'

'I'm the last resort and the only deterrent. I don't kidnap people.'

'How does that work?'

Jacob pushed his heavy face into Rook's personal space. When he spoke, his words came out slow, certain, and with the promise of future anger. 'If someone's actions threaten to reveal our presence to humanity, I deal with them. If someone commits an act that demands punishment, then I deal with that. Regrettably but finally.' Jacob held up his hand to stop Rook from speaking. 'I am not here to cover up crimes.'

Rook looked at Nicole while he decided how to respond to Jacob's explanation, but she was ignoring their conversation by studying whatever was on her computer as if she hadn't heard what Jacob had said. Which, Rook supposed, was one way to deal with your co-worker pointing out that execution was part of the job description.

'Okay, so you're in the dark too. Which, while great to know, doesn't get us closer to solving Caleb's death.' He waved his hands vaguely in the direction of the crime boards as he spoke. It was looking more like the arts and crafts project of a troubled toddler than anything you could use to solve a murder.

'I think you should come to mine for lunch, Rook,' Jacob said.

'You want to cook me lunch, Jacob? After I suggested you'd been murdering people on the sly, and before we meet a troll gangster?' Rook raised his eyebrows.

'I do. Carolina could only look after Michael for the morning, and I need to get back. It's time we had a chat about what I do, Detective Rook.'

CHAPTER SIXTEEN

They pulled up outside Jacob's house in time to see Carolina being walked out the front door by a heavy-set man in a blue suit. His face was twisted into a scowl, his hand gripping tight onto Carolina's elbow.

When Carolina saw Jacob and Rook, she pulled down the sleeves of her hoody to cover the red marks that were on top of old bruises. When the man saw them, he changed his expression into what Rook had to admit was a charming grin, leaving no trace of the rage that had been scrawled across his face a second ago. His hair was black, short and wavy, brushed back from a widow's peak. His light-green eyes danced on the line between anger and mirth. A big man, he looked like he'd once played rugby but had let himself go. He wore his extra weight with confidence, but his white shirt stretched across a paunch he hadn't had when he'd bought the shirt.

Carolina was about to speak when the man cut her off. 'Jacob, is it?' he said, extending his hand to Jacob.

Jacob gave a slight nod but didn't shake the outstretched hand, leaving it hanging between them while he regarded the man.

'I'm Darren Addy, Carolina's partner.' The man retracted his hand, tittering as if to suggest that Jacob was the one being strange but that he, Darren, was a big enough man to look past it.

'What's happening, Carolina?' Jacob said, ignoring Darren.

Darren, however, replied, 'She double booked herself, I'm afraid. Forgot she had some jobs to do for me. Now I'm picking her up.'

'What about Michael?' Jacob said, taking a half-step closer to Darren.

'It's lovely that she earns a bit of pocket money looking after your boy. But she has other responsibilities too. And to be perfectly frank, Mr Bennet, I think you need to get some proper care for him. Not sure Carolina can handle someone with that sort of temper.'

'Temper?' Jacob said, the fist of his right hand clenching like he was trying to crush an invisible stress ball.

'It was nothing I couldn't handle, but you should have a word with him,' Darren replied, running his hand through his hair and smoothing down some imaginary rumples on his suit. 'In any case, must rush. Nice meeting you both.'

He walked to his car, guiding Carolina by placing his hand on her lower back.

Inside, Michael sat at the dining table, wearing a grey tracksuit that struggled to contain his body. He was engrossed in the Lego in front of him, a mess of different shapes and colours that covered every inch of the dining table. There was no TV on or music playing, just the sound of the occasional shout from the nearby housing estates. Despite the silence, Michael gave no sign that he'd heard Rook and Jacob enter.

'Everything okay, Michael?' Jacob said, a forced joviality in his voice that failed to mask his concern.

'Yes, Dad,' Michael mumbled, still looking at his Lego.

'That's good,' Jacob said. 'Could you tell me what happened with Carolina?'

Michael continued playing with his Lego, and Rook realised he was building a wall with different coloured bricks.

'Why don't you tell me what happened this morning, Michael?' Jacob said, stepping across the room and placing his hand on his son's shoulder, a hand Michael soon enveloped in his own.

The big troll looked up into Jacob's face with his clear blue eyes. 'It was good,' he said, his voice trembling. 'We played Lego. Then we went to the park to feed the ducks. And then, then...' His wide face darkened.

'And then?' Jacob said.

'We were coming back and, and we saw Darren waiting outside. He was angry.' The words wobbled from Michael, each as unsteady as a fawn taking its first steps.

'What did he say?' Jacob said.

'He said Carolina was late or something, he... he grabbed her... I'm sorry,' Michael finished, his words petering out, his eyes filling with tears.

'Why are you sorry?' Jacob said.

'I thought he was hurting Carolina. I... I picked him up.' A huge sob caused his chest to start shaking and heaving.

'You picked him up?' Rook asked, shocked. 'How? He's pretty big.'

'With my hands?' Michael replied, eyebrows knotting in confusion.

'But you didn't hurt him?' Jacob asked, his words worried and rushed.

'Do we care?' Rook said. 'Sounds like he had it coming.'

'We care, Rook,' Jacob said. 'Because while Michael is sweet and kind and would never want to hurt anyone, he's strong. Very strong. And if he hits humans, he shatters their bones.' He moved closer to his son. 'Did you hit him, Michael?'

'I just picked him up and put him on the sofa.' He sobbed again. Rook fought a smile as he pictured the look on Darren's face as Michael lifted him off his feet and put him down on the sofa like a naughty child.

'That's good, Michael. No one is angry. There's nothing for you to worry about,' Jacob said, patting his shoulder. 'Rook is joining us for lunch, but we've run out of ketchup. Could you go to the shop on the corner and see if they have any – perhaps you could pick up some of those film magazines you like?' He reached into his jacket pocket and got out his wallet, taking out a £10 note and handing it to Michael.

'Are you sure?' Michael said. Suddenly the pain of his earlier encounter left his face, leaving only the ghosts of his tears and the beginnings of a smile.

'Of course. You can handle that, can't you?' Jacob replied, giving a rare smile that produced even more lines on his already craggy face.

Michael's head bobbed up and down excitedly, his face beaming. He paused briefly in the doorway, as if steeling himself for a grand adventure, before stepping outside.

When the door closed, Jacob said, 'I have some steaks we can fry up. Why don't you come into the kitchen?'

After Jacob cleared up the Lego, they went through the lounge into a narrow kitchen. Jacob took some steaks out of the fridge, along with a bag of chips, and turned on the oven. 'It's best if we let the steaks get to room temperature.'

'Is that right?' Rook said. Cooking was not his specialist subject. 'Steak is a big lunch for a workday.'

'You have some urgent leads you need to chase down?' Jacob replied, offering Rook a beer as he did so. Rook thought about turning the offer down, but his hand was already clasping the bottle before his mouth could move.

'You want me to have a word with this Darren Addy?' Rook said. Listening to the fear in Michael's voice had caused the anger to rise in Rook's chest, and he wanted Addy to pay.

Jacob shook his head. 'No, Michael wasn't hurt, and I doubt Addy is so suspicious of his strength we should worry. It's better it stays that way. If I need to, I will have a word with him.' Rook didn't want to know what Jacob *having a word with someone* who had hurt Michael entailed.

The kitchen was narrow enough that Rook could touch both walls at the same time without stretching. He couldn't picture Michael's bulk in such a confined space. But that was part of Michael's problem, wasn't it? He was too big to fit into the world around him.

'Did anyone ever tell you how Michael's parents died?' Jacob said, rubbing salt onto the steak.

'No.'

'No, and I doubt anyone else will tell you the story.' He turned on the hob so that blue flame engulfed the frying pan. 'Rowena called me. Told me some troll had killed his wife in Slough. So I went. Rowena was waiting inside the house, sitting on this broken-down old sofa while this tiny thing was screaming in a basket next to her. That was Michael. His mother was lying on the floor by his basket with her head caved in. She was a big troll, and heavy too. Not one of those tall, thin troll ladies who pass for human with a bit of make-up. She would have had to stay home during the day and only go out at night to avoid attention.

'Michael... Michael kept screaming, I picked him up and held him while Rowena told me how his father had always been violent and had finally taken it too far. I found him six days later drinking in some vile pub in Croydon. It's tough to kill a troll. Not just because of their strength and their size. But because their skin is so tough. Much tougher than a human's. Best tool I've found to use is a big hammer. Try to break their kneecap, then go for the head.' He clasped his fist around the handle of an imaginary hammer, raising it above his head. 'Which is how I killed him after he'd stumbled out of the pub and into the dark.'

Rook worried about how many times Jacob had carried out similar executions. It wasn't a comforting question to have about someone you worked with. Or someone who was cooking you lunch.

Some music drifted in from outside, where there were millions of people in London alone going about their happy lives, blissfully unaware of the world of the other species that existed in the margins. Rook thought about joining them and leaving all this behind. But then, who would find justice for Caleb?

His train of thought was derailed by a beaming Michael coming back into the house, holding a couple of magazines in one hand and a ketchup bottle in the other.

'Thank you, Michael,' Jacob said, taking the bottle from Michael's giant mitts.

'I've got change too,' Michael said, reaching into his pockets for a few pounds' worth of change. He put it down on the kitchen counter.

'Do you want to join us for lunch, Michael?' Jacob asked.

The troll shook his head. 'Carolina made us sandwiches.'

'Then why don't you have some game time with the tablet upstairs? You could put your headphones on so you can play it as loud as you like,' Jacob said.

'Thanks, Dad,' Michael said, turning round and making his way upstairs. Rook could hear each step he made.

'So,' Rook said once they were sitting at the dining table, eating the steak and chips, 'Michael's lived with you ever since?'

'There were attempts to find him somewhere more suitable. But he always ended up back here. And I was happy to have him.' Jacob's steak bled onto the plate as he cut into it.

'Why did you tell me this?'

'Because you need to know what I do and why I do it. I kill when there's no alternative. We couldn't let a troll like the one I killed go unpunished, not only because he deserved what happened to him, but because he was so big and so violent. What would happen if he started picking on humans? They would break and people would notice. He had to be killed.'

Rook chewed on his food. 'I understand what you do might be necessary. I don't have to like it,' he murmured between mouthfuls of meat.

Jacob's cutlery clinked against his plate as he put them down. 'No. But you cannot let your feelings stay your hand.' He was sitting upright, his body still, his voice deliberate. 'Should you find who killed Caleb, or if someone is behind these disappearances, then I will execute them. And you need to know this.'

'Can we finish lunch without discussing you executing people?' Rook replied, taking a drink from his beer.

'Yes, let's enjoy our steak. After all, we are meeting a dangerous criminal this afternoon. And, after that, I imagine our lives are going to get very interesting.'

CHAPTER SEVENTEEN

They waited outside the entrance to Sol's while Rook downed a black coffee, its harsh taste failing to clear his head or chase away the heavy steak and pint he'd had for lunch. The best he could say about the coffee was that it was hot. It was doing about as much as his winter coat and black suit to keep him warm, at least.

From the outside, Sol's was a feeble old shop that sold spare parts no one would ever need or want. Various odds and ends were strewn casually in the front window, their uses a mystery to Rook and none with labels or price tags. The street it was on was one of those empty side streets where the footfall had dried up years ago. He blinked into the unforgiving winter sun and picked at the bite mark Karl had left. The bandage had already come off, and the scab rubbed against his shirt.

'Something bothering you?' Jacob asked. His heavy brown coat was unzipped, the white T-shirt underneath showing his wiry, muscled frame. His stance gave no sign he was aware of the cold.

'Getting my head right,' Rook said. 'How serious is this Sol guy, anyway?'

'It's difficult for the other species to find regular employment. Some scrape by. Others have more ambition. Sol has a lot more ambition,' Jacob said, his broad shoulders shrugging under his coat.

'Ambition to do what?'

'Make money. Some of what he does is legal, but there's also drugs, protection, and dealing in stolen goods.'

Rook raised his eyebrows. 'Seems like quite the entrepreneur. How come I've never heard of him?'

'He's good at not making noise.'

'And if he didn't, you'd have words with him, right?'

'I would,' Jacob said.

'You think Sol's behind the burglaries of the jewellers and Purcell?'

'He is likely to have been involved or know who was. Let me ask the questions, at least to start. Sol is not someone you want to annoy,' Jacob said, emphasising the word "you" with a nod of his head.

Inside the shop a jumble of nozzles, bits of wire, and the occasional clock littered the unordered shelves. The air was thick with dust and dirt, the type of air Rook associated with the houses of shut-ins and hoarders.

He wondered why they bothered with the cash register. The shop couldn't have screamed "front" more if they'd had a sign outside reading, *This is a place of illegal activities. We do not want your business – please do not enter unless you want to perform a creative suicide*.

An old, thin orc with sunken cheeks and mournful green eyes was sitting behind the register. He was wearing a red check shirt that a charity shop wouldn't take and smoking on the bitter end of a cigarette. As soon as the orc noticed Jacob, he opened the heavy wooden door behind him.

Behind the door were some stairs, covered with rough red carpets and lit by one blinking light. The orc stumbled down them ahead of Rook and Jacob without engaging in conversation. At the bottom of the stairs was a black door, thick enough that the orc grunted with the effort of opening it.

The door led to a room so unlike the shop floor and the stairs that it might as well have been in a different building. Whereas the shop floor was a dingy and cluttered mess, this room was clean and bright. Rook's eyes had to take a moment to adjust to the light reflecting off the white walls. The room was dominated by a wooden desk, behind which sat a high-backed chair inlaid with red leather. In front of the desk sat two black utilitarian office chairs. The

desk was bare except for a sleek MacBook, which had its
screen folded down.

Although no one was sitting in any of the seats, the
room wasn't empty. A tall bald ghoul with a huge, hooked
nose and strong jawline was standing in the corner. His
dark suit highlighted his cigarette-thin figure and grey
skin. He stood, shoulders hunched, with the patience of
a vulture waiting for a carcass to appear.

'Hello, Max,' Jacob said. 'Sol making us wait, is he?'

Max's eyes moved to Jacob, but the rest of him didn't
move a millimetre. 'He'll be here soon,' he said, motioning
to the two empty chairs in front of the desk.

They sat and waited. Soon Jacob was drumming his
fingers on the arm of his chair and Rook was wishing he'd
stop. Rook glanced towards Max, but the ghoul remained
statuesque.

After a few more minutes of waiting, the door opened
and in walked Sol. Rook didn't need an introduction to
know who the guy in charge was. He was short for a troll,
although he was still a similar height to Rook. His wide
shoulders scraped the doorframe as he walked into the
room. His face was covered with as many lines and creases
as an unironed shirt. His white-blond hair was severe and
short, highlighting weary clear-blue eyes framed by bushy
blond eyebrows. He was wearing grey suit trousers, and a
smart blue shirt with the sleeves rolled up to his elbows.

He sighed as he slumped into the chair behind the desk, like a tired dad at the end of a long day.

'This the new Terry?' he asked Jacob, pointing a stubby finger at Rook.

Rook took a breath. 'Terry was my predecessor, yes. I'm Detective Rook.'

'So, why do you want to talk to me?' Sol spread his hands out expansively, as if to suggest he was an open book. Something Rook doubted to be the case.

'You can't guess?' Rook asked.

Sol looked at Rook, his fat lips pursed. 'I really can't.'

'Caleb's murder. To start with,' Jacob said, glancing at Rook, making it clear he should let Jacob take it from here.

'And why would you think I had anything to do with that?'

'We know Caleb was connected to at least one robbery,' Jacob said.

'Which robbery was that?'

'The robbery of some very expensive watches from a house in Chelsea.' Jacob eyed Sol like a wolf sizing up its prey.

'And this interests me because?' Sol said, tapping a single finger on the table.

'Do we have to go through all of this?' Rook interjected, his voice betraying his exasperation.

'All of what?' Sol said, turning away from Jacob to inspect Rook more closely.

'All of this "I'm nothing more than a local business owner" crap. Everyone in this room knows you're a criminal. And don't think that poorly disguised front upstairs is fooling anyone. I bet your laptop is worth more than all the trash in there. Maybe, in the future, your criminal activities will lead to you and I crossing paths in a less than friendly way. But, right now, in this moment, I'm struggling to care less about a few expensive watches when I'm looking into the murder of a kid someone ripped apart in his flat.'

'We might cross paths in an unfriendly way, might we? Why'd you think I'd have anything to say about a robbery some vampire may or may not have done?' Sol looked directly at Rook when he spoke, and the words came out slowly and with emphasis, as if each one was a punch and a threat. The weariness that had exuded from him when he'd entered the room was gone, and his lips were parted in a cold predatory smile, letting Rook glimpse the hardened criminal behind the avuncular pretence.

'Either you knew about the theft, Sol, or you'd be angry that it went ahead without you,' Jacob said, stopping Rook from saying something he would regret.

'Now, Jacob,' Sol said. 'If I were to be involved in something like that, would I be that unsubtle? I don't want to attract any attention to our shadowy corner of the world. In that respect, I'm on the side of the angels. Or whatever us lot get instead of angels.'

'You might not be behind it. But you might have been upset about it,' Jacob said. 'Young vampire started stealing from humans in a way that could attract attention. You might want to send a message.'

'Between you, me, and our new friend' – he jerked his thumb towards Rook – 'no, I wouldn't be happy if I heard someone was doing something that stupid. I wouldn't be happy at all. But would you, Jacob? To be honest, when I heard the young vamp had met his end, I thought it might have been you.'

'Not this time,' Jacob said.

Rook bit the side of his cheek at Jacob's words, almost drawing blood. 'So you knew about the theft of the watches,' Rook said. Out of the corner of his eye, Rook noticed Max tense in response.

'I only found out recently,' Sol conceded.

'When exactly did you find out?' Rook said.

'A few nights before he was stabbed.'

'Some might call that a coincidence,' Rook said.

The old troll shifted in his chair but kept his eyes on Rook. 'Might they?' he asked. 'Max, anyone said anything to you about it being a coincidence?'

'No, boss. No one's said a thing,' the ghoul said, as if he were rehearsing lines from a play he was bored with acting in.

'Funny that,' Sol said.

It was Jacob who asked the next question. 'Are we supposed to believe that you were fine with a young vampire bringing attention to you like that?'

'Fine, Jacob? No, I wasn't fine about it. I wasn't happy at all. But I didn't lay a finger on him. And no, before you ask, I didn't have anyone else lay a finger on him either.'

'Any reason you were so forgiving?' Rook asked.

'Maybe I'm a forgiving guy,' Sol said, his eyes doing their best to tunnel through Rook's skull.

For the first time since this meeting had started, someone laughed. It was Max. It was more a short huffing than a genuine laugh, but it made its point.

'What are you laughing at, Max?' Jacob said, without bothering to look at the ghoul.

'Ignore me. Something funny popped into my head, that's all.'

'I know why you didn't touch Caleb, not then at least,' Jacob said.

'Oh,' Sol said. 'And why would that be?'

'Because Caleb might have been the vampire who went through the window, but I doubt he was the one organising it. He was too new to town. And you want to talk to whoever was behind it.'

'You're absolutely right,' Sol said. 'We do want to have a word with whoever is behind this. When the time is right. But you don't begrudge us that, do you? After all, we're only keeping order in our own way. Just like you, Jacob.'

'And when will the time be right?' Rook jumped in again.

'I don't know,' Sol said, taking a deep breath that caused his chest to rise and fall like a tectonic plate. 'Perhaps when I'm not getting visits from some keen new detective?'

'You murder someone else over some robberies, you'll be getting more visits from me,' Rook said, struggling to keep the venom from his voice.

'Murder is killing a human,' Sol said, giving another chuckle that aped that of a fun uncle, but without the warmth or humour. 'Us other species? We don't count. You ever murdered anyone, Max?'

'No, boss. Can't say I've ever committed a *murder*,' Max said.

'See, no murders. To be frank, Mr Rook, I'm confused about why you care about this vampire's killing. It's been cleaned up. Humans know nothing about it. He's not going to be stealing any more watches. Let's move on. Live our lives.'

Rook stood up and leant his long frame across the desk, close enough that he could smell the spittle on Sol's lips and see the deep pores of his skin.

'I'm not letting it go,' he said, his voice a loaded whisper, 'because when someone guts a kid, it shouldn't go unpunished. And, if you were behind this, I'll make sure you'll pay. I don't care about some rich guy getting his watches nicked. Or some jewellers getting robbed. I could not give a fuck. But, if you don't stop playing this stupid game, I will care. I'll care so much that I'll spend all my days doing my very best to tie you to crimes and alert the normal police. I'll drag this operation out of the shadows, into the light. So that my higher-ups can't ignore it. And then Jacob here will have to pay you a less friendly visit.'

Sol rested back in his chair and stroked his chin while he weighed his options. It may have been Rook's imagination, but he suspected Max had somehow moved closer to them. A smile spread across Sol's lined face, like a warship parting the ocean.

'Well,' he said, 'that's me told. I knew Caleb. He came down from Manchester highly recommended in his line of work.'

'And what line of work would that be?' Rook said.

'Stealing stuff.'

'So you had him steal stuff for you? Like Purcell's watches?'

Sol waved his hand in the air like he was flailing at a fly. 'I had nothing to do with Purcell's watches. I used him to do much more discreet work. Sort of job that would never bother you police.'

'Like robbing a jeweller?'

Sol gave Rook another penetrating look, but his mouth said, 'Perhaps.'

'So, if you didn't set him up to steal those watches, who did?'

Sol sucked on his bottom lip. 'I don't know.'

'But you have an idea,' Jacob stated.

'I might be looking into it. But if you ever find out who was behind that mischief, you let me or Max know. We might save Jacob a job. Now, you two got any more questions?' Sol looked around the room.

Rook and Jacob looked at each other and shook their heads.

'Then you can both fuck off.'

CHAPTER EIGHTEEN

Fatigued from the long day, Rook's weary body welcomed his sofa's embrace with tired euphoria. Beer held tight in his right hand, his left reached into his jacket pocket, hunting for cigarettes. He was a millisecond away from lighting up before he caught himself. While he'd let the rest of the flat fall into a lazy mess since Sarah had left, the one line he'd yet to cross was smoking indoors. Even drunk, he'd always forced himself to go downstairs into the street.

He put his beer down on the coffee table that wasn't meant to be a coffee table. It was supposed to be a dining table. He'd got it when he and Sarah had first moved in. She'd wanted to look at the dining tables in a furniture shop. But he'd insisted he'd found a good deal online. Sadly, whoever had taken the pictures for the website had been a magician. They'd somehow made it look like a whole family was eating around the table and having a good time. Only when it arrived did Rook realise he should have checked its dimensions. It was a barely big enough to hold a couple of plates. Rook had been angry and then embarrassed when he'd discovered his mistake. Sarah had laughed until she cried.

They'd kept the table. For a while, it had been a fun token of their relationship. But now it sat covered in coffee stains and out-of-date magazines. The whole flat had been getting less spacious ever since the day Sarah had left, with a fixed smile and few tears. Rook had tried keeping the place tidy, but inch by inch, the clutter of his life had taken over. Like black mould on rotting wood.

Rook sighed and started scrolling through his phone, the content not registering in his brain as he flicked from image to image and story to story. He sent a non-committal message to his father. He knew he should see him soon, but he wasn't quite in the frame of mind to handle his father's quiet air of disappointment. He doubted his father would mind. They'd been playing the same game for years. Each would make occasional half-hearted promises to meet up, both confident that the other would not make it, both relieved when nothing happened.

He wondered if he should message anyone else. People he used to call friends or even his brother. See if they would drink with him. But that would mean putting himself through the wait while they figured out a way to say no.

Or, even worse, they would meet up and spend an awkward few hours realising why it had been so long since they'd last been in touch.

It was better to sit here with his beers, drowning in rubbish, and dwell on a case he couldn't solve. Then he'd be able to face Nicole with at least the appearance of a plan. He took out the pictures he'd taken from Caleb's flat, searching through each one as if he would somehow find some clue in the background. But all he saw were the fearless smiles and wild pupils of the young, drunk, and high.

Rook drained his beer, returned to his otherwise empty fridge, and pulled out another, then stumbled back to his sofa through the debris of his flat. Turning his TV onto a show he'd seen many times, he let his mind wander through the day he'd had, hoping some further insight would shake itself loose.

Once they'd left Sol's, Jacob had gone home to look after Michael for the afternoon. It was touching, seeing the orc everyone feared fretting over his son. Instead of returning to the quiet of the office, Rook had investigated the robberies of the jewellers – the ones he assumed Caleb had committed.

Rook had then visited the three different jewellers that had been robbed in the previous six months. One in Croydon, one in Kingston, and the other in Elephant & Castle. The last one had been the big score; they'd made off with stock worth over £150,000. Unless the owner was trying to fool their insurance company.

It had felt strange flashing his ID as if he were still a normal police officer, like he was pretending to be something he already was.

In general, people reacted in two ways when the police talked to them after a robbery: fatalistic or full-blown amateur Columbo. The fatalistic ones have zero hope that the police will catch the perpetrators and begrudge taking the time to talk about the crime. The amateur Columbos can't resist trying to solve the mystery and are all too willing to share their weird theories about how it might have happened. Unfortunately for Rook, two of the three had been amateur Columbos. Talking to them had taken up most of Rook's afternoon, but he'd got no new information. At least not from them.

The perpetrators had avoided being seen by the security cameras outside, and they'd taken the cameras in the store out with speed and precision. The only camera that had caught anything of interest was in the Elephant & Castle jewellers. A flash of a dark shape flitted across the screen for a second. The police had dismissed it as a camera error. Rook knew it was something else. He knew what he was watching wasn't some strange optical illusion or trick of the light or camera failing. It was a vampire moving at full speed.

How Terry had not flagged that as weird was mind-blowing. Even if he hadn't spotted the vampire, the lack of CCTV footage at any scene was noteworthy. In London, Rook doubted it was possible to go more than ten feet from any door without a camera catching you at least twice.

It wasn't until the final jewellers that Rook noticed a pattern. He had left the last jewellers and gone out into the cold London wind with his head ringing. The jeweller had fallen into the amateur Columbo camp. He seemed to suspect everyone from the Mafia to a homeless guy he sometimes saw who may or may not be on drugs.

Rook had escaped that conversation and was outside lighting up a cigarette when his perseverance paid off. He noticed the construction site across the road and realised that every shop had been within spitting distance of one of these.

This didn't have to mean anything. Property in London was such that a building only had to be derelict for a second and a developer would turn it into flats. Or, if it was already flats, tear it down and build more flats. The banging of construction was a constant source of headaches in the city.

The site itself was a brown patch of land containing a hunched crane and a few dirty white vans with *Bridge Construction Services* painted on them, and a lonely shed with *Security* written on the side. Rook noticed the few cameras purchased on the wire fence like crows in a grave-yard. He waved his police ID at the cameras, and after a moment's hesitation, the door to the hut opened. As soon as he saw the guard, Rook knew he was on to something.

The skinny guy was lost in a huge hi-vis jacket. Only a fraction of his face was visible between the jacket and the woolly hat, but it was enough. His ash-grey skin and pronounced jawline gave it away. The man in front of him was a ghoul.

'What do you want?' the ghoul asked, his voice muffled by his jacket.

Ignoring the tone, Rook asked, 'I've got a few questions about the robbery across the road. Why don't we go inside and chat?'

'Don't know anything about any robbery.' The ghoul stamped his feet, either to fight the cold or out of nerves. Rook couldn't tell.

'Maybe not. But let's chat, anyway. My name's Rook, by the way. What should I call you?'

The ghoul thought for a moment. 'Simon,' he said.

'Well then, Simon,' Rook said with his biggest, fakest smile plastered across his face. 'Why don't we go inside to chat?'

The hut wasn't much warmer than the street. An old space heater was trying its best, but the cold still bit Rook's hands and made his back ache. The hut was cramped. Three monitors showing the feeds from various CCTV cameras sat on a stain-filled desk, among old redtop news-papers and a bacon sandwich that was almost drowned in ketchup. Two cheap chairs huddled around the table, like tramps warming themselves around a fire.

Rook didn't wait for an invitation to take one of the chairs. Simon sat down opposite, rocking nervously in his chair.

'Quite a coincidence, isn't it?' Rook asked.

Simon looked to his monitors like he expected them to help and then whispered, 'What is?'

'Jewellers across the road gets knocked over by a vampire and here I find a ghoul looking after a construction site. A construction site with cameras that overlook the jewellers.'

Rook enjoyed seeing the ghoul's grey face tremble in shock. 'What's a ghoul?' he said, keeping his voice almost comically flat.

'A ghoul,' Rook replied, while reaching across to the bacon sandwich and picking the thick slice of white bread to reveal the raw rasher of bacon underneath, 'is someone who has their bacon raw.'

'Maybe I just like it raw?' Simon said, a hopeful inflexion on the end of his voice.

'Funny,' Rook said, dropping the bread. 'But I'm in no mood for this. You're a ghoul.' He pointed at Simon. 'And I know that the police looked at every CCTV camera on this street. Yet somehow yours didn't catch a thing. Despite having cameras pointing at the store.'

Simon looked to the floor and shifted in his seat like a schoolboy caught in a lie. 'Don't know nothing about that,' he mumbled.

'Really, you've got no idea how those two cameras, pointed straight at the jewellers, didn't pick up a single thing on the night of the robbery? I know there are a few more cameras around this site. And I bet they didn't catch a thing either. That so?'

'Don't know...'

'Don't know nothing,' Rook said. 'I guess there's a lot you don't know. Or, at least, you're not willing to say. But how about I help you out?'

Simon looked at Rook like an animal caught in a trap.

'I'm going to help you out,' Rook said, 'by telling you what happened. I think you work for a security company. Or a sort of one. I'm guessing that all the employees are one of you other species. And I'm willing to bet that the construction sites I passed at the other two burglaries I investigated today use the same security company. Now, wouldn't that be odd?'

Simon fidgeted with his fingers and avoided Rook's gaze.

'And I bet they turned their building sites into CCTV dead zones too. And this I'm very sure of: your boss is a guy called Sol,' Rook said.

A strangled 'Who?' escaped Simon's lips.

'Old troll, face like a bag full of walnuts. Don't pretend you don't know who I'm talking about.'

Simon sat frozen in response.

'Well, my talkative friend, I'm going to make you an offer. You can tell me exactly how this works or I'll go back to Sol. Tell him you told me all I know and see what happens.'

Simon's widening jaw told Rook he had hit home. The ghoul may not be the sharpest person Rook had ever interviewed, sitting in his cold hut with nothing but old newspapers for company, but he knew enough to fear Sol's wrath. It was cruel using Sol as a threat when Sol himself had already admitted to being involved. But Rook needed to know everything about how this operation worked. Hopefully, it would tell him more about Sol's business and give him some insight into what Caleb had been involved with.

'Listen,' Rook said, once he'd judged that Simon was suitably worried, 'Sol doesn't have to know. I only want you to tell me what you know. Then I'll be out of your way. But you better make me believe that you're telling me everything.'

Simon's mouth opened and shut a few times. Rook could see a fragment of uncooked bacon still caught in the ghoul's outsized, grinding teeth.

'You won't tell Sol anything?' Simon said.

'Not a word.'

'And then you'll leave me alone?' Simon asked, with the slightest note of hope that this would all go away and he could get back to his sandwich and papers.

'I'll forget you exist.'

Simon took a deep breath, the rising of his chest causing his oversized jacket to rustle.

'Okay, I don't know much. People don't tell me much. But I can tell you something.'

'And what's that?'

'We watch the shops.' He pointed to the feeds from the security cameras on his desk. 'Note down anything that happens.'

'Note down where?'

Simon leant forwards, slid a notebook out from under his jacket, and handed it to Rook. Rook opened it and found a diary noting when the jeweller's owner had locked up and left each night.

'You hand this into Sol?' Rook asked.

'No, never to Sol.' Simon's fear at hearing Sol's name shook his eyes in their sockets.

'Who did you talk to?'

'Don't know his name,' Simon said, but his voice lacked the conviction necessary to sell a lie.

'I'm not sure I buy that, my friend. Not sure I buy that at all. The deal was you tell me everything. Not just the odd bit of info you feel like giving away. Or I go to Sol.'

Simon was quiet, but Rook didn't push. It was time to let silence do its job. It was surprising how often it worked.

'Riothamus,' he said. 'It was Riothamus, but don't tell him I said anything.'

'Riothamus?' Rook said. 'Does he have a brother called Edgar?'

'I dunno,' Simon said. 'Maybe.'

'Tell me what happened to the cameras.'

'Riothamus drops by in the morning and tells us to change the camera's position. There's a gap in front of the door where the cameras don't touch, and one round the back where they come over the fence.'

Rook left the ghoul to his bacon sandwich and made his way home through the press of London at rush hour. *At last*, Rook thought as he polluted his lungs and the London air with cigarette smoke, *a good old-fashioned interview has led to a good old-fashioned lead*.

CHAPTER NINETEEN

The hammering from the building site rattled Rook's skull as he waited for Jacob. He took a gulp from his coffee and a drag from his cigarette and hoped that either the clangs of construction would cease or his hangover would disappear. Neither seemed likely.

After a few minutes more waiting than Rook could take, he saw Jacob stalk his way through the crowds of busy Londoners.

'You look tired,' Jacob said, once he had moved close enough to be heard over the noise.

'Feeling more human with every drag. No offence,' Rook said, taking a harsh draw of his cigarette that burnt his throat.

'None taken.'

'So, this is where Riothamus works.' Rook nodded his head towards the building site behind them. The builders were demolishing some old forgotten block of flats that stood within an otherwise commercial area. Men with broad backs and big bellies, wearing orange high-vis vests, crawled all over its decrepit structure, shouting and hollering as they pulled it apart.

Jacob nodded.

'What's with the Riothamus? Hardly common. Is it a troll name?'

'It's an old English one, I understand.'

'Are there any troll names? Or vampire names? Seems like everyone I meet has an English name.'

'Were you expecting to meet a lot of Draculas? Or Nosferatus?'

'Funny,' Rook said. 'I'm surprised you all use English names, that's all.'

Jacob sighed and scratched at his knuckles. 'We used to have our own names, all of us other species did. But then we also needed human names – it makes it easier to pass unnoticed. Occasionally they needed to be written down. And over time our original names became redundant. Now we only go by names in your language.'

'And Riothamus?'

'I assume his mother liked it.'

Small talk over, they went up to the gate where a red-cheeked and sweaty site manager came to meet them. Wearing a high-vis jacket over an ill-fitting suit, his too-short tie bounced on his paunch as he walked.

'I was told you were coming. Riothamus isn't in any trouble, is he?' he said, running pudgy hands through greasy black hair and giving Jacob a nervous glance.

'Of course not,' Rook said, happy to lie if it ended the conversation. 'We only need to talk to him.'

'Good, he works hard. He's clearing out the basement.' He jerked his thumb towards the five-storey building they were gutting behind them.

Rook and Jacob put on their hard hats and hi-vis jackets, which looked ridiculous over Rook's long winter jacket and Jacob's heavy brown coat. Rook couldn't hide his discomfort, but Jacob looked as stoic as ever. Paradoxically, this made him look even funnier. They descended a cracked wooden staircase into what used to be the basement of the building, where Riothamus was working alone.

The basement had once contained multiple rooms, but now that most of the internal walls had been demolished, it was one large space. The few temporary lamps placed in the middle of the floor weren't bright enough to reach the room's edges, leaving the space ringed in shadow. Rook coughed as the air, thick with dust, coated the inside of his mouth and nose.

Riothamus was demolishing a wall with casual swings of a sledgehammer. Each one threw up more dust into the air and sent echoes back towards Jacob and Rook.

As they got closer to the troll, Rook realised how massive Riothamus was. A full head taller even than Rook and built like a rugby player, he had a broad back and shoulders stacked with muscles Rook didn't know existed. Whereas the other trolls he had met had been chunky, there was nothing spare on Riothamus. He was all bone and muscle under a white T-shirt, orange hi-vis, and jeans. A hard hat, which could have swallowed Rook's entire head, was perched on top of Riothamus's enormous head.

As Rook and Jacob approached, the troll bent over, picked up a gigantic piece of masonry, and tossed it into a pile like it was paper. Only then did he turn around to look at Rook and Jacob with his pale-blue eyes.

'What's with the human, Jacob?' he asked.

'I'm surprised you haven't heard. This is Rook, our new police.'

Riothamus regarded Rook like a bear staring down a fox. 'You must have been pretty bad at your job to slum it with us other species.'

Rook ignored the jab. 'Have you worked in construction for a while?'

'That's right,' Riothamus said, slowly, as if admitting doing the job he was currently doing at that very moment might lead him into a trap.

'You do some building works on the side, such as bathrooms?'

'Sometimes,' Riothamus said. 'Why?'

'Because you also do another type of work on the side, don't you? Stealing expensive jewellery. Don't pretend you don't. I know you're involved in a few burglaries of jewellers. And I'm betting you've recently done some building work in a very expensive house in Mayfair. A house that, not long after, a vampire broke into and nicked some very expensive watches from. Nicked in a way that would be a mystery if vampires didn't exist.'

'You got a point?' Riothamus said, the weak glow of the temporary lamps casting shadows across his face, emphasising the line of his jaw and hiding one eye in darkness. He stood stock-still, his huge hands wrapped around the handle of his sledgehammer, his legs wide, with heavy worker's boots on his feet. His indifference to Jacob and Rook clear in every sinew, Riothamus's whole body radiated certainty and power, and Rook felt as nebulous as the air in front of him.

In a different time, Riothamus would have been a warrior king or a monster in a Viking legend, capable of killing ten men or more in single combat. But here he was, hidden in the basement of a construction site, keeping his presence unknown to humans, like a polar bear kept captive so long it had forgotten the existence of snow.

'You see, we know you used Caleb for at least the robbery of the watches. We found an Omega at Caleb's place. A very expensive Omega. Have to say, it stood out in his squat.'

Riothamus's grip tightened on the handle of his sledge-hammer, but he stayed quiet.

'Stealing from the jewellers isn't the problem,' Jacob said, tilting his head upwards to meet Riothamus's gaze. 'Those didn't attract attention. The burglary of the house? Having Caleb steal the watches in such a hard-to-explain way? That couldn't be ignored.'

'Have you come to kill me, Jacob? Here at work? You think this skinny human can provide you enough help?' Riothamus's lip curled into a smile.

'No one has to know any more, of course,' Rook said, interjecting to prevent a fight. A fight that, no matter who won, Rook was certain would be painful, even fatal, for him. 'Caleb is dead. Caleb had the watch, so that investigation can end if I decide. It's not like anyone else is looking.'

'Why would you do that?' Riothamus casually swung the huge sledgehammer over his shoulder with one hand.

'Because, like pretty much any detective, I don't want to be talking about the theft of some overpriced watches when I have a murder to solve.' Rook steeled himself, aware that his next question could pour gasoline on the fire he'd just tried to put out. 'Unless that's why you killed him? With Caleb being out of the way, you might have thought yourself safe from punishment.'

'You think I killed Caleb because I fear a visit from him?' Riothamus said, glowering at Rook and pointing the head of his sledgehammer at Jacob.

'Or because he'd kept a watch for himself,' Jacob said, stepping towards the towering Riothamus. His face was calm and he kept his eyes on Riothamus, despite now being inches from the sledgehammer.

'If I'd found out he'd stolen from me, Jacob, I wouldn't have been surprised. He was a thief.' Riothamus kept the sledgehammer pointed at Jacob, without any apparent effort. 'But I would have been angry. And I would have made him return it to me. I would have left him alive, but he wouldn't be fast anymore.'

Rook sighed and gently put his hand on Jacob's shoulder, moving the orc away from Riothamus and hoping neither noticed the shaking in his right knee. 'Now, boys, I know you're both very scary individuals. But let's not stage a death match in the middle of a construction site. Jacob isn't here to kill you, Riothamus. If he was, I promise I wouldn't be here with him. But I am a detective, and I need to ask these questions. And I need to ask you one more, but I'd prefer it if you put your sledgehammer down.'

Riothamus didn't let go of the hammer completely, but he did lazily drop it down to his side, so that the head of the hammer was resting on the floor as he gripped the shaft in his right hand. Rook decided against pressing the point.

'Do you want to tell me where you were on the night of Caleb's murder?' Rook asked.

'At home. By myself. That enough for you?'

'Not really. But it'll have to do for now.'

'It will. So, if you two have got nothing else to ask, then I'm going to get back to work.'

'There is one more thing, Riothamus,' Rook said, causing the troll to exhale in frustration. 'What can you tell me about your brother?'

'My brother?' Riothamus said, a look of surprise flitting across his face.

'That's right. Edgar, I believe.'

'What about him?'

'I understand he went missing last year.'

'Not much to say about Edgar.' Riothamus looked around the room he was busy demolishing, his gaze resting on a far wall.

'You aren't going to talk to us about your missing brother?' Rook asked.

A short exhale escaped Riothamus's nose, putting Rook in mind of a bull snorting before he charged. 'Caleb was looking into those of us who have gone missing,' he said, the words coming out slowly, each one weighed in his mind before being allowed to fall from his lips. 'He was asking questions. He tried official channels. And now he's dead. Executed in his flat. And now an executioner comes to my work asking questions about Edgar. You understand why I'm suspicious?'

'I didn't know about the disappearances, I've never heard of your brother, and I didn't kill Caleb,' Jacob said.

'That might be true. It might not. But it's not like I can take your word for it, is it? Now you should leave. Or we will have that death match in a construction site.'

The huge troll went back to breaking down a nearby wall, each smash of his hammer reverberating through the room.

Chapter Twenty

Perhaps the frustration of Riothamus stonewalling him over the disappearances had got to Rook more than he liked to admit. Or maybe he just needed to do something normal again as an antidote to the strangeness swirling around his life. Whatever the reason, Rook had been too tired to lie when his father called that afternoon. He wasn't sure if it was surprise or disappointment he'd heard in his father's voice when they'd agreed on a time and place to meet.

The time was seven, and the place was an old-fashioned curry house in Kingston. Unsurprisingly, Rook arrived first. Sitting down at a table in the corner, he ordered a pint for him and his father. The restaurant was cramped, and the blood-red wallpaper covered in ornate gold patterns only made it seem even less spacious. Soft lighting and smells of curry, beer, and sweat bathed the restaurant in a warm glow welcome on a cold night.

Rook was halfway through his pint when his father turned up, scanning the restaurant like a lost child searching for its parents in a crowded room. He hadn't been on time for anything since Rook's mother's funeral. He shuffled towards Rook's table in his old green Barbour coat over a charcoal-grey suit jacket that didn't quite match his trousers. Rook had seen him a few months before the Incident that had led to Rook being suspended, but he'd aged even since then.

His face had become gaunt, his body skeletal. The only mass on him was his bushy eyebrows, which were turning as grey as his thinning hair. It was a wonder he had the strength to propel himself forwards.

They muttered awkward hellos and then got straight to ordering their food. The customary poppadoms helped them avoid talking for a while, but at some point, conversation broke through the barrier of silence.

'Still wearing that,' his father said, flicking his finger towards the winter coat hanging on the chair next to him.

Rook looked at it as if appraising it for the first time. 'It's a bit faded, but it's still good.'

His father's thin lips parted to reveal his yellowing teeth. 'I know your mum bought it for you, but I don't think she expected you to keep it forever.'

'It was the last thing she bought me.'

'Then you should look after it better,' he said with a sad-eyed smile. 'But then, you never were great at looking after your clothes. Your brother would always look so smart, but even when you were dressed the same as your brother, you would always have your shirt untucked, or your collar misaligned. You remember?'

'I've seen the pictures,' Rook said, hoping that his father would take the hint and stop this line of questioning, which would be a first.

Luckily, the waiter ended this attempt at conversation by coming to the table with their food. The beers and poppadoms had sharpened Rook's hunger, and he tucked into his curry with gusto.

'You still on suspension?' his father asked after watching Rook eat for a minute.

'I'm through with the official police force. I've been moved on to somewhere else.'

'What does that mean?' His father took a mouthful of his curry.

Screw it, Rook thought. *If you're going to lie, lie big.* 'Well, because of what happened they couldn't have me back. But...' He took a gulp of beer and rubbed his chin. 'They found me a role in the Home Office. Said they didn't want to lose someone of my skills. So now I do undercover investigations for them. Look, I still get to keep my old ID.' Rook took his ID from his jacket pocket.

'Is that right? Home Office. Can you tell me what sort of thing you're investigating then?'

'Let's just say, there are some crimes that need to be kept secret, even from the police, but that still need to be investigated. I investigate them.'

A smile crept across the worry lines on his father's cheeks. It wasn't the broad smile Rook remembered from childhood camping holidays, but seeing it reminded him that there hadn't always been a chasm between them.

'Sounds like it's all worked out okay.'

'Could be a lot worse, I suppose,' Rook conceded, thinking back to the two weeks he'd spent stuck, drunk, in his apartment during his suspension.

'You're not missing being on the police force, then?' his father said, crunching into a poppadom.

'Missing it?'

'You used to love it. I remember you were working all the time, especially when...'

Rook didn't need him to finish the sentence. He was talking about after the murder of his mother. She'd been walking home one night and ended up stabbed in a side street, her handbag and jewellery stolen. A mugging gone wrong. Rook assumed his mother had fought when she should have acquiesced. After all, he got his bad temper from her. They'd never found the killer.

As soon as he'd finished the mandatory bereavement leave, Rook had dived back into work, working every hour he could, volunteering for every second of overtime. He'd even missed a memorial evening at his mother's firm as he was working some murder in Islington. They'd never solved that case either.

At first, when he'd made time to see his family, they'd ask if he had any news on his mother's case. Later, his father or brother would ask him something more general about his work, but it was clear they were fishing. Then they'd stopped asking at all, but Rook could still hear the questions forming in their minds. Looking back, he couldn't tell when this burst of activity had drained him. He just knew that every day it became harder to drag himself into work.

'Guess I lost my love for the job,' Rook said.

'What about this new job? Can you tell me anything about it? Or is it all too hush-hush?' His father attempted to waggle his eyebrows conspiratorially. It looked like he was having a seizure.

'Can't say much, I'm afraid. But I'm still a detective.'

'Are you enjoying it? Are you happy?'

Rook shoved food in his mouth while he thought of what he could be enjoying. The investigation was going nowhere, his partner was an executioner, and everyone he spoke to distrusted him at best and hated him at worst.

'I'm working on a case, Dad,' he said, taking a drink. 'I'm putting one foot in front of the other. What more could I ask for?'

CHAPTER TWENTY-ONE

R ook stumbled home, taking drags off his post-meal cigarette, smiling at the drunken sounds ringing out from the pubs and bars around him. His breath crystallised in the cold air, but the curry, beer, and time he'd spent with his dad still warmed him. To his surprise, after the initial awkwardness and questions, he'd enjoyed himself and had meant it when he'd said they should do it again soon. He suspected his father had too.

Rook found his way from the high street, still loud and busy at this late hour, to the quiet residential streets where he lived. Soon the joyous shouts and pounding music of late-night bars receded, and he was wandering down an empty street close to his flat. Well, not quite empty, as his drunken steps took him past a tall figure resting against a shuttered shop window. Someone a lot taller and much broader than Rook. A troll, in fact.

He was wearing a heavy black jacket over a green sweatshirt with the hood pulled over his head, but even in the poor light his bone-white skin and light blue eyes gave him away. That and the fact he was closer to seven feet than six and had hands that could palm a basketball.

'Hi...' Rook slurred.

'What?' the troll said, his heavy brow furrowing as he spoke.

Rook stammered an apology and forced his body forward. He was still cursing his stupidity at being surprised to see a troll outside of work when he heard hard footsteps hitting the pavement behind him. Rook glanced over his shoulder and, sure enough, the troll was following behind.

'Shit,' Rook muttered. He kept walking, trying to will his clouded mind into something approaching clear thought. It could be a coincidence that there was a troll following him, the only police officer aware of the other species' existence around. That would mean the troll was most likely following him to mug him. This wasn't that bad. Rook could tell the troll that if he didn't fuck off, he risked a visit from Jacob.

Rook slowed his pace and glanced over his shoulder again. The troll slowed to a hesitant pace in response.

'Fuck,' Rook said, under his cold breath. If the troll wanted to mug him, he would have kept walking. That meant the troll probably knew who Rook was. He clenched his fist as he worked out his next steps. He considered running, hoping he could either make it home or to the safety of a busy street.

'Bollocks to that,' he said under his breath. Sometimes the best idea was a bad idea.

Rook turned around, set his feet wide, took a deep drag of his cigarette, blew the smoke high into the sky, and shouted, 'Oi, troll, what do you think you're doing?'

The troll stopped dead, his breath curling into the night like smoke from a dragon's nostril. Thirty seconds passed and all he could hear was his own heartbeat and the distant noise of late-night traffic.

'What?' the troll said.

'You heard. Why are you following me?' Rook said with more confidence. He'd taken the initiative from the troll, and he wasn't giving it back.

'I'm not.'

'You were walking down this street by chance, then?'

The troll stood there without responding, facing Rook with his head bowed.

'Don't worry,' Rook said. 'I'll make it simple for you. I'm going to go home now. You can follow me, but then you better be willing to kill me. Otherwise, I will find you. And then your life will become interesting, violent and short. That understood?'

His voice was confident, but he could feel his heart rattle inside his ribcage. Without waiting for a response from the troll, he turned and walked away before his reserves of bravery ran out. His ears strained to hear the troll's footsteps but heard only the occasional sounds of distant streets.

He risked a look back as he rounded the corner. The troll was still standing there, watching Rook depart. His breath flooded his lungs in big gulps. In a stroke of luck, Rook soon passed a backstreet full of darkness, bins, and rats. Perfect for someone who needed to take an adrenaline- and beer-fuelled piss.

Afterwards, he calmed himself with yet another cigarette. It coated his mouth with the taste of dry ash, but he didn't stop taking drags until he'd smoked it down to the filter. After he'd gathered himself, Rook dragged himself home, dreaming of his safe flat and warm bed. He was smiling as he made his way up the stairs to his front door.

Then his smile vanished.

CHAPTER TWENTY-TWO

Whoever had broken into Rook's house hadn't bothered picking the lock – they'd ripped the door straight out of the frame. For a normal person, this would be a great time to call the police, but Rook never entertained it as an option. He'd faced down a troll in an empty street and he wasn't backing off now. He stepped through the doorway with a snarl on his face and anger in his chest.

'You should clean this place up, Rook,' a bored voice said. It came from a tall ghoul in a well-tailored dark suit who was resting his body against a wall, his long fingers flicking through a magazine Rook had left about. Rook swore inwardly when he realised it was Max, Sol's number two. He doubted that Max had torn his door from its hinges. That was likely the troll currently taking up about two-thirds of Rook's sofa.

The troll was sitting in a black shell suit that would make a shuffling sound as he walked. His white trainers rested on Rook's tiny table. His head was shaved and an unkempt beard covered his face. A face that hadn't looked towards Rook since his arrival.

Max finished reading whatever article it was he was reading, then threw the magazine onto the coffee table, almost hitting the troll's feet. He looked down his sizeable nose at Rook, his grey eyes zeroing in on him like a hawk that's seen a rabbit.

'It's time you and I had a chat,' Max said.

'Why did you have someone follow me?'

'You mean Tim?'

'Didn't catch his name, told him to fuck off.'

'Bet that confused him. People don't often say things like that to Tim. But we only wanted him to let us know when you were on your way. I hope he didn't worry you too much,' Max replied, his voice full of mock concern.

'Not in the slightest.'

'Glad to hear it.'

'You could have waited outside.' Rook moved farther into the room, which elicited a sideways glance from the troll lazing on his sofa.

'It was cold, and Wilson likes to put his feet up.' Max waved a hand at the troll, who nodded contently.

'You mind skipping the chit-chat, getting to the point, then fucking off?' Rook said.

Max stretched out his arms in a parody of a peaceful gesture. 'Now, now, Detective. You upset my boss, Sol, yesterday and he wants Wilson and me to make sure you understand more of how our world works and what your position in it is. It doesn't even have to be all bad for you, so you may want to be more polite to us; a bit more open to our presence.'

'Perhaps I'd be more polite if I hadn't come home to find that some bear in a shell suit had broken the lock off my door and made himself at home. In any case, how did I upset him? We'd already spoken about the jewellers.'

'We had, Detective, we had. And if you had left it at that, all may be well.' Max sighed theatrically. 'But then we found out you'd been investigating the robberies themselves. Even questioning our not-so-bright employees about matters they know next to nothing about. That upset us, Detective, it truly did. You could also have been a touch more...' – Max searched for the right word – 're-spectful, at our office.'

'How did you find out what I'd been doing?'

'We are very close with our employees, and they do not keep secrets from us. I was just speaking to young Simon myself, and he practically volunteered the information.'

'I think it's time you left. You and your pet troll.' Rook pushed himself into Max's personal space. The ghoul's smile didn't wilt nor his eyes blink.

'Oh, I am sorry you said that, Detective. I thought we were getting on so well. So well indeed.' Max stepped away from Rook and gave Wilson a polite nod.

Wilson grunted as he raised himself to his feet with an exaggerated effort, the room shrinking around him as he stood. Rook was still taking in Wilson's size when the blow snapped his ribs. Wilson had swung with such casual violence that Rook was on his knees and gasping for air before he'd had time to register the punch.

'You see,' Max said, coming closer to squat down next to Rook. 'I need you to understand something. To grasp the realities of your situation. You seem to think you're a tourist in our world; that you can go back to your scruffy flat and forget we exist. But that's not the case, Rook; that's not the case at all. You are part of this, and you need to know what that means. There's nothing to protect you. No other police to help. No courts to turn to.'

'You mind getting to the point?' Rook said, spitting the words from his mouth, along with his blood.

'Keep talking and Wilson will crush your hand so bad it won't be able to hold your dick. Be quiet and listen carefully. Terry understood. And you need to understand too. Stay out of our way. If Sol's interested in something, then you better make sure you aren't. In fact, we'd like you to make sure that none of our business interests or activities come to light. You do this, and you may even earn a bit of cash. Sol paid for Terry to drink himself half to death, and that can't have been cheap. Maybe you could buy yourself a new door with a better lock. Now, Wilson and I are going to report back to Sol, and you can think about what I've said.'

They left, leaving Rook to drag himself to his kitchen. He didn't bother finding a glass. He poured the whisky straight down his throat.

Chapter Twenty-Three

'You okay?' Nicole said. She'd watched Rook wince and groan since he'd struggled into the office but had held off from asking questions until he'd taken a few gulps of his morning coffee.

'Nothing a coffee won't fix,' Rook lied. He hadn't decided how he was going to respond to Max's "offer" from the night before, but he knew he wasn't ready to tell Nicole about it. The pain in his ribs was begging him to accept, but his pride was putting up a fight. Rook gazed at the whisky tumbler that Terry had left behind and wondered if he'd hold out. Maybe Terry had got the right idea. Turning a blind eye and getting drunk during the day wouldn't be the worst way to spend whatever remained of his career.

'How was your curry last night?' Nicole asked as Rook put down his coffee in front of her.

'Okay. Food was good, we had a few drinks. He asked about what I did.'

'Oh, what did you tell him?'

Rook grinned sheepishly. 'Said I worked at the Home Office, in a secret investigative role. Figured it would keep him happy and I could easily avoid answering further questions.'

'Good answer,' Nicole said, picking up her own over-sized coffee mug in both hands and taking a sip.

'What did you tell your parents?'

'I told them I was working for a logistics division of MI5. They get to think I'm working in a state-of-the-art office for the intelligence services, while I get to enjoy all this glamour.' She smiled and looked around the tiny London flat they called an office, where the only natural light came from the small windows behind her.

'Nicole, why are you here?' It was a question Rook had been meaning to ask for a while, and now seemed like the time.

'Excuse me?'

'I was wondering... I mean... I know why I'm here. Even before I shouted at that twat and became an embarrassment to the force, my career was going nowhere. But you're competent. And you're not an asshole like me. How did you end up working here?' Rook said, keeping his voice light as he noticed Nicole's lips purse.

'I'd worked with Steele on various projects. He present-
ed this opportunity to me, and I accepted.'

'Why?'

'I realised I could do some good for those who needed
it,' she said, with a shrug.

'Okay, what about Marlowe?'

'What about Marlowe?'

'You wanted to do good. I get that. But I can't imagine
Marlowe being motivated by altruism. What's his deal?'

'He told me that he was interested in studying the other
species. He believes that by coming to a better understanding of their physiologies, he could help them and help
humanity. I don't fully understand the science behind it
myself.' Nicole picked up her coffee mug, but it couldn't
hide her Cheshire cat grin.

Rook realised she desperately wanted him to ask her a
follow-up question, so he played along. 'What is it you
aren't telling me, Nicole?'

'Okay, since you interrogated me, I'll tell you.' She put
her mug down and dived straight into telling Rook what
she knew, clearly glad to be sharing a story she had been
sitting on for a while. 'I did some digging on Marlowe. It
turns out he wasn't employed when he took this job. In
fact, he left his previous position – a senior research role –
under something of a cloud.'

'What sort of cloud?'

'Well, it was all very hush-hush, and even I couldn't get all the details. But from what I found out, he played fast and loose with the rules in a medical trial. Altered the doses and decided who should and shouldn't get a placebo in a double-blind trial.' She raised her neat eyebrows to emphasise the salacious nature of the gossip she was imparting.

'Why did he do that?'

'I'm not a doctor, so I couldn't tell you the ins and outs of it, but apparently, he thought it was necessary to get better or more interesting results. Whatever it was, he didn't face any criminal charges for it. But it halted an already faltering career dead in its tracks.'

'And Steele still hired him?'

'We are the department of second chances,' Nicole said, raising her arms, palms upwards, as if in praise. Which was true for Rook and Marlowe apparently, if not Nicole. It made Rook uncomfortable to think of any similarities between himself and Marlowe, but they were clearly more alike than either would probably admit. He wondered if someone had given Marlowe the same speech he'd given Rook about being a loner no one believed.

His musings were cut short by two bangs: the first of the door burst open, the second when it slammed against the wall.

A vampire wearing blue jeans and a black balaclava and jacket sped into the room, knocking Nicole off her seat before Rook had time to stand up. They were carrying a baseball bat. Thankfully, they didn't use it.

Next through the door was probably an orc, as they weren't big enough to be a troll, as fast as a vampire, nor spindly like a ghoul. They were dressed the same as the vampire and were also wielding a baseball bat. Unfortunately for Rook, they *were* happy to use it. On him. Smashing it into the side of his chest. Breaking the ribs opposite to the ones the troll Wilson had busted up the previous night.

Rook was gasping for air on the floor when the troll entered the room. The troll was also wearing a balaclava, but Rook couldn't figure out why they bothered with a disguise. It was clearly Riothamus. Rook could tell from his size, shape, and the way he was standing like he was challenging the world to a fight.

While Rook and Nicole were on the floor, the trio grabbed the computer towers. Then they bolted. A few seconds later Rook heard the rev of an engine and the shouts of passers-by as the thieves sped away.

The burglary took less than three minutes. Rook pushed himself to his feet, wondering how many broken ribs a man could have and his lungs still work.

He was about to make a grim joke, but it caught in his throat as soon as he walked around the table to Nicole. She was completely still, her body trembling as she laid on the floor as if stuck by glue.

'Hey,' he said, bending down and putting his arms on her shoulder. 'Let's get up.' He eased her back into her chair. Her eyes were glazed over, unfocussed, and so wide it looked like her cheekbones might snap. It was as if her brain had given up on processing visual inputs while it dealt with the shock of what had happened. Her hands were in her lap, right hand holding her left, trying to stop it from shaking.

Rook left her in her chair and went back to the kettle. *Funny thing about us British*, he thought. *Despite the national stereotype, most of us prefer coffee to tea. But as soon as there's a crisis, we turn to tea for comfort. Preferably with a biscuit*. So that's what he got, taking all the packets down from the cupboard and putting them in front of her. Her hand shook its way towards the chocolate bourbon.

'How do you take it: milk, one sugar?' he said, showing her their rarely-used tea box.

'Two, please,' she replied in a voice he had to strain to hear.

'We should get a sofa in here. Something to relax in; make the place comfier. And some better biscuits.'

'We've been broken into by some guys with baseball bats and you want to talk home furnishing and snacks?' Nicole said, nibbling her bourbon.

'You're right, we should start with getting a better lock on the door. Do you mind if I smoke? I know it's against all sorts of rules. But special circumstances and all.'

'Only if I can have one.'

'Didn't know you smoked,' Rook took a crumpled cigarette packet from his pocket and smoothed it out.

'Special circumstances,' she said, her voice bitter.

They opened the window, the winter air causing Rook to give a shiver that rattled his broken ribs. He handed Nicole a cigarette and a lighter. It took her three attempts to light the cigarette. After a couple of drags, a big wet tear formed in her left eye and plunged down onto the street below.

'Fuck,' she said, and then with more vigour, 'Fuck, fuck, fuck.'

'They going to get something we should be worried about from those computers?'

She shook her head. 'When they turn it on from a different location, the hard drive will wipe itself. Don't worry, it's backed up once a week offsite, so you shouldn't lose much. It's...' She pointed her cigarette at the street in a stabbing motion as she tried to find whatever it was she was trying to say.

'You asked me why I took this role. Why I decided to work in this shitty office? It wasn't only to help. I wanted to do... something useful. I'd done well in school, gone to a good university, got a good degree, and then went into the civil service. I'm smart. I know I'm smart. And I'm great with computers and figuring out problems. I'm just not good at getting people to listen to me. Or notice me.'

Nicole paused, but Rook didn't prompt her. He gave her a moment to take a drag of her cigarette and look out at the street. Normal people were shuffling about beneath them, going about their business, but no one looked up at Nicole and Rook smoking above them and no one had seemed bothered by the break-in. It had only been another background noise on a busy London street – another event occurring in someone else's life – so not worth bothering about.

'If there was a group,' Nicole said, 'I'd always be on the outside. I never had that ability to click with people. It's like I've spent my whole life a second late to the conversation or on the edge of the joke. I thought it would change when I got to the civil service. That people would value me for my work, but no matter what I did or said, I'd be overlooked. If I had an idea, it would be used but only once someone else had got the credit. Maybe they'd give it a snappier title, have better delivery, or use a different font. But if the project went ahead, I'd be left behind.'

She tapped her cigarette with a trembling finger to get rid of the built-up ash. 'But then Steele took an interest in what I was saying. And I thought I might end up working with him some more; might actually be valued... But one day we had what he called "an open and frank discussion". He told me my career in the civil service was going nowhere. I wasn't ever going to "fit". But, with my background in computer science and logistics, I could do some real good here. I had my doubts, of course, but I respected him, so I accepted. And now... now I let my dad be so very proud that his daughter works for MI5. And I hate myself more each day for lying.'

'Nicole, I've only known about this world for a few days, and I've already seen how much you do to help. So what if your dad is proud of you for the wrong thing? He should be proud of you. You help more people here than you ever would working for some incompetent minister in Whitehall or the spooks in MI5.'

Nicole smiled without showing her teeth and took another drag of her cigarette, causing her to splutter and cough. 'You think they'll get much for the computers?'

'They won't sell them. There are better places to steal computers from. What they wanted was on *those* computers.'

'We'll have to tell Steele. Then they'll have to be caught and...' she trailed off.

'Then Jacob gets sent in and they likely die. Over some computers. Computers they can't even use.' Rook could hazard a guess about who had helped Riothamus carry out the attack. But he'd need confirmation before he shared his ideas.

Rook stubbed his cigarette out on the cracked wood of the window frame. His ribs on one side ached where Max had broken them, and on the other where he'd been hit by a baseball bat. He pictured himself going back to his flat, watching the whisky pour into the glass, and then enjoying every sip and gulp until he passed out.

'Fuck this,' Rook said.

'Fuck what?'

'People do stupid shit, Nicole. But don't let it drag you down. I'll find the idiots who did this. And I'll even find out what's happening to these missing people and who killed Caleb.'

'You sound confident,' Nicole said, dispelling the last of her tears with a disdainful swipe of her hand.

'No. I'm mad.' Mad enough to tell a ghoul where he could shove his offer.

CHAPTER TWENTY-FOUR

The cold afternoon air felt like rough shards of ice pressing against Rook's skin. He drained his take-away coffee and threw the cup in the bin, wondering if anyone inside Sol's had noticed him loitering outside. The street was empty, and he wasn't inconspicuous in his suit and long coat.

Rook lit a cigarette and his mind drifted to his earlier call with Nicole. He had suggested she take a day to get over the previous day's attack, but she had gone straight back into the office and was busy organising new computers and a new door. Rook couldn't detect a single note of unease or fear in her voice. She'd shaken off her ordeal and was now back to work. Rook wasn't sure whether he should be impressed, worried, or both.

He stubbed out his cigarette and took a deep breath that sent shockwaves of pain through his beaten-up chest. His ribs still ached from the damage from Wilson's fist and the previous day's baseball bat.

The shop was as murky as he remembered it, with shelves covered in useless odds and ends. The same orc was sitting behind the till. His thin face twisted into a grimace as Rook entered.

'I'm here to see Sol,' Rook said.

'He's not in,' the orc muttered, green eyes shifting around the room, looking everywhere but at Rook. Rook almost felt bad for him. He'd probably been having a peaceful day until Rook had ruined it for him.

'Is that right? Maybe I should send Police Officer Lassiter around again.'

'I'll go down and see,' he said, shuffling quickly through the door at the back. *Good*, thought Rook. *It looks like sending Lassiter to see Sol this morning has had the desired effect.* It had been a risk, but he couldn't let what Max had done stand. He'd called one of his few friends left on the force and asked for a favour: knock on Sol's door and ask some questions about the burglaries, making it appear that Sol's actions were on the police's radar. About an hour ago, Lassiter had called him to say that the deed was done, and that Rook owed him a bottle of whisky.

A moment later, the orc opened the door. 'He says you can come down,' he mumbled.

Sol was sitting behind his desk, his head resting in one of his massive hands, his mouth curled in contempt. His rumpled light-blue shirt was hanging loosely from his massive body. Rook wasn't surprised to see Max standing in the corner, stick-thin and ash-grey in his dark suit – like an undertaker without a funeral. He gave Rook a broad grin, revealing a set of oversized ghoul teeth. Rook ignored him and took his seat.

'I take it you coming round after that copper came snooping isn't a coincidence,' Sol stated, tapping the table with enough force that each touch of his finger caused a loud thud.

'What do you think?' Rook said, letting his long frame lounge in his chair and his smile widen all the way across his face. He radiated a smugness that had to be as annoying as a scab on a testicle.

'And you think because you had a copper come round, you can come flouncing in here and expect me to give a shit?'

'Pretty much. Yes.'

'And no part of you is worried that we might ask Wilson to come down and finish what he started the other night?' Sol growled.

'I think that having a member of Her Majesty's constabulary visit your clear front of a shop upstairs got your attention and you're not sure what to do. But don't worry, Sol. I can help you.'

'Is that right?' Sol said, lips curling and nostrils flaring. The old troll's muscles shifted under his shirt like the movement of continents. Rook tried to forget how easy it would be for Sol to rip him apart.

'It is. You thought that having tall and skinny here' – he yanked a thumb towards Max in the corner, who chuckled at the jibe – 'come around to mine with his giant friend to scare me into your pocket was a good idea. Guess you figured that, because I'm working with the other species, I don't have any influence.'

'You think you do?' Sol cut in.

'Enough to get the real police to look at your dealings, should I wish. They won't know what you are, of course, but I could share information on the jewellers you've been robbing and some more crimes when I put my mind to it. I could even ask someone to look at your taxes. And won't that draw attention? All it will take is for your name to be on one report and people higher up than me or you will take notice. Then I'll get the word to shut this whole operation down. They won't even ask me to investigate or see why you were being investigated...'

'Careful, Rook, or you may find it harder to get out of this room than you expected,' Max said as he inspected his nails.

'Don't be hasty, Max,' Rook said. 'Should anything happen to me, I've left very specific notes with those I work for about the meeting we're having now. If you're suspected of killing me, it will not go well for you.'

Silence fell across the room. Sol rolled his eyes towards Max, and Rook could tell there was a wordless conversation going on between them.

'Fine. We can agree to stay out of each other's way,' Sol said, turning his stern gaze back to Rook.

Rook took a breath and steeled himself before he attempted to push his advantage further – possibly too far.

'Oh, that's not it. You're going to do a couple of things for me.'

'Be careful how you tread,' Max said in a voice a touch louder than a whisper.

Sol waved one of his bear-paw hands at Max to quiet him.

'Tell me what it is you want and go.'

'Three people broke into our office yesterday. And I want their names.'

'We had nothing to do with that,' Sol said.

'I know, but I got a picture of the van they used from a nearby CCTV camera.' He pulled the picture out from his jacket and placed it on Sol's desk. 'And it looks pretty similar to the ones I saw at your construction sites. Even has *Bridge Construction Services* written on the side.'

Sol tilted his head towards Max, who came forwards and picked up the picture.

'What do you want to happen to these people when we find them? A beating? A maiming? Worse?' Sol said, like he was reading out a menu at a run-down café.

'Just their names, nothing else. Don't even approach them.' Rook stood up and straightened his jacket. 'Let me know as soon as you have anything. I expect you can get results fast.' He turned around and swept out of the room.

Rook held his nerve until he got out of the shop, despite his ears reverberating with the sound of his heart beating against his ribcage. But the moment he stepped outside, he raced around the corner into a dirty side street and frantically lit up a cigarette he needed but wouldn't enjoy.

A cough alerted Rook to Jacob's presence. The orc stepped away from the shadows of the wall and into the light.

'How long have you been waiting for?' Rook said, gasping between coughs and drags of his cigarette. Jacob had offered to come to the meeting with Rook. Rook had declined, believing it would be better long-term if he faced Sol alone, so Jacob had agreed to meet him afterwards. If nothing else, it had given Rook the confidence that Jacob would know where he was should something go wrong.

'Not long – you're out quicker than I expected. And with none of your limbs broken,' he said.

'I got what I wanted. Didn't think it was a good idea to stick around.'

'Wise decision. Do you think Sol will come through?'

Rook took a few puffs of his cigarette, letting the harsh taste fill his mouth. 'I don't know. But if it doesn't cost him anything, he may humour us.'

'If you had wanted, I could have had a more direct conversation with him,' Jacob said.

'That's not going to be a solution for every problem, Jacob,' Rook replied, stubbing out his cigarette.

Whatever Jacob was about to say was interrupted by the orc's phone vibrating. He pulled a face, like the phone had offended him by daring to make a noise, as he retrieved it from his pocket. Rook couldn't hear whoever was on the other end, but he could see Jacob's deep-set eyes narrow and his heavy jaw set in a picture of pure rage.

'We'll be there in ten minutes,' Jacob said, shoving his phone back in his pocket and storming off. Rook did his best to follow while wondering what the hell was going on.

CHAPTER TWENTY-FIVE

J acob rattled through the London streets in the tin can he called a car, his green-tinged skin turning white around his knuckles as he gripped the wheel. Rook tried to get Jacob to tell him what had happened, but Jacob would only tell him that Michael was hurt, and they had to get back to his home. Rook winced with each jolt, the seatbelt digging into his bruised ribs, and silently prayed they wouldn't crash.

Jacob didn't worry about where he parked and ended up half on the curb, the front of the vehicle covering the pavement and the back hanging out into the road.

The front door to Jacob's house was closed but not locked. The lights were on in the living room, but no one was there, and nothing was disturbed.

'You left Michael alone?' Rook said.

'Carolina was with him,' Jacob said as he hurried into the lounge.

Rook was worrying they had a missing troll on their hands, when they heard a sob from upstairs.

They moved up the stairs in silence, as if they feared to intrude on Michael's sorrow. There were three rooms: the bathroom; the room next to it, which had its door shut (Jacob's, Rook presumed); and a room with its door open but the light off – Michael's room. The shaking sobs grew louder as they got closer.

'I'm going to turn the light on now. Is that okay, Michael?' Jacob said when he reached the doorway.

Michael let out a low moan and Jacob switched the light on, revealing the massive figure of the troll lying on the bed, looking at the ceiling and crying. He was wearing blue tracksuit bottoms and a grey T-shirt that he had probably grown out of a few years ago at least. The bed was long enough that Michael could lie down without folding his legs and just barely wide enough that his shoulders hung slightly over its sides.

Rook almost smiled when he saw the bedspread: it was sky blue and Disney-princess-themed. The parts of the bed not concealed by Michael were adorned with various princesses and the occasional catchphrase like 'let it go' from Disney movies. The drawn curtains were dark blue and heavy. A white wardrobe with its doors shut loomed over the room. On the bedside table sat a bronze-coloured lamp beside a Captain America action figure. A child's bedroom, Rook thought, with a six-and-a-half-foot troll living in it.

'Are you okay, Michael?' Jacob said, concern written into the crevices of his brow.

Michael glanced towards Jacob and Rook, but then looked back at the ceiling. The bruises on his face were wet with tears.

'What happened? Where's Carolina?' Jacob said.

'Her boyfriend came for her.'

'Darren? What happened?' Jacob asked again. His voice was quiet but had the hint of an edge, like a knife concealed in a gloved hand.

'He was angry. Said that Carolina had been spending too much time here. She hadn't been paid enough.'

'What did Carolina say?' Jacob said.

'She tried to say something, but he shouted at her. I asked him not to...' He started sobbing again, trying to wipe away the tiny tears with his heavy hands.

'And she left straight away; didn't even lock the door?' Jacob said.

'She didn't want to,' Michael wailed. 'He made her.'

'No one is mad at you, Michael. Or Carolina. Everything will be okay. Tell us what happened next.' Jacob leant down next to the bed and put his hand on Michael's giant paw.

Michael swallowed. 'We were watching TV together. There was a banging at the door and Carolina went to answer and they started shouting. Then he was in the room, shouting at me. I didn't know what I had done wrong, Jacob, but I said sorry, but he said' – Michael rubbed his forehead with his meaty fingers as he tried to remember the exact words – 'she shouldn't be spending time with stupid freaks like me when he was around. I tried to say sorry. He laughed and kicked me in the face.'

'In the face?' Rook interjected, unable to stop himself.

It was Jacob who responded, 'You were lying down to watch TV, weren't you, Michael?'

Rook remembered how he'd first seen Michael lying in front of the TV, looking up at it with rapt attention. The thought of him being kicked by a violent thug caused Rook's fists to itch and his temperature to rise. He had never been good at keeping his temper, a family trait he'd inherited from his mother. Seeing Michael cry left him feeling the familiar pricks of rage throughout his nervous system; every fibre and sinew demanding action.

'He kicked me a lot,' Michael said, shaking his head.

'Is that all that happened?' Jacob asked, giving Michael's hand a squeeze.

'He dragged Carolina out and left me.' Michael's watery blue eyes looked up at Jacob. 'I'm sorry, Dad. I didn't know what to do.'

'It's okay, you did well. You didn't hurt him. He doesn't know how strong you are.'

'But... I didn't stop him.'

'That's okay, we can sort that out. Can't we, Rook?'

'Of course,' Rook said. He didn't know what he could do, but he would need to do something. Rook glanced at Jacob and realised that sorting out Addy wasn't his biggest problem. While Jacob was all concern now, Rook suspected that concern would soon turn to vengeful anger.

'But for now,' Jacob continued, 'why don't you wait up here while Rook and I talk downstairs? Then we'll go out.'

'Out?' Michael asked.

'Yeah, how does a pizza and a movie strike you?'

A big smile spread across Michael's face. 'Sounds good, Dad. Thanks.'

'Okay, Michael. Let me finish up with Rook first.'

With that, Rook and Jacob left the room and went downstairs, leaving Michael behind them, still shaken but happier than when they'd found him.

'Don't,' Rook said when they were back in the living room.

'Don't what?' Jacob said, his voice calm.

'Don't go after Darren. Leave it to me.'

'And what, exactly, will you do?'

'I'll talk to him. See if Carolina will press charges. Trust me, I will make sure he regrets this.'

'What are the chances of him seeing justice? Of getting what he deserves?' Jacob said, his deep-set eyes wide and fierce, his fists clenched by his side.

'You can't go after him, Jacob. Trust me, I know from bitter experience. If you lash out, it could backfire – no matter how much he deserves it. Let me figure out what to do.' Rook knew his words fell on deaf ears the moment they left his lips. He could only hope that Jacob would calm down enough to let Rook help before he did something himself.

Jacob stared at Rook, his jaw clenched. 'You should leave. I have to take care of Michael,' he said, going back upstairs to see his son.

CHAPTER TWENTY-SIX

Nicole greeted Rook with a fragile smile and a half-hearted hello. She was sitting in front of a brand-new computer, a twin of which was on his desk. She'd also replaced the office door with a far sturdier jet-black model that looked about half a foot thick. Rook didn't know if you could get a troll-proof door, but Nicole had clearly tried.

'You've got everything fixed pretty fast.'

'I'm a logistics expert managing a clandestine office. What good would I be if I didn't have supernatural powers of requisition?' Nicole said, motioning around the office with a wave of her hand.

Rook gave a weak chuckle. 'Thanks. I don't suppose you've got the extra CCTV footage I asked for?'

'Of course. It sometimes takes me longer to get CCTV footage than the police, particularly if it's from private sources. But I get there in the end.'

Rook switched his computer on, and Nicole had indeed sent him the footage he needed. He started working through the CCTV to corroborate the alibis he'd been given. Sadly, they all checked out. Multiple cameras had picked up Nathan walking back from Caleb's at the time he'd said. That alone didn't rule him out, though. It wasn't like they had a precise time of death for Caleb, after all. But he was noticeably not covered in blood. Cameras also captured Abby at the petrol station, buying cigs, blood-free as well. The cameras confirmed that not only had they left the street, but they'd also gone back to their homes. Rebecca was seen stumbling into the street when she'd said she had too. She still could have killed him, called Jacob, and somehow got rid of her bloody clothes by the time Jacob had arrived. But that seemed far from likely and too pre-planned for such a vicious killing.

Rook wasn't surprised. The case had been nothing but dead ends at every turn. Other than the addition of the disappearances, he had hardly touched the crime boards since he'd got them out of the storeroom. A few marks here to denote an alibi or add more to the timeline, or a new line of enquiry. But other than that, all that was on there were a few pictures and a list of questions. What was meant to be a way to visualise the crime and spark theories had become another piece of clutter.

Riothamus still didn't have an alibi and could have been angry about Caleb keeping hold of the watch. But Rook couldn't place him near the scene. So, unless he'd hidden his seven-foot frame in the boot of a car and waited for hours for Caleb to turn up, and to be left alone, he was unlikely to be the culprit. Anyway, Riothamus seemed more like the club someone to death type rather than a frantic stabbing sort of murderer.

That left the disappearances. Rook couldn't rule out the possibility that these people were leaving their lives without warning or notice. It happened, especially when people felt alone and ignored. People could also kill themselves in quite ingenious ways that made discovery impossible. It was one mystery of modern life people didn't like to think about. Around 200,000 people a year go missing in the UK, and there are currently around 6,000 people who have never been found. If humans were that prone to going missing, the other species would be doubly likely to. They already lived on the edge of society, ignored and unwanted.

But, even without Caleb's involvement and subsequent murder, Rook was convinced there was something more sinister about these disappearances. The people had all vanished too completely and too suddenly for Rook not to be suspicious. Sadly, until he found a connection between the supposed victims, it was hard to take the case any further.

He continued to look at the crime boards, hoping that something would leap out at him. But he found it hard to concentrate as his mind kept wandering to what Jacob was planning for Carolina's boyfriend. He was about to confide in Nicole but decided against it. If Jacob had wanted Nicole's help, he would have asked for it. Rook would just have to hope he could defuse the situation before Jacob did something that couldn't be undone.

A message from Max interrupted Rook's train of thought. Sol's man said he had info on the people who'd broken in, and they should meet and discuss it at a café close by.

A short walk later and Rook was in a café he couldn't stand. It was a trendy, independent place, with exposed brick walls, wooden tables, and baristas being driven mad by swing music that Rook assumed was ever-so-cool, but grated on his ears.

Max walked through the door ten minutes after the meeting was meant to start. Standing bolt upright in his fitted dark-grey suit, the bald ghoul surveyed the café until he found Rook, and a lazy smile spread across his face. He held a finger up to let Rook know he'd be with him in a minute and then went to the counter.

Rook watched how the baristas reacted to Max with interest. One of them gave his ash-grey skin and oversized jawline a second glance, but that was it. To everyone else, he was just someone with a skin tone a couple of shades outside the normal range. Nothing a skin condition or genetic disorder wouldn't explain. Only someone too deep into conspiracy theories would jump to the conclusion he wasn't human. How many times had Rook seen an orc, troll, ghoul, or vampire and not realised?

'Glad you could meet me here, Rook. I do love the coffee,' Max said, sitting down opposite Rook and taking a sip of what looked like a latte.

'I'm happy to meet wherever, Max. If you've got useful information for me. Now, tell me what you've found out, or do we have to sit listening to this awful music together?'

'Oh, it's like that, is it?' Max replied, putting his hand on his chest to mime shock. 'I thought we could chat. Maybe strike up a beautiful friendship. The ghoul and the detective, solving crimes together while they bond.' He made a dry noise that might have been a chuckle.

'Yeah, my ribs are still hurting from that little chat we had the other night. So I'd rather get on with it, if it's all the same to you.'

'I will tell you what I've discovered, and I'm sure you'll be impressed with the thoroughness of my work. But first I should give you some advice. A word to the wise,' Max said.

'Should you?' Rook said, rubbing the stubble on his chin and staring at Max.

'Oh, trust me, hearing this could save your life.' Max took another drink of his coffee and waited for Rook to respond.

'Fine. Give me this oh-so-important advice.'

'Well, since you asked so nicely. You see, I liked what you did the other day. Turning the tables on us. It was smart. Even a touch funny to see the boss get wound up after you left. Made the day a bit different. I even enjoyed finding out who had used one of our vans and broken into your office. It was like being a private detective in one of those novels. Although, when I ask people something they normally tell me the truth pretty quickly. On account of me having their legs broken if they waste my time.'

'This getting to a point anytime soon, Max?' Rook cut in. 'I've almost finished my coffee.'

Max rolled his eyes, mock-irritated by Rook interrupting his conversational flow. 'I'm getting there, Detective Rook. I'm getting there. You see, you need to understand something about this relationship. We've done this for you. This type of work doesn't cost us much. Doesn't cost us much at all. We can write it off as the cost of doing our sort of business. Until…'

'Until what?' Rook said.

'Until that cost of business becomes too high,' Max said, lifting his long grey hand parallel to his head to make his point. 'Then you go from a small problem now and again, like a pimple that keeps coming back, to becoming a problem that needs dealing with, like cancer. And we would have to deal with you in a certain way. A final way. You may think you have some protection because of your position, or because you're human or whatever. But the fact is, if you disappear, and you would disappear, how many people notice? I'd put a lot of money on it not being many. And then your bosses would face a choice. Do they kick up a fuss because you died? Or do they let it go because you're not worth the fuss?'

'You going to tell me who broke into the office or are we going to continue this delightful chat?' Rook said, hoping his indifference showed he either didn't see the truth in Max's words or just didn't care about them.

'Okay, okay. Ignore my free and heartfelt advice. Well, I did some checking and, yes, that was one of our trucks. It had been taken from one of the construction sites we've been working on. I checked the footage, and lucky for you we caught all three on camera when they dropped it back. The cameras were pointed the wrong way when they stole it but, lucky for us, a hard-working ghoul noticed and set them right by the time the van was returned. I can send you the footage if you don't believe me.'

'Send the footage later. Give me their names now.'

Max did. And Rook swore.

Chapter Twenty-Seven

The green tinge to Rebecca's skin paled as soon as she opened the door to see Rook. She was about to shut it in his face when he shot his hand out and said, 'Wait. If I wanted to take you in, don't you think I'd have brought Jacob with me?'

Rebecca lived in a block of council flats, with long corridors lined with identical yellow doors. The floors were dirty, and the walls were covered with graffiti that someone had attempted to remove. Even in his ill-fitting suit and coat, Rook felt like a peacock in a chicken coop as he waited for Rebecca to let him in.

'Then I suppose you can come in,' she said, leaving the door open and moving back inside. She was wearing tastefully ripped black jeans and a dark T-shirt from a Specials tour, which emphasised every angle of her frame.

Pictures of various family members and friends adorned the walls. A dark-blue sofa faced an old TV. Next to them sat a dining table currently holding a bouquet of purple flowers in a glass vase. A delicate gold-coloured, old-fashioned clock sat on the mantelpiece, ticking the seconds. Someone had dumped a pillow and a white duvet bearing a pattern of roses on one end of the sofa – the only items in the flat that appeared out of place.

Through the door to the left of the room there was a poky kitchen, on the other side of which was a dark room Rook assumed was Rebecca's bedroom. An air of sadness settled across the sparse furniture like dust in a disused library.

Rebecca curled herself into the sofa after moving the duvet and pillow onto the floor. It left Rook nowhere obvious to sit, other than next to her, so he pulled up a chair from the dining table, took his notebook out, and sat down opposite her. Both his position in the room and the chair itself made his body itch with awkwardness.

'Why would you want to take me in? Or whatever?' Rebecca asked with a lazy shrug and a pointed look on her face.

'Are you really going to pretend you don't know, Rebecca?' Rook shrugged. 'You broke into our office. Smashed a bat into my chest. I think you might have broken a rib, by the way. Don't deny it. You were seen getting out of the truck you *borrowed* from Sol. You know why I'm here.'

'Yeah, sorry about the baseball bat. I got carried away. Well, maybe just a bit.'

'Thanks for the apology, I guess. Why did you do it? I take it the computers didn't give you anything useful.'

'Not a damn thing,' she said.

'Did you think you could just switch them on and find out our secrets?'

'We know this ghoul – he's good with computers. Thought he could find a way in. Didn't work though.'

'Of course it didn't. Nicole is, without a doubt, very smart. Why did you do it in the middle of the day? Why not wait until night?'

'We figured you locked them up in a safe or something at night. Given they must have information about the other species and whatnot on them.'

'Well, you'd be right about that,' Rook lied, shifting in his seat and making a note to run that idea past Nicole as soon as he got back to the office. 'What were you looking for, anyway?'

'We want to know what's happened to those of us who went missing.'

'I'm looking into that.'

'Really,' she said, tilting her head. 'And what have you found out about it?'

'I know three people have disappeared. A vampire called Benjamin, an orc called Jeremiah, and a troll called Edgar.'

'There are more than that,' she said, looking away from Rook and at the pictures on the wall behind him. She took a deep breath, then the words poured out. 'Clara Patton – a vampire who lived by herself in Croydon and had arthritis – went missing first. We think she went missing around twenty months ago, in June 2020. Then there was Pauline Coulson. She had a cough she couldn't get rid of. She disappeared five months later. Sean Davies – a ghoul who worked as a cleaner for some big law firm in Canary Wharf – probably went missing four months after that, March 2021. Then there was Edgar, Jeremiah and finally Benjamin, all taken in the last nine months. Although, it is hard to be sure of the dates; it normally took a while for anyone to notice someone was gone.'

'How come you know some of these people were ill, Rebecca? Did you know them?' Rook said, still taking notes of who had gone missing when.

'Not well,' she said, crossing her arms across her chest.

'But you knew them. How?'

'They were all regulars at the centre.' Rebecca bared her teeth to bite her lip.

'You met them there?'

She nodded, her wild black hair bobbing up and down.

A confused moan came from the darkened room that Rook had assumed was empty. It took a couple of more moans for Rook to work out that whoever was in the room was calling out for Rebecca.

'I'm sorry.' Rebecca sighed, her sharp shoulders sagging. She pushed herself off the sofa and made her way to the other room.

Rook could hear her whispering reassuringly to whoever was in there. In minutes the moans subsided, and Rebecca returned.

'My mother,' she said, after sitting back down. 'She's not well.'

'What's wrong?' Rook said.

'She's dying. We orcs don't get many illnesses or diseases. But we do get one particularly nasty one.'

'What is it?'

'We call it The End. Your body breaks down. The longer you live, the worse it gets. Your reward for lasting as long as Mum has is to go half-blind, mostly deaf, and be almost completely bedridden.'

'Is there anything you can do for her at the health centre?'

'The health centre can't handle anything major. It can't do much more than first aid. Marlowe looked at her, stuck her with needles, took some samples. But he shook his head and gave her some powerful pills. Said it would take years for him to understand The End, never mind treat it.'

'Is there nowhere that can look after her?'

'You think there's an old care home for orcs?' Her eyes burrowed into Rook and he felt like a bug under the sun's glare. 'Somewhere nice by the sea where we can feel a pleasant breeze in our hair while we cough a lung out of our mouths? Most humans can't afford to die in dignity. You think we get that luxury?'

Rook tried to think of something clever or consoling to say, but nothing came. She was right, of course. Letting people die in the shadows was something society was happy to allow. Or, at least, was willing to ignore. Sure, you might feel sad when you saw an advert for some charity on TV about the old and the sick dying alone. But then you'd take a drink and carry on whatever it is you were watching.

'You said all those who disappeared had been to the health centre,' Rook said, ashamed to have to turn the conversation back to why she'd broken into the office and cracked him with a baseball bat. 'If you had their names, why break into my office and steal the computers?'

'We need to know what's happened to them. Find out if there were any more.'

'And you thought there would be a kidnap list on the computer? Were you hoping to find a spreadsheet called *Kidnappings and Other Crimes* on there?' Rook said, condescension and irritation written all over his face.

'No need to take the piss. We were desperate. Nicole set up the centre. People from the centre are going missing.

Figured the why of it would be on her computer,' Rebecca replied, body stiffening into a more defensive posture.

'You think Nicole is behind people being taken? Nicole? Have you met her?' he asked, with a forced chuckle to emphasise the ridiculousness of Rebecca's accusation.

'She's been to the health centre a bit. She set the place up. Sure, she seems nice. But then, you never really know anyone, do you? Especially not a human.' Rebecca said the word human with thinly-disguised venom.

'Whoever is behind this, it's not Nicole.' Rook shook his head.

'Maybe,' Rebecca replied. 'I still want to know who is.'

'So do I. Why didn't you tell us about these disappearances?'

'Caleb tried.'

'He spoke to Terry. That's not the same as speaking to me. I know you don't know me, but please trust me on that. Anyway, there wasn't anything in the notes about Pauline, Clara, and Sean.'

'We didn't know about them then. It was only when me and Caleb were talking about it later that I realised they'd all been at the centre.'

'When did this conversation take place?'

'If you must know, it was after we'd had sex,' she said, still staring at Rook.

'I meant what date, but thanks for the detail,' Rook said.

'You're welcome for the mental image.' Her face broke into a vicious grin. 'And it was about two or three weeks ago.'

'Then he was killed a couple of weeks later. Who else knew?'

'Can I trust you?' She leant forwards, examining every millimetre of Rook's face.

'You can.' He held her gaze.

Rebecca cocked her head to the side and continued to regard Rook with unblinking eyes, but didn't respond.

'Really? You're actually thinking about this?' Rook's voice failed to mask his exasperation. 'You realise how many problems you've already caused me by not talking to me? How cool I'm being about the whole breaking-into-the-office thing you did? How I'm not telling anyone else what you did? Please, there's nothing else I can do to show you that you can trust me.'

'Well... You don't seem completely awful. But if I'm wrong about you, my friends could end up dead.'

'Fine,' Rook said, exhaling. 'How about I guess? Riothamus and Karl know. After all, they were with you on your ill-advised bit of burglary. How about Abby or Nathan? They know?' Rook asked, jutting his head forwards and raising his eyebrows.

Rebecca's body deflated as she swore under her breath. 'Okay, I'll tell you. Rio and Karl knew. I don't know about

Abby and Nathan. They weren't meant to know. But Caleb couldn't always keep his mouth shut.'

'What about Rowena? You try to speak to her?'

'She told us that Benjamin was in Manchester. But Caleb asked around; no one up there had seen him. Said she didn't know about the others. Like the rest of them, he left without saying goodbye. You don't think that sounds suspicious?' Rebecca said, shaking her head.

'Of course I do. I just didn't know about it, otherwise I would have investigated.'

'As I said,' Rebecca replied in a terse voice, 'we had told Terry and we didn't know we could trust you. Given what happened to Caleb, we had good reason.'

'Do you think, now that I'm not doing anything about the break-in to my office, or the vicious attack on my ribs by you and your baseball bat, that you could trust me just enough to help me out with whoever killed Caleb?'

'You don't think it's related to the disappearances?' Rebecca said, cocking her head to one side.

'It could be. But that wasn't the only way he was pissing people off.'

'Do you mean the stealing or the sleeping around?'

'Whichever you think was most likely to get him in trouble.' Rook tapped on his notebook with his pen.

'Stealing might have got him in trouble, but he never seemed worried about it. He'd been a thief for a while. Vampires are suited to it, moving as fast as they do.'

'What about his sex life? Was he sleeping with any married women? Anyone not a fan of his lifestyle?'

Rebecca hesitated and Rook noticed her feet fidget. 'No,' she said.

'Who did you think of before you said no, Rebecca? Was it Abby, by any chance?'

'You don't think she killed him?'

'I don't,' Rook said, but it wasn't true. He'd been a detective for too long not to know how crazy jealousy made people. And she was also the last person to have seen Caleb. Though her alibi was solid, as far as he could tell. 'Were there others?'

'Probably, but none I know of who would have an issue with him. He was trying to have fun, you know. He didn't want any complications, and he was always honest about his intentions. Only Abby struggled with it.' Rebecca pushed a wild strand of black hair out of her face. 'I'm sorry,' she said, looking away from Rook.

'Sorry?' Rook said, wrong-footed by her sudden change of conversational direction.

'For hitting you with the bat; for scaring Nicole. For all of it. We had to do something.' She screwed her face up and closed her eyes as she tried to get the words out.

Rook looked around at the door that led to the dark room where Rebecca's mother was going to spend her final days. 'You were desperate and took the only option you thought you had left. And desperate people need help, not punishment. And – whether or not you believe it – I'm here to help.'

CHAPTER TWENTY-EIGHT

'Why are we going to see Ms McCloud?' Nicole asked, breaking a silence that had stretched from the muffled "good mornings" they'd exchanged when she'd picked Rook up over half an hour ago. While he would have preferred being picked up after he'd had his litre of morning coffee, he was happy it was in Nicole's car, with its spacious interior and comfortable seats. She'd also had the good manners to let the first part of the drive pass in silence, sensing that Rook wasn't a morning person and would need some time to get into the talkative mood.

'Got a few questions I'd like her to answer.' Rook yawned, his eyes struggling to stay open in the face of the cold morning light pouring through the windscreen.

'Questions about what?'

'I need to know if she knows anything about these disappearances.'

'You could have asked her over the phone. Or got me to ask her?' Nicole said, giving Rook a quick side glance.

'Yeah, that's how we always handle interviews. A phone call through someone else, maybe an email. I was going to do it with WhatsApp, but I didn't know the emoji for "Are you in any way involved in the disappearance of at least six people? Questioning face, winky face,"' Rook said, with a laugh.

'Hilarious. Remember, Rowena has some influence in this world, and you've only been on the scene for a few minutes.'

'And you're worried I'm going to cause you problems.'

'Pretty much. Do you think she's involved? She's basically the queen of the other species.'

'She might be. Sounds like she was wrong about Benjamin.'

'Or she received bad information. She's in charge of all the other species in the UK, Rook. She wasn't out pounding the streets of Manchester looking for one vampire.'

'Maybe, but it's a lead, and I can't ignore a lead just because it could get messy.' Rook looked out the window and watched brown fields appear as the concrete of London's outskirts receded.

'That list of people who went missing. You can't be sure the connection is the health centre,' Nicole said.

'Right now, it's the only connection we know of,' Rook said, regretting it as soon as he noticed Nicole's jaw clench.

'I didn't get that place set up so people could get hurt, Rook. It's there to help. A lot of people go to it. It's the only one of its kind in the country. And if it works and doesn't attract attention, we'll roll it out in other cities. It's not surprising that it connects any group of the other species in London.'

'I know, Nicole, I know,' Rook said, holding his hands up as if fending off an attack. 'But it doesn't mean we should ignore it. Someone could be watching the health centre.'

Nicole let the conversation fall into silence. Rook felt bad about making her feel uncomfortable. He felt worse about not telling her he already knew who'd broken into their office. One day he would have to tell her what he knew. But he couldn't be sure she wouldn't bring Steele into this, and that would mean deciding what to do with Riothamus, Karl, and Rebecca. Rook couldn't blame them for taking extreme measures. They had a just cause, and were being ignored. Rook understood why they would respond with violence.

Soon they departed from the main road and descended into a narrow valley covered in a dense forest of dead trees, their bare winter branches reaching out to claw at them as they passed by. The road changed from tarmac to dirt under the wheels of Nicole's sleek black car as it made its way to its destination.

Their destination was a country house that had seen better days, probably before the First World War. Once, it would have been the seat of some lord, home to a hundred staff, and used to host lavish parties. But those days were long gone. The rooms that would once have been full of staff or well-to-do guests had been boarded up, moss had grown on the stone lions that guarded the drive, and much of the brickwork was crumbling.

Rowena was waiting for them at the bottom of the staircase that led up to the entrance. She was dressed in a long coat the yellow of autumn leaves, tied with a wide red belt, the vibrant colours standing out against the cold winter's day. Rook and Nicole approached her, both wearing crow black, their slow steps quiet on the muddy ground.

'Thank you for driving all the way out here,' Rowena said. Her lips pursed and her stare locked on to Rook.

'It's no problem,' Nicole replied. 'It's good to be out of the city once in a while.'

'I quite understand. I only go to London when I must. It grew too modern for me. It's the price we orcs pay for our long lives – the world changes around us until we no longer feel welcome in it,' Rowena said, sweeping around and walking up the steps.

The grand doors at the top of the steps opened into a bright-white hall with doors at either end, each a lighter shade of white than the walls. Rook didn't know what he expected behind the door they followed Rowena through, but it wasn't what he found. A high-ceilinged room, which may have once held ladies' tea parties, was now an office. The windows that covered one side of the room had frames that had long since lost a battle to black mould. The room contained six cheap desks spaced out evenly, each covered with coffee rings and hosting a computer monitor, notepads, and various bits of office debris.

Behind each desk sat a ghoul, troll, vampire, or orc. Each one was in comfy warm jumpers, jackets, and even scarves, which made sense, given the cold bit as hard in this room as it did outside. The aroma of awful coffee and conflicting lunches brought in from home hung in the air, reminding Rook of every busy office he'd ever worked in.

Rowena moved through the room until she was stopped by an aged vampire with lambchop sideburns, a brown cardigan, and a mug that had *I'd rather be birdwatching* written on it in a simple blue font. Like all the vampires Rook had met, he was thin, with the type of white skin that would turn a painful red in direct sunlight.

Rowena gave all her focus to the vampire, leaving Rook and Nicole stranded as the office workers did their best to look at them out of the corners of their eyes.

'Excuse me,' said a quiet, apologetic voice behind Rook's ear. It was a female troll, about the same height as Rook, with long white-blonde hair and a willowy frame hidden in a big jumper with a fox sewn across its front. She was standing, with her broad shoulders hunched, holding a large cup of black coffee in her long fingers.

'I'm sorry,' Rook said, moving out of the way.

She hurried past Rook, making her way to an empty desk and coughing as she sat down.

Nicole and Rook exchanged awkward glances while they waited for Rowena to finish her discussion – something she appeared in no hurry to do. When the conversation finally ended, Rowena indicated for them to join her in her office.

Rowena's office was spacious and ordered with the precision of an engineer. A dark wooden desk was placed in the centre of the room, a slim computer screen on top of it. Two office chairs were on one side of the desk, behind which sat a black leather chair that towered over the room like a throne. Two windows stretched from the floor to the ceiling of the far wall, in front of each was a tall houseplant trying to warm itself under the bleak winter sun. Next to one wall was a slim sideboard made from the same wood as the desk, on top of which sat a bronze-coloured kettle, delicate white teapot, old-fashioned tea strainer, and four identical white teacups and saucers laid out in a strict line. An ornate bronze spice rack that must have held over thirty different herbs in clear bottles – none labelled – sat against the wall.

Rowena placed her coat carefully on a brass peg on the back of the door, ensuring she maintained its perfect lines.

Then she made her way to the spice rack, ran her finger along the middle row of bottles, and asked, 'Would you like some tea? I have quite the collection.'

They refused and sat silently while Rowena selected her herbs and began to make tea for herself. Soon, the kettle was whistling and she was pouring the tea. Then she took her seat, placing her white cup and saucer on a silver coaster and steepling her hands under her chin, making her head the point of a triangle.

Rook and Nicole sat down on the somewhat less comfortable chairs opposite. Nicole sat with her legs crossed, her back upright, and her smile wide. Rook struggled to feel comfortable in the tiny chair.

'Well,' Rowena said, 'now that you're here, would you like to tell me what you couldn't over the phone?'

Nicole jumped in with, 'Certain oddities have come up and Rook wondered if you could clear them up for him. I also thought it would be good for him to get a better understanding of how things operate.'

Rook wondered if that last part was true but replied, 'Thank you, Nicole. I'm here because of something Caleb was looking into prior to his death.'

'Oh really?' Rowena said, in a tone Rook associated with smug teachers looking to trap some upstart student. 'And what was that?'

'He believed that some people – members of the other species – had been kidnapped. When he was told that one of them had been seen in Manchester, he did some investigating on his own but couldn't find them.'

'Mr Benjamin Guster. I remember. His description was sent to my representatives and employees across the country. He was believed to have been seen in Manchester,' Rowena replied, picking up her teacup by its delicate handle, using only her thumb and forefinger.

'Why "believed to have been seen"?' Rook asked, leaning forwards in his chair as if ready to pounce on Rowena's answer.

'Pardon?'

'Surely if you're looking for someone, there is no "believed to have been seen" about it. If you think you've found someone, you go up and ask them if they are who you think. They say yes and job done.'

'Is that so?' Rowena said with a slow blink. 'I said "believed" because it's not like I investigated the matter personally. I do, after all, have quite a few other duties.'

'And what would those duties be?' Rook asked, causing Nicole to flinch.

'Running a secret community that provides for a few thousand trolls, orcs, vampires, and ghouls,' Rowena replied, a smile on her face but acid in her voice.

Nicole leant forwards. 'Ms Rowena and this office are the administrative centre of operations relating to the other species, organising everything from healthcare to finance,' she said, leaning forwards as she did, her voice eager.

'Finance?' Rook asked.

'We have several investments in equities, bonds, and property. We orcs live for a long time. It gives us a long-term view that is beneficial when it comes to money. We have enough finances to keep what we can going. Even if it's not an overabundance.'

'I thought Nicole handled the healthcare and the other admin.'

Nicole shared an apologetic look with Rowena, like a travel guide apologising for a tourist's unfamiliarity with local customs.

'Rowena runs everything to do with the other species – she is their government. But when she needs to interact with our government, or other official institutions such as banks, she comes to me and Steele. This includes special projects such as the health centre, which I set up with Marlowe's aid. You can't set up something like that without interacting with the state on some level. You need equipment and medicines, and these can't be purchased off the black market or just fall off trucks. I have to use quasi-official channels to make the necessary arrangements.' A note of pride entered Nicole's voice.

'I see,' Rook said. 'So, Rowena, you're saying a missing person being found in Manchester wouldn't be a priority for you.'

'I'm afraid not,' Rowena said. 'One of the drawbacks of a secret population is that we are hard to trace. Not a lot of paper trails, and that does mean people tend to be challenging to find. Often we think someone has gone missing when, in fact, they have simply moved. Secrecy has made us private.' Rowena took her elbows off the table and let herself relax into her chair.

'I imagine it would. But I do have one more question. How come you knew who I was talking about?'

'Excuse me?'

'When I said someone was missing but was found in Manchester. You knew I was talking about Mr Guster. If it was such an inconsequential occurrence, why would you remember him?'

'Are you accusing me of something, Detective Rook?' She said, arching her eyebrows.

Rook smiled his blankest, most annoying smile. 'What could I possibly be accusing you of?'

They waited for Rowena's answer, Rook remaining still while Nicole fidgeted with her hands.

After some consideration, Rowena said, 'I knew who you were talking about because once I heard about Caleb's death, I asked my employees for any information they had on him. One of them flagged his request and the response.'

'That makes perfect sense. Did you turn up anything else?'

'If there was anything useful, I would have sent it through.'

'Please send me everything through, regardless. You never know when something incidental may corroborate a more important fact or theory.'

'I will have someone send the details on. And you say Caleb was looking into what had happened to these people?'

'He was, until someone gutted him.'

'It is not uncommon for one of the other species to go missing. As I mentioned, often they have left for somewhere else. Sometimes they turn up dead. Sometimes they have slipped through the cracks of an uncaring world. Yet you think this young vampire has uncovered a conspiracy?'

'At this stage, I try not to *think* anything. But given what happened to Caleb, I have to believe there's a possibility someone murdered them too.'

'I'd be careful how you approached these matters outside this office, Detective Rook,' Rowena said, placing her hands on the table and leaning forwards again.

'How do you mean?' The condescension in her tone set Rook's teeth on edge.

'Our community keeps to itself, and while we have become secretive by necessity, we are also scared.'

'Scared of what?'

'Persecution, genocide, and extinction,' Rowena said, enunciating each word clearly. 'Most of the time, a lid can be kept on that fear, and we go about our daily business as people do. But if you talk about people going missing, about murderers in our midst, you could throw a match into that tinder box of fear and rage, and I'm not sure I could control what happens after that.'

'But what if there's a serial killer out there? Preying on the other species?'

'Then find them, but find them quietly, Detective Rook. We other species have every reason to fear fear itself. We are hanging by a thread. Anything that disrupts that could be the end of us.' Rowena stood and moved to the spice rack that held all those different tea leaves and herbs, her eyes losing their sharp focus and her voice its edge. 'It's exhausting,' she continued, 'shepherding my people through this human world. Making decisions I don't want to make. But it's still my duty. Yours too, if you have the stomach for it.'

'What do you mean by that?' Rook asked.

'You aren't a real police officer anymore, Mr Rook. You may still have a police ID and you may even still investigate crimes, but your job isn't to find criminals. It's keeping the peace. Keeping all the other species' rage and fear buried deep under the surface.'

'Oh, I'm all for keeping the peace, Rowena. But I'm also going to find out what happened to those people, and who killed Caleb.'

'All I ask is that you be careful,' Rowena said, still gazing at the spice rack. 'Because, if you're not, you could burn our world down.'

CHAPTER TWENTY-NINE

Rook had finished his third beer when his phone went off like a siren.

'Get yourself to 14 Spencer Street now,' Nicole stated, her words rushed, urgent, and fighting to be audible over the roar of London traffic.

'What's happened?' Rook asked.

'I'll explain when you get here.'

'Could you give me a lift? I've had a few.' Rook put his about-to-be-opened fourth beer back on his tiny coffee table.

'A few? It's eight o'clock,' Nicole replied with more than a hint of reproach in her voice.

'It's quarter to nine, and I've only had three. But I don't like to be driving after one. So unless anyone is in immediate danger, either you can pick me up or I'll get a taxi.'

'I'll be there in twenty.'

***

Nicole was true to her word, her Mercedes arriving in front of Rook's house precisely twenty minutes later.

'You need to watch that drinking. I don't need you turning into Terry.'

'Terry was drinking whisky at work. I had a couple of beers after. There's a big difference,' Rook said, ducking into the car.

'Every bad habit starts somewhere,' Nicole said as they pulled away.

'I'm aware,' Rook said, painfully aware of the box of cigarettes in his jacket pocket. 'Anyway, why all the drama?'

'I have set up a system of alerts for whenever the police enter a witness description that may be of someone from another species. About an hour ago, a guy was hospitalised, and a neighbour described the suspect as "having funny-looking skin, almost green-looking". I got an alert and we're on the move,' Nicole replied as she navigated London's night-time traffic.

The realisation of what had likely happened crawled over Rook's skin like an army of spiders trapped under his shirt.

'That guy called Darren, by any chance?' he asked, pulling at the shirt collar cutting into his throat and irritating the scab that had formed over the vampire bite.

'How did you know that?' Nicole looked sideways at Rook.

'It wasn't a lucky guess. That orc we're looking for. I'd put good money on it being Jacob.' The words dropped into the car like lead weights. Rook cursed himself as he looked out the window at the people either going out for the night or coming back after a long day. He hoped he still had time to calm Jacob down; to stop this from escalating.

'Why is Jacob beating people up? How does Jacob even know this guy?' Nicole asked, eyes bulging and hands clutching at the wheel like she was about to rip it off.

'Darren's girlfriend, whom I'm pretty certain he beats, looks after Michael for Jacob. We got back to Jacob's a couple of nights ago and Darren had attacked Michael. It shook the big lad up a bit.'

'He hit Michael? Who would do that?' Nicole said.

'A piece of shit who beats his girlfriend.'

Nicole sucked on her lips. 'Jacob still can't go off and beat him. He isn't a vigilante.'

'No, he's a state-sanctioned killer.'

'Hilarious. If Steele thinks Jacob's gone rogue, he'll... Well, I don't know what he'll do, but it won't be good.'

***

Darren lived in a nice block of flats with clean carpets and working lifts, and only a hint of weed in the air. It was easy to tell which door had been his because it had a gaping hole in the middle and shards of wood strewn across the floor within.

They could see Carolina through the hole in the door as she approached: her hair tied back, her face a tear-stained red, and a bruise almost closing her eye.

She led them through to the living room, which Rook guessed would have looked sparse but well-kept before the fight had left it covered in glass and bloodstains. A sofa sat in front of a coffee table and a TV, which had an Xbox with one controller beneath it. A chair lay prone on the floor like a drunk who had fallen over and given up trying to stand again.

The windows would have given a great view of South London, if it hadn't been too dark to see anything but their reflections. The bloodstains on the white carpet had formed into strange shapes. Some fanned out in a spray; others pooled in gruesome red blobs. Each told a story of Darren's beating.

'What are you doing here?' Carolina said, falling onto the sofa like her legs had given out.

'As well as working with Jacob, I'm also police.' He pulled out his ID. 'So I thought I'd come and see if I could help you out and find out what happened. Have you met Nicole?'

Carolina gave a quick shake of her head.

'She works with Jacob and me.'

'Hello,' said Nicole, shifting uncomfortably. 'I take it your dustpan and brush is under the sink like everyone else's?'

Carolina nodded, her one good eye confused.

'Good, then I'll get started cleaning up,' Nicole said.

Carolina was about to protest, but Rook waved it away.

'Trust me,' he said, taking a seat opposite. 'If Nicole wants to help, you'd be better off letting her. It's my job to find out what the hell happened. I know it's rough right now. But we need to know, if we're going to help.'

A sob left her lips.

'How did you get that?' Rook asked, motioning towards the bruise spreading across her face.

'Darren,' she said in a muffled voice.

'I'm sorry,' Rook said. 'Was it before Jacob arrived?'

'We'd been arguing about something.' Carolina stared at the black screen of the turned-off TV. 'It was stupid. Darren, he gets angry. I should have let him calm down. But I kept talking and he lashed out. He didn't mean for this.' She touched her cheek. 'He's clumsy.'

'I'm sure he is,' Rook said, his voice flat. He could tell that Nicole was about to say something, but she stopped when she saw him raise his eyebrows. 'Is that when Jacob arrived?'

'He came through...' She looked back at the wooden debris all over the floor. 'He came through the door. I didn't know he was that strong.'

'Could he hear your fight from outside?'

'I don't know, maybe. He didn't say.' Carolina looked up at Rook, one eye big and wet with tears, the other a mess of a bruise. 'He didn't say anything. The whole time he was here, he didn't say anything. He went at Darren and kept hitting him. Darren did smash that bottle.' She pointed to some green bits of glass still on the floor. 'And stabbed Jacob in the face. Tried to stab him in the face, anyway.'

'He missed?' Rook said.

Carolina pursed her lips. 'I didn't think so. I saw... I saw the bottle stick. But when it left, his face wasn't bleeding. I must be wrong. Guess I'm not seeing so well,' she said, letting out another sob.

'There's nothing right about Darren hitting you. You know that?' Rook said.

Carolina stared out the dark window in response.

'This isn't the first time I've had a conversation like this. Part of the job. The pretty rubbish part at that. Sometimes – most of the time – the woman makes the decision she must make. Gets the help she needs.' Rook's shoulders sagged.

'He's not that bad. It looks worse than it is,' she said.

'Are you enjoying feeling like this?'

'No,' she said, her body almost drowning in the sofa.

'If you want any help – someone to call, somewhere to stay – let me know.'

'Actually...' Nicole cut in as she swept up the last of the glass and put it in a plastic bag. 'You should let *me* know.' Carolina looked up like she'd forgotten Nicole was in the room. 'I have access to a range of places to stay across the city and beyond. I can get you a prepaid phone and whatever else you need in a heartbeat.'

'She really can,' Rook said, noticing Carolina's furrowed brow. 'She's kind of the queen of organising things.'

To Rook's surprise, Carolina agreed to exchange numbers with Nicole. As they were leaving, Rook noticed the gleam of a shard of bottle glass Nicole had missed. It had somehow got itself almost entirely underneath the sofa, completely separated from the rest of the glass Nicole had cleared away. Rook bent down to pick it up. It was jagged and stained with blood. Jacob's, Rook supposed.

'Oh,' Nicole said. 'I can't believe I missed that.'

She reached out to take it from him, but Rook shook his head.

'It's okay, I'll keep this.' Both Nicole and Carolina gave him confused looks, so he continued, 'May be useful as evidence, of a sort.' That seemed to satisfy them. He wrapped it up in some kitchen roll and put it in his coat pocket.

'He did have it coming, didn't he?' Nicole said, once they were back on the street and the frozen night air was whipping at their cheeks.

'Without a doubt,' Rook said, lighting up a fresh cigarette and watching its sad ember burn.

'You think she'll leave?'

'I hope so. But, even if she does, she might go back.'

'No!' Nicole said, with a mixture of shock and concern.

'It normally takes a few attempts to leave for it to stick. The human heart can be a treacherous fucker. Especially when it's being poisoned by someone else. But let's be hopeful. Women get out of situations like this all the time. It takes a lot of time and effort, but they do.' Rook decided not to tell her about the things he'd seen when they didn't get out. Sometimes he'd been called in because the woman had snapped and given the man what was coming to him. But most of the time, that wasn't the case.

'What will you do about him and Jacob?' Nicole asked.

'I need to have a chat with Mr Darren Addy. I want to end this tonight.'

CHAPTER THIRTY

They didn't talk as they drove to the hospital; the only sound was the irregular beat of Nicole's worried fingers tapping on the steering wheel. The carpark was half empty when they arrived, and Rook hoped it wasn't a busy night in the hospital. He wanted as few witnesses as possible for what he was about to do.

'You sure you don't want to wait until tomorrow morning to do this?' Nicole asked.

'No,' Rook said, stepping out of the car. 'I want him tired and off balance.'

'You need me to wait, to drive you back?'

'I'll find my own way, thanks,' Rook said, watching her try to hide her relief at his answer.

Nicole drove into the night, leaving Rook standing in front of the brutal architecture of the hospital. Jacob would be a while, so Rook killed time by prowling up and down, past the ashen-faced patients who had snuck out for a smoke. His hand went towards his cigarettes numerous times, but he always stopped himself. Smoking in front of a hospital was like spitting in the face of fate.

There were few places as forsaken as the front of a hospital at night. Stranded under bad street lighting, surrounded by others stuck in a place they didn't want to be. Everyone waiting for answers that may not come and may well not be the ones they wanted to hear. While some were chatting in ones and twos, most were standing by themselves on the edge of where the shadows met the streetlights. Rook tried to guess from their faces whether they were here for some minor reason or if it was something more serious. There was no way of telling.

Jacob moved past the muttering bystanders, his face hidden by the grey hood of the sweatshirt under his coat. Rook didn't see any blood on him and wondered if he'd washed it off or if he'd bothered to wear different clothes when committing the assault.

'Why am I here?' Jacob asked as he planted his feet in front of Rook.

'This is the hospital Darren Addy is recuperating in,' Rook replied.

'That isn't an answer.'

'You could have come to me, you know, Jacob, before sorting out Darren Addy yourself,' Rook said, arms held out to the side, palms to the skies.

'Would you have talked to him? Suggested he stops hitting Carolina? Said please? What would have happened? Anything at all?'

'I wouldn't be outside a hospital trying to clear up your mess,' Rook said, his voice showing his fatigue and his frustration. 'You look okay at least. Carolina said Addy cut your face with a bottle.'

'I'm an orc. It was a shallow cut. It healed while I was still beating him,' Jacob said, striding past Rook, into the hospital.

The nurse behind the reception desk was slouched in her chair, dragged down by the weight of a long day. Her eyes fell on Rook and Jacob with all the joy of a dying animal seeing a vulture circling above.

Rook could see an inch of brown roots in the blonde hair tied tight behind her head. Her thin face could have belonged to an old-looking twenty-year-old or young-looking forty-year-old. It was impossible to be sure.

'What can I do for you?' she asked, and Rook could hear the need for a cigarette and a drink in her voice. The nurse – Sara, according to her name badge – sighed as Rook pulled out his ID, every ounce of her body willing him to stop bothering her.

'I need to speak with Darren Addy,' Rook said.

'I'm not even sure he's awake.'

'I'm sorry,' Rook said, and meant it. 'But we need to talk to him. It's about his case. And it's urgent.'

'Take a seat. I'll talk to his doctor,' she said, dragging herself to her feet.

Rook got himself some coffee from the machine and collapsed down in the rough plastic seat next to Jacob. The waiting room was full of uncomfortable blue plastic seats that were fixed to the ground. A couple of ancient TVs hung from the ceiling, one with a cracked screen and the other playing some public service announcement about smoking.

They were alone other than a woman with a wrinkled face singing under her breath as she rocked side to side, wearing a coat that was at least three sizes too big.

'Do you understand how much trouble what you've done could cause?' Rook said, his voice a low, hoarse whisper.

'He hurt Michael.' Jacob's right fist clenched.

'You didn't think giving me a heads-up would have been a good idea? Maybe see if we could sort something else out. So we didn't end up here?' Rook glanced around the waiting room.

'There isn't another punishment for attacking one of us. He can't go to prison for attacking Michael because trolls don't exist. But I can make sure he regrets it. What would you have done?'

'Probably something stupid. You still should have left it to me,' Rook said, looking at the TV with the cracked screen and wondering what right he had to judge Jacob.

After all, it wasn't like his own temper had never got him into trouble before, with far less provocation.

Jacob leant forwards and put his domed head in his hands, pushing back his hood as he did. 'I grew up in the circus.'

'What?' Rook said, wrongfooted by this sudden twist in the conversation.

'More like a freak show. There was my mother, the woman who healed herself; a troll lady, "the strongest woman in the world"; a ghoul who would freak out the punters by eating raw meat; and an assortment of other garden-variety oddities. We would tour. People would pay their money to gawk and laugh... Mother would cut herself and people would watch as she healed right in front of their eyes. Great slashing cuts across her chest. One night, a group of boys who'd been drinking – as young men like to do – decided that pointing and staring wasn't enough fun. They came back in the night and cornered my mother. They wanted to see if it was a trick.'

Jacob pressed two fingers against his temple and moved them in soothing circles, his expression pained.

'They did this by giving her some bruises and cuts she couldn't have planned for, to see if she would heal from those. After that, they thought they'd find other ways to have some fun,' he said, spitting the last word. 'I found her not long after they'd left. She was still shaking. I remember her tears. First time I had seen her cry. We were going to leave town soon. So we had to be quick to do what needed to be done.'

'What needed to be done?'

'We found her attackers. We executed them. We burned their bodies a few towns over.'

'You know,' Rook said, looking sideways at Jacob, 'we'd get on a lot better if you'd stop telling me about people you've killed.'

'There isn't a lot in the way of justice for us on the outside of your society, Rook. We have to take it when we can. Otherwise, we're left screaming in the shadows. We don't have the luxury of mercy.'

'I've brought you here, haven't I?'

Loud steps on the hospital floor alerted them to the doctor's arrival. A thin man, he walked towards them in green scrubs and a slight limp, his right foot dragging across the floor to catch up with his left.

'I understand you want to talk to my patient?' he said, running his hands through salt-and-pepper hair that high-lighted brown eyes cracked with crow's feet.

'I'm afraid so, and I'm sorry for the rush, but it's impor-tant to his case,' Rook replied.

'Will you promise to be calm and not disturb him? He's been through quite an ordeal,' the doctor said, head cocked to one side like a bird.

'Of course,' Rook lied.

The ward was dark and smelled of sweat, antiseptic wipes, and God-knows-what-else. There was only one other patient on the ward, who was fast asleep or co-matose. Rook pushed past the cheap plastic sheets that acted as curtains to reveal the dark corner in which they'd put Darren Addy in. His meaty arms lay by his side and wheezes seeped out of his mouth. Rook sat on a beaten-up chair next to the bed, leaving Jacob to loom over the sleep-ing Darren.

Darren's face was a study of brutality. A lamp on the bedside table gave off a yellow glow, showing each painful mark Jacob had made. Stitches held together the parts of Darren's face that weren't covered in a patchwork of black bruises.

Rook gave Darren's shoulder a shake. His good eye opened, first in confusion and then in terror when he saw Jacob staring down at him.

'Please, Mr Addy,' Rook said, raising his police ID. 'If I'd brought Jacob here to kill you, I wouldn't have bothered waking you up. I'm not a sadist. Which makes me unique in this room.'

A strangled 'WWha—?' escaped Darren's lips, his good eye stretched wide like it was scared to blink.

'Please, don't strain yourself by talking. It's best you lis-ten. I don't know what's going through that Neanderthal brain of yours right now, but I need to know you aren't going to do anything silly like press any charges against Jacob here. You can answer me.'

'I won't,' Darren rasped.

'Good. Now, I wish I could leave it at that. But something tells me you aren't to be trusted. So, I need to ensure you understand your situation. Have you ever heard of the 007 Law? Like James Bond?' He didn't wait for Addy to answer the question. 'Of course not. Its actual name is Article 7 of the Intelligence Services Act. It means that, under special circumstances, agents of the Crown, such as spies, can murder someone if it is justified. The fun part of it is, it's pretty much the agents of the Crown who decide if it's justified.'

An uncomprehending 'Huh?' came out of Darren's mouth.

'Don't speak unless I ask you to. Just listen and keep looking at Jacob.' Rook motioned to Jacob, who was standing completely still.

'All you need to know right now is that there's a law that allows the British Secret Service to murder people without oversight.'

'But... police,' Darren mumbled.

'Jesus fucking Christ, Darren. I did not ask you to speak. I know there's some brain damage going on in there but shut up. Yes, I am police. But I'm not ordinary police. I work for a special branch of the Home Office, alongside Jacob here. Now, I know you're wondering why Jacob could be so special. Well, he has some abilities that come in useful. Do you remember cutting him with that bottle back in your apartment? As you can see, that cut is already gone. But, to make sure you get the point, Jacob here will give you another demonstration.'

As he spoke, he pulled the shard of glass out of his pocket and removed it from its cocoon of kitchen roll, holding it up towards Jacob. The orc's deep, cavernous eyes looked through Rook, and he worried that Jacob was about to refuse. But Jacob took off his jacket, sweatshirt, and T-shirt to reveal a torso that was nothing but muscles and hair. He reached out and took the shard from Rook's hand, pushed it deep into his flesh with a grunt, and dragged it across his chest from underneath his left collarbone to his left nipple. A thick line of dark blood bloomed where the glass cut its trail.

Rook noticed Darren flinch as Jacob cut himself without so much as a groan escaping from his lips.

'Wait for it...' Rook said. Within a minute, the skin started to scab and knit itself together, the wound closing while there was still blood dripping from the glass. A moment later, Jacob brushed off the scab, revealing bare, unbroken skin.

Jacob placed the bloodied shard on the table. Darren was so transfixed by the glass that he didn't react when Rook touched his shoulder.

'Now, Darren. Let's recap,' Rook said, leaning over him. 'You will retract any statement you've already made to the police, and you will not be pressing charges. You will tell your family and friends you got in a car accident or lost a bar fight. I don't care. But if we hear you have breathed a word about my indestructible friend here, we will find you. And we will end you. It may look like an accident, or we may make you disappear, but it will be a very painful experience and there will be no investigation into it. Also, you're going to give Carolina some space. If we see even the ghost of a bruise on her face, even if it is an honest-to-God accident, we will pay you another visit. Now, nod if you understand.'

Darren nodded, causing a spasm of pain to bloom on his face.

'Good, then we can go, and you can pray you never see us again.'

CHAPTER THIRTY-ONE

'We live in London,' Nicole said, wrinkling her nose in disgust. 'One of the culinary capitals of the world. I know for a fact you pass all sorts of places offering all types of delicious healthy food on your way to work. Yet you pick the filthiest bacon sandwich I've ever seen to eat at your desk?'

'I'm a traditionalist,' Rook replied, wiping ketchup from his chin. *And I'm shattered from spending the night scaring a girlfriend-beating prick into silence*, he added to himself.

'You'll have a traditionally British heart attack by the time you're forty.'

'Not like I've got a pension that'll be worth anything, anyway.'

Nicole laughed and turned back to her computer, leaving Rook to pore over his notes for the hundredth time.

In a normal murder investigation, there would be reports coming in as officers conducted interviews and canvassed the neighbourhood. But as it was, he was alone with his notes and waiting for his next interview.

There were two cases here: the murder of Caleb and the disappearances. And he was making little headway with either. Caleb had been investigating what had happened to those who'd vanished, and he'd been killed. Seemed straightforward enough. But the disappearances appeared to be methodical and clean. It was hard to believe whoever had been behind them was the same person who'd got so stab-happy at Caleb's. And why wouldn't they make him disappear too? To send a message?

'You think the business from last night is behind us? Do I need to tell Steele?' Nicole interrupted.

'I think we're good,' Rook said, hoping it was true. 'Addy is a bully who has met a much bigger bully and he's scared. I'm more worried about Carolina, to be honest. Did she contact you?'

'She did. I got her put up somewhere for a while.'

'That's something good at least.'

'Any news on the break-in?' Nicole said, getting up to make herself another coffee. She was doing her best to keep her voice casual, but her nervous movements betrayed her.

Rook considered telling Nicole that he knew who had attacked the office, and why. How they were desperate and that she should look past it. But he couldn't be sure that wouldn't make everything worse. First, he would need to make sure it wouldn't happen again, and that meant talking to Karl and Riothamus. He'd like to think Rebecca had got through to them. But Rook wasn't sure it was possible to get Riothamus to calm down. The image of the giant troll single-handedly destroying walls with a sledge-hammer stuck in his mind like a splinter.

'I'm meeting someone at lunch who could shed some light on what's happened,' he said, which was true in a way.

Nicole took her coffee back to her desk, where she sat down and started working on whatever it was she was working on. Rook hoped she was getting further than he was, as he went back over his poorly written notes in the hope something would pop out.

Eventually, the clock rolled around to midday, and it was time to go see Karl. After a brief fight through London traffic, he pulled up outside The George – the same pub they'd been to before.

The pub was empty of people and stank of stale beer. The only sound that cut through the muffled silence was the synthetic siren calls of a couple of slot machines, beck-oning the desperate to part with their cash. Karl sat at one of the corner tables hidden from the rest of the bar, pint in hand and denim jacket tossed over a chair. Rook got himself a pint and went to join him.

Karl greeted him with his familiar lopsided smile that emphasised the long scar running down his face. 'Rebecca says you're pissed off,' the vampire said.

'About what?' Rook said. 'Pissed off that you and your friends broke into my office, scared my co-worker, and hit me with a baseball bat? Or pissed off that my very own vampire CI not only didn't tell me about the attack but was directly involved? Or maybe it's that the same CI has been absolutely sod-all use in finding the killer of one of his friends?'

Karl put his hands up in a mollifying gesture. 'Yeah, we're all sorry about Nicole. We were hoping she wasn't in.'

'But you weren't so concerned about me getting hit with a bat?'

'Not particularly, to be honest,' Karl said, taking a sip of his pint.

'You're not worried about me talking to Jacob.'

'Not as worried as I'd be about pissing off Riothamus.' Karl laughed.

'You telling me that's why you went along with it? Because Riothamus told you to?'

'Nah,' Karl said, shaking his head and curling his lips. 'I did it because I wanted to know what happened to Jeremiah and the others.'

'I told you I'd investigate it. And I am. It would be easier if you would all keep out of my business. What can I do to make you trust me on that?'

'Well, not turning us in after the attack was a start. But even if we trust you, it doesn't mean we trust humans. After all, do you know who killed Caleb yet? Have you really been looking?'

'Yes, I've been looking, you little prick,' Rook retorted, hitting the table with enough force to make the beer jump in his pint glass and to earn a disapproving look from the big guy behind the bar. 'But it's kind of hard when no one will tell me anything and everyone seems hell-bent on doing some seriously stupid shit at every opportunity. Stupid shit like stealing the computers we were working on.'

'You got anywhere with all that looking? Do you have the slightest clue who killed Caleb?' Karl needled, a punchable smirk plastered across his face.

'I've ruled out a few possibilities, which is how investigations usually begin,' Rook said.

'Come on, it's something to do with the disappearances that Caleb was looking into.'

'That's one angle, yes. But not the only one. Now, perhaps you could be a good CI for once and give me some information. Think of it as a kindness for overlooking you biting me and breaking into my office.'

'Fair enough. What do you want to know?'

'What aren't you telling me about Caleb?'

'Like what?'

'Like about his thieving.' Rook let the irritation seep into his voice.

'I know he did some for Sol. That's how he got the cool squat all to himself,' Karl said.

'Sol wasn't the only troll he worked for though, was it? I know he worked for Riothamus too. And he didn't hand over all of what he stole either. Did you know about that?'

'Caleb was holding out on Riothamus?' Karl scratched a single finger along the scarred side of his face. 'He never told me. And if he had told me, I'd have told him to stop being stupid. But Riothamus didn't know about it.'

'How can you be so sure?'

'Because Caleb still had his limbs, last I saw. And he was helping Rio find his brother,' Karl shot back.

Rook sucked on his lips. Karl was right; it was unlikely to be Riothamus. 'Do you think Caleb would have stolen from Sol?'

Karl gave a short, dismissive grunt and looked at Rook like he had suggested Caleb was an alien. 'Put it this way, if I even thought he was stealing from Sol, I'd leave London myself. Just to be safe.'

'What about Caleb's relationships?' Rook said, looking at the vampire in front of him and beginning to despair of getting any useful information from him.

'You think Caleb was killed because he slept around?' Karl said, clearly unimpressed with the suggestion.

'Love is the oldest motive there is,' Rook replied, taking a drink.

'Yeah, but everyone knew the score with Caleb. He never went with anyone who had a boyfriend, and he was upfront with not wanting anything serious.'

'You mentioned boyfriends. Did anyone else like Rebecca, Abby, or anyone else Caleb was sleeping with?'

'Well, Nathan has always had a bit of a thing for Abby. Think they may have even got together a few times, but she wasn't interested. But I can't see him killing Caleb over it. Just like I know Abby got pissed off with Caleb too, but I doubt she killed him.' Karl's eyes betrayed his worry that he was throwing a friend under the bus of Rook's investigation.

'Whenever I'm interviewing anyone, they always say "so-and-so wouldn't have killed him over it" or "it wasn't that big of a deal, really". But people get murdered over inconsequential shit every day because to the murderer it isn't stupid or inconsequential. You take any group of people, you will find one person who's thought of killing another over something dumb.' Rook looked around the bar, imagining the faces that would fill it when it was full and wondering how many of those people were hiding murderous intent behind strained smiles. 'Anyone else you can think of, now that you're feeling chatty?'

'No,' Karl said.

'But you'd tell me if you did?' Rook didn't hide the sarcasm in his voice.

'Yeah, I would, okay? But I'm telling you, it's to do with the disappearances. Caleb got too close. So he was killed.'

'Then why not make him disappear? Why leave his body?' Rook said, tapping on the table to emphasise his point. 'Listen, I get why you attacked the office. You were desperate. You didn't think anyone was doing anything for you. But I am. So don't do any more stupid shit just in case Caleb's murder was related to the disappearances. You're a prick, make no mistake about that, but I'd rather not have to find you too. I've got enough work on right now without you adding to it. Stay out of my way, okay?'

Karl picked up one of the blue beer mats, the action so quick the mat seemed to appear in his hand by magic. He held it between his thumb and finger and tapped it against the table five times, edge down. His eyes watched the beer mat, but his mind was clearly elsewhere.

'No,' Karl said, slamming the beer mat down and snapping his eyes back to Rook.

'No? You're telling me no?' Rook said, clutching his pint glass so hard it was a miracle it didn't shatter.

'That's right,' Karl said, baring his teeth in a rough, slashing smile. 'I'm going to figure out what happened to Jeremiah. He was like my brother, and he's gone, and it took far too long for anyone else to give a shit. You say we can trust you, and maybe we can. But that doesn't mean I'm going to stop looking for my friend. Us other species need to look after ourselves. If you want to threaten me with Jacob or whatever, you can. But my answer stays the same.'

Rook wasn't sure if he was impressed by his passion or dismayed by his stupidity. Before he could decide, his phone jumped in his pocket.

'You've got to come back to the office,' Nicole said as soon as Rook answered, her voice fast and urgent.

'You okay?' Rook said, his chair skidding along the floor as he stood up.

'Yes, I'm fine,' Nicole said, as if Rook's question was stupid and annoying. 'Someone came to the office, and we've figured something out. It's not the health centre that connects the disappeared. It's where they were taken after.'

In the interest of discretion, Rook ended the call. He was sure Nicole's voice was loud in his ear, but Karl was looking at his pint and showing no sign he'd heard her.

CHAPTER THIRTY-TWO

Rook came back into the office to find Nicole sitting with a pen in hand and a pad full of meticulous notes in front of her. She'd pulled her chair away from her desk just enough to be at a slight angle, giving her a better view of the female troll in Rook's chair. The troll's tall frame was hunched over a green coat in her lap, her face obscured by long, straight white hair. She had dropped a voluminous beige handbag at her feet, its zip broken open, contents threatening to spill out. She had used blusher to downplay the inhuman whiteness of her skin and her clear-blue eyes were blinking nervously, as if she were struggling to acclimatise to bright lighting. Rook could tell that, behind her bulky, purple knitted jumper, she had a thin frame, but the shoulders of an Olympic swimmer.

'You work with Rowena, don't you? I don't think we were introduced. My name is Rook,' he said.

'It's Alice. I'm sorry, am I in your chair?' She began to get up, but Rook motioned for her to stay seated and rested himself against the kitchen counter. He hung up his coat and asked if anyone would like a tea or coffee. They both declined, so he went to put the kettle on for himself.

'I understand you've got some information for us regarding these disappearances,' he said, pouring the water into his mug and taking a moment to enjoy the smell of an imminent caffeine hit.

'I've told Nicole,' Alice said.

'That's great. But I'd love to hear it directly from you, if you don't mind.'

Alice's bottom lip disappeared into her mouth as she bit it in worry. Only when Nicole smiled at her did Alice speak.

'I don't think Ms McCloud told you everything the other day.'

'Why do you think that?'

'Because I don't think she's telling anyone the whole truth.'

'And what is the whole truth?' Rook asked.

'About a year and a half ago, I got a call asking about a missing vampire called Clara. So, I set up an investigation,' Alice said, her head down, watching her feet push her handbag as if trying to cajole the zip shut. 'We have people around the country who work for us, and I sent them a description with pictures to follow. One of us disappearing isn't unheard of and it's not like we can put pictures on the news. A day or so later, Ms McCloud calls me into her office and asks me to stop. She told me someone had already looked into it.'

Alice lapsed into silence, so Rook asked, 'But you weren't sure?'

'No one in our office had looked into it. I checked.' She gave her coat another squeeze. 'Then a few months later, another name came up. Pauline. I was about to start an investigation, but when I went to log the case, the disappearance was already recorded. With a note that read *Matter resolved. No further action required*. I went to Ms Mc-Cloud. She said that Pauline's disappearance had already been brought to her attention, an investigation had been completed, and I shouldn't worry anyone else about it. And that, in the future, any calls involving serious matters should go through her.'

Again, Alice fell into silence, the only noises the engine growls and human shouts from the street outside. She looked up to stare at the crime boards. Nicole had turned them towards the wall, sparing Alice the grisly pictures of Caleb's corpse. But it was clear Alice knew their significance. Rook wanted to help her, but the most useful thing he could offer was patience and time.

'I tried to tell myself I was being silly, but something about how Ms McCloud responded stuck with me. It just wasn't like her. For a while I was able to forget about it.

But then you came to the office and we were all gossiping about why you could be there. I didn't say anything, but all I could think about was Pauline and Clara. I wanted to know what had happened to them, so I went back through our database.' She looked at Nicole, who smiled encouragement. 'But no information had been added. Then, when I expanded my search, I found six records involving the disappearance of someone, including Pauline and Clara. All had this same note, but with no sign anyone had investigated.'

'Six?' Rook said.

'Clara was the first. The last was in November last year,' Alice said, fretting with her hands as if trying to remove some invisible string that was binding them together.

'Jesus.' Rook sighed. 'Do you have their names?'

'Alice has given us names and dates of when the matters were logged into the database,' Nicole interjected. 'I've written them down, ready for the crime boards.'

Nicole had indeed written each down, in neat handwriting Rook could only be jealous of. The names confirmed those Rebecca had already given him. The earliest Clara, the latest Benjamin Guster, in November last year.

'And from that, you've been able to establish a connection?'

'I was,' Nicole said, smoothing back her hair, 'At first, I looked back through our records and realised that, yes, they had all been to the health centre, but that wasn't the only connection. They had all gone for further investigation.'

'Further investigation?' Rook said.

'Yes, the nurses at the health centre are trained to handle basic issues and offer basic help. Suggest which over-the-counter medicine to take or similar. But if there's something they can't handle, it gets flagged for further investigation.' Nicole's face sagged with the weight of what she was about to say. 'And that's when they go to see Marlowe.'

'And he can carry out tests and give a more in-depth response. I remember. How does Marlowe see them again?'

'Sometimes he will go into the health centre to see them, but if he needs to do more complex tests, they are taken to his lab.'

'Who takes them? I can't imagine they take an Uber to a secret lab.'

'Carver.'

Rook took a big drink of his coffee, which was hot enough to burn his tongue. 'All these people went to see Marlowe, never to be seen again? And this is the first anyone has noticed?'

Nicole shook her head. 'They were seen again. I've checked our records, and they were all seen at the health centre multiple times prior to their disappearance after seeing Marlowe.'

'But they all saw Marlowe,' said Rook.

Nicole was about to respond, but stopped when she caught Rook's glance towards Alice. They'd already said more than they should in front of a civilian, even one who'd been so helpful.

Instead, Rook continued, 'I appreciate you coming to us with this, Alice. Few people have had this much trust in me since I started this job.'

'It's not you I trust. It's her,' Alice said.

'Me?' Nicole said.

'I see how much you've done for us since you started working here. You started up the health centre; people are getting better housing. In the past, we did what we could, but it was getting harder. Everything was getting more expensive; everything required more forms of ID and a digital presence. We couldn't do anything without some-one on your side helping. And, until you came, no one really was. You are improving our community. I respect that – any troll should.'

A smile appeared on Nicole's face, despite her best at-tempts to stop it.

'What do you mean,' Rook asked as Nicole strug-gled to find a response to Alice's compliment. '"Any troll should"?'

'Most think that trolls have violence as the bedrock of our culture. Wars and killing... like most humans do. But we don't, we don't at all,' Alice said with a warm smile that seemed to go round the side of her face all the way to the big earrings she was wearing. She transformed from the hesitant person sitting in Rook's chair. Her posture improved and her hands started moving as she spoke, clearly enjoying the change of topic from crime to troll culture. 'We value community spirit above all else. It was a hard life in the frozen top of the world. And we needed to pull together, so that is what our culture is based on. In fact, one of our most important myths is about the hero Cal-Dalen digging out the northern sea so we could find food. Although the old tales seem childish in this human world, we should still respect those who help the community. Like you, Nicole.'

'Thank you,' Nicole said with an awkward smile, suddenly struggling to look Alice in the face.

'If you have no more questions, I assume I can go,' Alice said, picking up her handbag.

'Thank you for coming in,' Nicole said. 'If you think of anything else, feel free to come back.'

Rook had nothing to add, so he opened the door for Alice.

'So,' Nicole said when they were alone. 'That is quite the breakthrough, isn't it?'

'It could be,' Rook said, standing up to turn the crime boards back around. 'Well done for noticing the connection to those who required further investigation. You're a regular Ms Marple.'

'Ms Marple? That's who you want to compare me with? An old white woman?'

'Hey, Ms Marple had a 100% record,' Rook said as he added the names and dates Alice had provided to the crime boards.

Nicole made herself a large cup of coffee and sat down to look at the crime boards. 'You think it has something to do with Marlowe and Rowena? I can't believe it's true. Or maybe it is true, but there is some reason we can't see. Like they are all living somewhere secret, or something. I can't imagine Rowena being involved in anything to hurt the other species. And they were all seen alive after seeing Marlowe.'

Rook wasn't sure if Nicole believed what she was saying or if she just really wanted to. In either case, he didn't want to shatter the glass house of her illusions with the bricks of his dark thoughts. He didn't want to guess what role Marlowe and Rowena had in all of this, if any. But, as he looked at the crime boards, he could only see an escalating pattern of crime building to the bloody crescendo of Caleb's murder.

CHAPTER THIRTY-THREE

R ook picked his way through the beer cans and lumps of frozen dog shit that littered the street on the way to Riothamus's house. He'd almost decided against coming at all. But he couldn't have Riothamus leading break-ins and doing anything else crazy as Rook was trying to close a case. After Karl's refusal, Rook didn't hold out much hope that Riothamus would calm down. But he had to try.

Riothamus lived in a well-kept red-brick terrace house with a black front door, and a front garden that comprised one neat patch of grass cut into a perfect rectangle. A bird feeder filled with black seed stood on the grass. The few brown birds on it fled at Rook's approach.

He was about to knock on the door when it opened, revealing not only Riothamus but also Nathan, the vampire from the magic shop who'd gone back to Caleb's the night of the murder. Nathan looked like a sick child next to Riothamus. The vampire was wearing ripped jeans and a faded green T-shirt beneath a scruffy brown coat he hadn't fully buttoned up. When he saw Rook, Nathan puffed his chest out and bared his teeth in a pointed smile.

'Looks like the police come to bother you, Riothamus. Hope you haven't been a naughty boy,' Nathan said in a faux South London accent that he thought was funny. Behind Nathan, Riothamus involuntarily rolled his eyes – an odd expression on the troll's serious face.

'Move along, Nathan,' Rook said.

'Maybe I should stay. Stop you from harassing my friend here?' Nathan responded, jerking his head towards Riothamus. Rook tried to picture exactly how the vampire runt would protect the seven-foot-tall troll behind him.

'Leave,' Riothamus said from behind Nathan, giving Rook the satisfaction of seeing Nathan's face curl up in displeasure.

Nathan looked around the empty street, then darted out the door, a blur of bad clothing as he brushed past Rook. He moved so fast Rook wouldn't have been able to grab him even if he'd wanted to. By the time he'd turned around, Nathan was already on the street.

'Oops,' he said, giving a mock salute. 'If any humans see how fast I am, Jacob might come and kill me.'

Rook faced Riothamus, whose frame filled the door, each oversized muscle highlighted through his plain white

T-shirt. An odd moment of understanding passed between them: despite their differences, they both thought Nathan was a tit.

'Sorry about that. He just turned up. Rebecca said you would come,' Riothamus said, stepping into his house.

He showed Rook into a lounge so small it was a miracle they both fit into it. On one side of the room was a green sofa that was past its best. Stitches marked where it had been repaired with thread close to the sofa's original colour, but not quite matching. The sofa faced a TV sitting on a stand that was a couple of sizes too big for it. Heavy green curtains hid a window that would have looked out onto the bird feeder in the garden. A dark wooden sideboard rested against a wall, on which three roughly-hewn rock sculptures sat. It was a room that only expected to hold one person, so two felt like a crowd.

'You want to tell me why Nathan was stopping by?' Rook asked as Riothamus sat on the sofa. Rook had stayed standing, hoping this would be a brief visit.

'Social call,' Riothamus said.

'Is that right? You don't seem close.'

Riothamus gave a shrug, his shoulders moving like boulders under his T-shirt.

'Now, Riothamus,' Rook said, deciding to jump straight into his reason for being there. 'I know you've talked to Karl and Rebecca. I'm even willing to look past the attack at my office. But I'll need some assurances from you. And I think that's fair.'

'Fair?' Riothamus responded, glaring at Rook. 'Our people are being taken. My brother has gone. And you talk to me about fair?'

Rook held his ground under the troll's glare. 'I think it entitles me to know why Nathan was at your house, don't you? I'll even make it easy for you and ask it as a multiple-choice question. Was Nathan here a) because he wanted to get in on your little burglary sideline or b) because of the disappearances?'

Riothamus rubbed his hand over his brow and down his face as he struggled with the idea of speaking to Rook. 'Both,' he said, eventually.

'So, he knows about the disappearances. And that you're looking into them.'

'He said Caleb told him. I'd have had words with Caleb about that if he were still alive.'

'You don't trust Nathan?'

Riothamus leant back in the sofa, spreading himself out as he weighed his words. 'He's unreliable. I've done some stuff with him in the past, but he gets too excited when he's involved in anything like this. You saw him showing off outside. He's too indiscrete. I had to move onto someone else.'

'Was that someone Caleb?'

'Yeah. He came recommended.'

'What did you tell Nathan when he came asking questions today?' Rook asked.

'I told him I wasn't planning any burglaries right now, and that we weren't looking into the disappearances right now.'

'Either of those things true?' Rook said, raising his eyebrows.

'Well, I'm not doing either of those things with Nathan,' Riothamus rumbled. 'Do you want to ask me not to search for my brother and the others who are missing? Karl already told you no, and I'll give you the same answer. Then you can leave.'

'I will ask you that, but first I want to ask you about Edgar,' Rook said, swallowing his frustration at Riothamus's denial of a question he hadn't even asked yet. 'You can at least answer me questions about that. After all, as well as not pursuing you for the break-in at the office, I've tied the theft of the watches and all the break-ins at the jewellers on Caleb, and Caleb alone. No one will know of your involvement.'

'You want to know about Edgar?' Riothamus said, looking towards the stone statues on the sideboards. 'Not much to tell. He worked in construction like me. Kept himself to himself, even from me. Did a few jobs for Sol too. Then he got sick and went to that clinic. Later he disappeared.'

'When was that?'

'June last year. I talked to his work. To the few people he called friends. There was no sign of him. I went to his home. Almost everything had been taken.'

'Almost everything?' Rook said.

Riothamus sighed and sat down. 'He left those.' He looked towards the stone sculptures. 'They're Durin stones. Trolls get them when we come of age. One is mine. One is my father's. And one is my brother's. I got Father's when he died; I found my brother's at his place after he disappeared. Everything else had been taken.'

Rook walked over to the stones. At first glance, they looked like oddly-shaped rocks. They were about a foot in height and appeared heavy. Rook would be the first to admit he didn't have the most refined tastes when it came to art, but the stones appealed to him. Some parts were rough; others smooth. While the shapes seemed random, there was clearly some sort of form within. Whether that form spoke to strength, endurance, love, or something else entirely, Rook couldn't say. But their significance to their creator was clear.

'Doesn't seem like something he would leave behind,' Rook said.

'He wouldn't. But I guess whoever took his stuff didn't think it was worth carrying.' His words hung in the air.

'I'm sorry, Riothamus,' Rook said, still looking at one of the sculptures.

Riothamus didn't respond; he just stared at the stones, lost in thought.

'Now,' Rook said, taking his eyes from the stones and standing up straight. 'I'm going to ask you the question you've already said no to. Will you promise not to do anything about the disappearances while I conduct my investigations?'

'You know the answer to that question. No. Don't make me repeat myself. I'm not known for my patience.'

'Well, neither am I. And I need you to stop. There are new leads I'm following up. But I can't have you stirring up trouble for me.'

Riothamus leapt to his feet, suddenly towering above Rook. He placed one hand gently on the detective's chest and moved so close his lips were centimetres from Rook's nose. Although Riothamus wasn't exerting any force, Rook could still feel the pressure of each fingertip and was in no doubt as to the power that lay behind them. 'You want me to forget my brother was taken? Is likely dead? You think I should give up on looking for him?' Riothamus said, his voice like the first tremor of an earthquake.

'No, I want you to let me look for him and not get in my way. Only for a week or so at most,' Rook said, forcing himself to ignore the threat of imminent violence dominating the room.

'No,' Riothamus stated, his hand leaving Rook's chest, his face still inches from Rook's. 'Now leave.'

Chapter Thirty-Four

Rook left Riothamus's house shaken and filled with anger, his entire body tight with impotent rage – rage he had to bottle up if he was to continue his investigation before something else happened.

He considered going straight at Marlowe to get answers. If there was anything going on with the health centre, he would be behind it. But he wanted to speak to Carver first. If Marlowe was involved, Carver would be too. Going to Carver might also have the bonus of rattling Marlowe. And Rook would rather interrogate a spooked Marlowe than a confident one.

Rook also wanted to understand how Carver fit into this world. He had no particular skills that Rook was aware of and he couldn't quite picture Marlowe putting out an ad in the local paper reading, *Help wanted. Must have a clean driving licence and be willing to cut vampires up into bits.*

Nicole had got Carver's address, so not long after leaving Riothamus's house, Rook and Jacob were waiting in an alley outside of Carver's place. It was a suitable spot as they could see Carver's, but he would not see them when he came home. They were hidden by shadow next to some bins, discarded fast-food boxes, and the occasional scurrying rat. It smelled like the inside of a rotting kebab. While the alley provided cover, it did not protect against the evening cold, and Rook's hands shook as he brought yet another cigarette to his lips.

'You know much about Carver?' Rook asked Jacob, who was wearing his usual heavy coat and brooding expression.

Jacob shook his head. 'I know he helps Marlowe; no more than that.'

'That's all anybody seems to know,' Rook said.

Rook first noticed Carver as he drove past, parking a bit on from his place. They waited until he had entered to make their move.

Carver lived in a basement flat, accessed by going down a set of stairs slippery enough to make Rook lose his footing a couple of times. Rook knocked three times on a brown door in need of repainting or replacement. He could hear Carver's footsteps come closer to the door, opening to reveal his grimacing face and uneven teeth.

'Why are you here?' he said.

'We've got some business we need to discuss. Thought it best if we did it at your place,' Rook responded.

'Why's he here?' Carver spat, jerking his head at Jacob.

'He cares about you.'

Carver's laugh was all edges and implied violence. 'I suppose I could tell you to fuck off. Not like you've got a warrant.'

'I don't need a warrant,' Jacob said.

Carver stared at Jacob, sniffing as if he had smelled dog shit, then went back into his flat, leaving the door open for them to follow. His home was a poorly lit blank. They were standing in the lounge/kitchen, which contained a single red sofa that faced an oversized TV, and a wooden table in one corner surrounded by four seats. There wasn't a single ornament, picture, or other evidence of personalisation in sight.

Carver walked to the fridge at the far end of the kitchen and got himself a bottle of beer, opened it, then sat down in one of the wooden chairs, one hand clasping his drink, his other elbow resting on the table. He was wearing the same suit he'd worn to dispose of Caleb's corpse, but his shirt was untucked and the jacket crumpled from a long day in the car. He wiped the sheen of sweat off his brow and took a swig from his bottle.

'Guess you aren't offering either of us a drink then,' Rook said as he and Jacob took the two other chairs. He sat across the table from Carver while Jacob pulled out the seat right next to Carver.

'Why are you in my home, Rook?' he said.

'I was hoping you could guess,' Rook replied.

Carver gulped his beer, then smiled, revealing teeth the colour of melting sludge. 'You think this is my first time talking to the police? That I'll tell you anything? If you want me to say anything, then you tell me what brings you to my door. Or you can leave. You and that.' He fired a sneer at Jacob.

Jacob met Carver's stare. 'If he leaves, I will stay. And we will not be talking.'

'Sounds fun,' Carver said, suppressing a flinch.

'How did you get involved in all of this?' Rook said.

'All of what?'

'You know...' Rook shrugged. 'The other species... all of this?'

'Why do you want to know?' Carver said, slicking back his hair with his hand.

'It interests me, Carver. Curiosity is a curse of the profession.'

'I met Marlowe while I was doing a stretch inside,' Carver said, glancing again at Jacob.

'Really?' Rook replied. 'What was Marlowe doing in a prison?'

'Well, he obviously wasn't doing fucking time, was he?' Carver said, lashing out with his voice. 'I was sick. Prison doctors couldn't figure out what was wrong with me. Somehow, the case was rare enough it came across Doctor Marlowe's desk. He came to see me a couple of times over the next few months while he figured it out. We chatted a bit. When I got out, he offered me a job.'

'Why was he so keen to offer you a job?'

'Said he needed someone he could rely on.'

'And someone willing to chop up dead bodies,' Rook countered.

'There have been perks,' Carver said.

'Well, now that that mystery is settled,' Rook replied, 'you can tell me what you know about Caleb.'

Carver sniffed. 'What about Caleb?'

'You kill him?' Jacob said.

'You think I killed him, then came round a few hours later to deal with the body?'

'Would be a good way to throw off suspicion.'

'Why would I care about that? Why would I want to kill him?'

'Because he thought you were involved in kidnapping and killing some of us,' Jacob said, his speech slow and quiet.

'Don't know why he'd think that,' Carver said, taking a noisy glug of his beer.

'Because,' Jacob said, 'everyone who disappeared was taken to see Marlowe. By you.'

'Because Doctor Marlowe gives you freaks free health-care, you think we're kidnapping you? Think you'd be a bit more grateful.' He forced a false, gasping laugh from his mouth.

'Six people were taken by you to see Marlowe and, although they were taken back home on that day, have since gone missing. Looks like a pattern to me,' Rook said.

'Your problem, Rook, is that you still think the other species are just funny-looking *people*.' He pointed at Jacob like the orc wasn't conscious. 'That we're all the same underneath. But that's bullshit. They aren't people, Rook. Those creatures you say went missing. They crawled away to die alone. Lots of animals do that.' Carver punctuated his speech with loud slurps of his beer.

Jacob stood up, his chair scratching on the wooden floor. 'Actually, Mister Carver, I think I will have a beer,' he said, stepping towards the fridge. Carver stood and grabbed Jacob's shoulder to try and stop him, but a slap from the orc sat him back down. The slap echoed throughout the room so loudly that the following silence seemed to rush in like a wave. For a moment, all three men were still, each waiting to see if the moment would shatter into further violence.

Jacob sniffed and made his way to the fridge, but Carver did nothing more than seethe in response. His eyes were black lumps of gleaming hate. Jacob grabbed a bottle of beer and opened it, looked directly at Carver, and took a deep drink.

'Living as long as orcs do gives us a different perspective than you humans,' Jacob said as he walked back to the table and sat down. 'Playing the long game is our natural state. That means I can take your insults in my stride. But don't forget who I am and what I am capable of, Carver. And know that if you are involved in the murder of that young vampire, or a single one of these disappearances, then I *will* come for you. And it won't be to take you back to prison.'

'What can you tell us about Clara Patton, Pauline Coulson, Sean Davies, Edgar Silas, Jeremiah Fochs, and Benjamin Guster?' Rook said, hoping to regain some sort of control of the conversation. For all his faults, Rook wasn't sure Carver would be likely to respond to threats.

'Who are they?' Carver said, his hand rubbing the red mark Jacob had left on his cheek.

'You know those names, Carver. You drove them to see Marlowe. What you need to tell us is how they ended up disappearing.' Rook leant across the table, closing the space between himself and Carver as much as he could.

'Maybe they had an appointment with the doctor. I picked them up, and I drove them back. Not like we talked.' Carver said, turning his face away from Rook and finishing his sentence with a nervous rasping laugh.

'So, you knew where they lived?'

'Guess I did.'

'You see why we're talking to you, then?'

'Because you're police and you've got no actual evidence. You're fishing. So, unless this orc' – he spat the word – 'is going to beat some information out of me, you can leave.'

Jacob got to his feet and began to move towards Carver. As soon as he did, Carver tried to put some distance between himself and Jacob but ended up backing into the wall behind him.

'No,' Rook said, 'no one is going to beat anything out of you.' He stood up as smoothly as he could, praying he could solve this without it coming to that. 'We'll be seeing you, Carver. Tell Marlowe I said hi.'

CHAPTER THIRTY-FIVE

Jacob had been unhappy with how things had gone at
Carver's. In his mind, Carver was involved in something and if it required beating the information out of
him, then that's what they should do. It was an old-school
way of thinking even when Rook had joined the force, and
he wasn't comfortable letting Jacob loose on a suspect now
– even a suspect as repulsive as Carver. Rook needed proof
first. After all, he was still a detective. Kind of.

'Proof,' Jacob had said when Rook told him. 'What
proof do you think you will find? You don't have a team
of scientists to bring you DNA evidence. Or even another
police officer to aid you. You think you're building a case
that you could take to a jury. But there's only your word
and what you're willing to do. And you need to decide
what that is.' With that, Jacob had stormed off into the
night, leaving Rook to drive home by himself.

He wandered over to his fridge, grateful for the couple of bottles of beer he found. He opened one and flopped onto his sofa, the cushions welcoming his shattered body like a warm embrace. Christ, he needed something good to look forward to. It was one of the things he missed most about Sarah, his ex-girlfriend. She'd always had something new planned, somewhere fun to eat or go. Left to his own devices, he'd be stuck inside drinking beer and thinking about a case, his career, or some other great disappointment in his life. Rook couldn't remember if Sarah having to drag him to these places was one of the reasons she'd left him, or if he only assumed it was.

He thought about contacting her, just to talk to someone about something, but couldn't bring himself to do it. He didn't need her bright enthusiasm shining a light on his dark mood. So instead, he messaged his dad to arrange another curry.

Without thinking, he pulled the photos he'd taken from the wall of Caleb's squat out of his pocket and started to look through. There was nothing new to be seen in them. No fresh evidence that would crack the case wide-open. They were only pictures of a now-dead vampire with his friends, smiling with a freedom Rook couldn't recognise.

Perhaps Jacob was right. Maybe there was no way to get the proof to make an airtight case. But then, what should he do? Ask Jacob to execute his best guess for the murderer? Have him beat Carver for information?

He wondered how those early detectives at Scotland Yard managed. The ones when the police force was just another gang. Detectives like Frederick Abberline, who'd chased Jack the Ripper. They hadn't had much in the way of backup and forensics. Of course, they'd never caught the Ripper. Perhaps they just gave it a guess and hoped they never found out about the times they'd sent the wrong person to the gallows.

The ringing of his phone cut through his reverie like a chainsaw. He answered without looking at the number.

'What the hell do you think you're playing at?' the voice screamed down the phone. A voice so wet with vitriol that Rook thought he could hear the spittle hit the phone screen.

'Good to hear from you, Marlowe,' Rook replied. 'How can I help?'

'You can help by not bothering my employees,' Marlowe shouted.

'I take it you're referring to my conversation with Mr Carver,' Rook said, enjoying the man's anger. Angry people made mistakes – as Rook knew all too well.

'I'm talking about your harassment of him, Rook.'

'Harassment seems a bit strong, Doctor Marlowe.'

'Does it? Does it really? I don't know why. You turn up at his house, uninvited and unexpected, late in the evening with that orc. An orc who assaults him.'

'Jacob decided to calm the situation down and used the minimum force necessary to do so. Sometimes it's needed in this line of work,' Rook replied, hoping his bureaucratic tone would drive Marlowe to new heights of anger. An impotent growl told him it had.

'Jacob's a thug. You shouldn't be taking him with you to talk to humans.'

'Jacob goes where he wants. And we can both talk to Steele about this if you have any further issues you want to raise.'

The threat of Steele seemed to give Marlowe pause. *Interesting*, Rook thought.

'Fine, but that doesn't explain why he is being followed.'

'Followed? By who?'

'Don't play dumb, Rook. I know you're not the best educated, and you are police, but even you aren't that stupid. Yesterday, Carver noticed a car following him all the way from London to five minutes from our lab. Don't pretend you didn't have something to do with it.'

'Maybe he's paranoid. Is there a reason someone would be interested in what you and he are doing? Anything you wouldn't want him caught doing?'

'You still think you're a police officer?' Marlowe said, his voice half laughing and half screeching. 'You're a security guard with a desk and an ID. Your job is to make sure none of the orcs, vampires, ghouls, or trolls step out of line and make sure they are punished when they do. You shouldn't be concerning yourself with anything that we're doing. If this is too confusing for that simple ex-proper-copper brain of yours, remember... if you find yourself interrogating a human, stop.'

'What if that human has committed a crime?' Rook asked.

'The only "crime" you need to concern yourself with is if any of the other species step out of line. Then you sic Jacob on them like a rabid dog. That's it.'

Rook placed his beer bottle down on the table, his hand shaking with sudden anger. 'You remember why you hired me, Marlowe?'

'I hired you because you were convenient.'

'You hired me because I shouted at some pricks who were bullying a homeless guy and wouldn't apologise to them. If you, or your fucking pet Carver, have anything to do with those people disappearing, I will come for you.'

'Oh, grow up, Rook. They disappear all the time. It's not like anyone is keeping track. They aren't like us. They aren't built like us. They don't think like us. And they don't act like us.'

'That's not a denial, Marlowe.'

'Of course it's a fucking denial. Now leave me alone,' Marlowe said, hanging up.

God, I hate that guy, Rook thought. He hated every inch of him. And now he was sure Marlowe and Carver were involved in the kidnappings. And he was going to nail them for it. Holding that thought, he picked up his beer and took another drink. Then he blinked, then smiled, then laughed.

Marlowe was right. They didn't always act like us, and they weren't built like us. Rook looked back over the pictures laid out on his coffee table. As he suspected, one person was missing from all these pictures. The killer.

CHAPTER THIRTY-SIX

'Would have never guessed you lived in such a fancy house,' Rook said.

'It's okay,' Nathan said, his lips barely moving as he stared at Jacob, who was roaming the room and inspecting its contents.

'It's more than okay, Nathan,' Rook said. 'This is a better place than mine, and I don't mean because it's tidy.'

It was true too; Nathan had a great place. It was a spacious two-bed flat in Clapham, with a modern open-plan kitchen-diner big enough to include a neat kitchen island. Even some of the equipment looked high-quality, with a stylish set of knives resting next to the slow cooker. Posters of old magicians, like Houdini and Keller, decorated the walls. Each one looked out from his poster with fierce mesmerism. The only exception to the magicians was a picture collage filled with Nathan's friends on various nights out.

It was one of these that Jacob was now examining, a frown carved into his face. Nathan's scrawny body was resting against the kitchen counter in coolly distressed jeans and a T-shirt.

'Thanks,' Nathan replied, fiddling with his hair. Rook could see that the peroxide blond was growing out to reveal his dark roots.

'But seriously, no offence, but how do you afford this place? That magic shop pay this well?' Rook said.

'You come to talk property prices with me?' Nathan's bone-white face scrunched up like a teenager who'd been told he had a curfew.

'I'd like to know too,' Jacob cut in. Nathan flinched at the sound of his voice.

'A friend is letting me use it,' Nathan replied.

'That's a good friend,' Rook said, moving closer to the other end of the counter from Nathan.

'Guess so,' Nathan said.

'Would you mind closing that window? It's freezing in here. You are aware it's winter, right?' Rook asked, pointing at the wide-open window behind Nathan.

Nathan shook his head. 'I like the cold.'

Rook could see Jacob start towards the window, but he held up a hand to stop him.

'It's fine,' Rook said, pulling his jacket tighter to his chest.

'Great, now what are you doing here?' Nathan said.

'I'm going back over people's statements, trying to see what I can uncover,' Rook said, taking his notepad out of his pocket.

'Clutching at straws, you mean,' Nathan said, his lips parting so Rook could see his sharp white teeth.

'Something like that. Caleb had lots of pictures on his wall too.'

'So? People like pictures.'

'Can you take me back through what happened the night of Caleb's murder, please?'

'I told you. I went back to his place with him and Abby. Left a bit after, went to bed.'

'I still don't get that.'

'Get what?' Nathan asked, sullen eyebrows quizzical.

'Your going back with Abby and Caleb. They were clearly going back to have sex, and everyone knows you like Abby. Were you hoping to get in on the action or get in the way?'

'We've been friends for a long time, that's all.'

'And you were going back with them when she was going to have sex? That's not something I do with my friends. What were you going to do when they were going at it? Make yourself a cup of tea?' Rook said.

Nathan's face contorted in disgust. Whether directed at himself or Rook, Rook couldn't say. Rook took a step towards the collage on the wall. All the pictures were of various young people partying and having fun. He could see Abby in more than a few. He smiled when he noticed Rebecca firing withering looks at the camera in a couple of the pictures, and then there was Karl smoking, looking like the wannabe rock star he was.

'Do you know what's funny about these pictures, Nathan?'

'What?'

'You're hardly in any of them. You only creep into the background of a few. Caleb had a lot of pictures up too, but he was in a few of them. More than a few, to be honest.'

'Guess I'm not as in love with myself as much as he was.'

'I guess not. You weren't in any of those photos either.'

Nathan was silent; a silence filled by Jacob drumming his fingers on the kitchen counter.

'You were telling the truth about going back home after leaving Abby and Caleb, though. CCTV proves it. Got you walking right up the street, right to the front door. And for a while, that ruled you out as a suspect. You were alibied.'

'Because I didn't do it,' Nathan said, his eyes darting to and from Jacob's drumming fingers.

'But then…' Rook said, ignoring Nathan's interruption, 'I remembered how fast vampires move and how very good they are at climbing. You evolved as treetop hunters, I believe?'

'That's what I'm told. Not like I was there, was I?' Nathan's voice was as tentative as a man trying to burgle a hornet's nest.

'Not sure I would have remembered how fast you were if I hadn't seen you show off in front of Riothamus's place, to be honest. So I thought, just because I didn't see you come out of your door again, doesn't mean that you didn't go out another way. A human couldn't get down from your window into the alley behind, but you could. And sure enough, there was a CCTV camera across the road that caught you going out of your window and up over the rooftop at about ten past one. It then catches you coming back in the same window just over an hour later. Plenty of time for you to get yourself to Caleb's and back.'

'CCTV, really?'

'London is the most monitored city outside of China,' Rook replied, a fact he'd heard but never checked.

'I went out. Doesn't mean I killed Caleb,' Nathan said.

'You telling me you went out for a bit of night-time rooftop ramble? Don't take the piss, Nathan. You killed him. And I'm guessing you killed him because you were jealous. Caleb got the girl you wanted, and he was doing jobs for Riothamus, who didn't want to work with you. A cool kid getting all the attention you wanted, while you're the type of hanger-on who will tag along when the girl he likes goes back with another guy. What's messed up, though, is that you couldn't have known Abby had left. Were you willing to kill her if she was still there too? Or were you going to wait until she left in the morning? Could have been a hell of a wait.'

Rook saw Nathan's glance towards his knife holder. Jacob had seen the same thing, quietly moving in front of it. Nathan's chest deflated as he exhaled.

'I wouldn't have killed her,' he said.

'Then what would you have done if she was still there?'

'I had a plan for that,' he said without conviction.

'You had a plan? People who kill in a jealous rage rarely plan.'

Then Nathan did something Rook wasn't expecting. He laughed. He laughed and looked at Rook with something approaching contempt.

'You think that's why I killed him? I thought you might have some actual importance, but you're as in the dark as everybody else. For a detective, you're fucking slow. Even now, you still can't figure out what's really going on. I did what had to be done. Jacob, I thought you would understand that, but I guess you're as out of the loop as this human.'

'Whatever,' Rook said sharply. 'You can tell us all about your motives later. Jacob, let's take him in.'

'Take him in?' Jacob said, his face a picture of irritation.

'Yes, we take him in and get a full confession. Make sure we know everything,' Rook said, pulling a pair of handcuffs from his pocket and moving towards Nathan.

'That's not how this works,' Jacob said, placing his hand on Rook's shoulder.

'You're going to execute him right here, right now?' Rook said, turning to face Jacob down.

'He confessed. He's a vampire. I'll snap his neck. It won't take long.'

'I'll let you two figure this out,' Nathan said with a giggle.

And then Rook felt the movement of air around him as the vampire sprung past him. Nathan didn't fly, but he moved so fast that he may as well have. In the time it would take Rook to blink, the vampire had danced behind his back and was out of the window. The window wasn't even big, but Nathan had moved like a cat to contort his body through it.

Rook swore and walked up to the window, but Nathan was already gone.

'Should have closed the window,' Jacob said, joining him.

'Guess so,' Rook replied. 'What did he mean by us being in the dark, Jacob?'

Jacob shook his head. 'He could have been lying.'

'I doubt it. People don't tend to half confess to murder. Jealousy had a part to play. Otherwise, why cut him so many times after you've slashed his throat? But there's something else for us to find out. He's working for someone. Possibly Rowena. And I need to question Nathan about it. It's possible he's involved in the disappearances and killing. And maybe she is too.'

'Why not just go to Rowena directly?'

'Because she is a politician, and we need more evidence if we aren't going to get stonewalled.'

'What if we don't get the evidence?'

'Then I'll have to talk to her anyway. But it will be more difficult and could just lead to her destroying any evidence we would otherwise find.'

'You understand what I must do after he is found and has talked?'

'We can't execute people in the dark, without knowing what happened and why. There has to be some sort of procedure,' Rook said, still gazing out of the window onto the alley below.

'If you don't want me to kill him, don't look for him.'

'I can't do that either.' Rook turned away.

CHAPTER THIRTY-SEVEN

Rook was bolt upright in his bed before he realised he was awake. His alarm clock said it was six in the morning, but his body felt like it was still the middle of the night. Someone was banging on his door, hard enough that he was worried they were going to break his new lock.

'Please, come in,' Rook said as Rebecca pushed past him as soon as he'd opened the door.

She had gone straight into his living room and was now standing there, her slim body trembling in a long black coat. Her mess of thick black hair was tied back, showing the worry on her angular face.

'He's gone,' she said.

'How do you know where I live?' Rook asked, his eyes still acclimating to the light.

'What?' Rebecca said, shaking her head in frustration and clenching her fists.

'I'm sorry,' Rook said. 'It's the middle of the night and you're going to have to give me some context. So, who's gone and, seriously, how do you know where I live?'

'Karl's gone. And I know where you live because we had him follow you.'

That little shit, Rook thought. He must be the worst CI anyone had ever had. Not only was he not giving Rook information, he was also spying on him.

'Why are you sure he's gone? And please sit down. You're stressing me out standing there.'

Rebecca looked at Rook's sofa, moved some old newspapers out of the way, and selected the least messy part to sit on. Rook stayed standing and fought his urge to fidget as the adrenaline released into his system mixed with the weariness he felt in every muscle and sinew. The futile hunt for Nathan had led to long hours of walking and talking, and it had already been late when he and Jacob had called it a day.

'He was supposed to get in touch yesterday afternoon. But he hasn't called. No one else has heard from him in the past couple of days. I waited all night outside his place. He didn't show up.'

'Is there any other reason he would be out? Could he be staying with a friend?'

'Do you think I wouldn't have thought about that?' she snapped. 'He's been taken.'

'By who?' Rook said, but the answer formed in his mind like a long shadow.

'He was following Carver.'

Rook's back snapped upright as if he'd had coffee shot straight into his veins. 'Why was he following Carver?'

'He'd overheard you on the phone with Nicole. How all those missing had been taken somewhere after the health centre. Figured it was the people taken to see Marlowe.'

Rook pressed his hands to his skull and fought an urge to shout. 'What the fuck, Rebecca? You said you were going to wait. I asked you all to wait,' he said, his voice terse.

'He was only following him.'

'He was spotted. Carver realised someone was following him. Marlowe told me. I thought he was being paranoid.'

'They've taken him. They're going to kill him like they killed Caleb,' Nicole said, a note of terror clear in her voice.

'Nathan killed Caleb,' Rook said, shaking his head.

'Why would Nathan kill Caleb?' Rebecca replied, her eyes narrowing to disbelieving squints.

'Not sure. I thought it was about a girl, but he said it was about something else. It was probably both.'

'Do you have him in custody or something?'

Rook shook his head. 'He got away. Nicole has the word out. We'll bring him in soon.'

'You think he could have got to Karl?'

'Possibly, but we should start by seeing the psycho ex-con he was trailing.' Rook thought about sharing his suspicions about Rowena's role in all this but decided against it. The simplest solutions were sometimes the right ones, even when you were dealing with vampires and trolls. Karl was following Carver. Carver was probably the one who'd taken him.

'Well then, it looks like I'm going to see Carver,' Rook said. 'I better call Jacob.'

'I'm coming too,' Rebecca said, sticking her chin out.

'No, you're not. You need to rest.' Rook took a deep breath and tried to clear his head. 'I'm sorry, Rebecca. I shouldn't have said anything about asking you to wait. You've done more than anyone to help find the truth. None of this is your fault and you should be proud you tried. But now you need to let me do my job and do it knowing that at least you will be safe.'

'I... I don't want to go home,' Rebecca said.

'Fair enough. You can stay here. No one knows you're here. There's some food in the fridge. And I'm sorry about the mess.'

'It's okay, it's not the first bachelor pad I've been in.'

Rebecca took the throw draped over the back of the sofa, gave it a shake to remove at least some of the crumbs from it, and wrapped it tight over herself as she lay down. Meanwhile, Rook called Jacob. He answered within a couple of rings.

'I'll be there in fifteen,' Jacob said, no trace of tiredness in his voice.

Rook forced himself into a cold shower, threw on his suit and long coat, and then poured some strong black coffee down his throat. Once outside, he lit up a cigarette, its bitter taste forcing his mind into something approaching an alert state. He tried to come up with a scenario where this ended well for Karl. He couldn't. Whatever the outcome, the next twenty-four hours were going to be brutal.

CHAPTER THIRTY-EIGHT

As they descended the hill towards the vineyard, they saw pinpricks of light bleeding out of the windows of Marlowe's office into the early morning gloom. Three cars were parked outside: a sleek black Audi SUV, a new-looking hatchback, and a car even less roadworthy than Jacob's.

'Guess that's Karl's?' Rook said, pointing at the scruffy car.

Jacob nodded, parking the death trap he called a car. Rook had suggested they take his, but Jacob refused.

They walked towards the building, the soft crunch of the gravel under their feet the only sound to trouble the early morning air. The lights inside would have made their approach invisible, had anyone been in the foyer to see them.

Rook tested the door handle of the glass doors. They opened without resistance. He shared a glance with Jacob, who nodded, and they stepped inside, making sure they didn't make any unnecessary noise.

Marlowe's study was empty, dark, and silent. Rook and Jacob were drawn by the faint glow beading from the corridor that led them to Lab One. Reaching the corridor's end, Rook took a steadying breath and thrust the door open. The scene within seared itself into Rook's consciousness, indelible and raw.

Marlowe stood in a blood-covered surgical gown, scalpel in hand and sweat on his brow. Carver was next to him, a smile like an open wound on his face and holding a gun – a gun he was pointing lazily at Rook.

'Apologies for the gun, Rook,' Marlowe said, his tongue flicking out of his mouth to wet his lips. 'But we heard you come in, and you can never be too careful when dealing with these things.'

'And we were worried you would lose your temper when you saw what we have on our table,' Carver said.

What they had on the table was Karl's corpse, displayed naked and in pieces. Various tubes were jammed into his flesh. His left leg had been cleaved in two, revealing the flesh and bone below the knee. His chest opened so Rook could see ribs, and a segment had been cut from each cheek to show off his sharp incisors. The all too human stench of blood, cauterised flesh and sweat filled Rook's mouth, nose, and throat, and he had to force himself not to gag.

It was Jacob who responded first. 'I'm going to kill you. Both of you. I am going to tear you apart,' he said, his fists tense, his body coiled.

'Not now you won't,' Carver sniggered.

'You think that gun can stop me?' Jacob said.

'It can stop him,' Carver replied, jerking his gun towards Rook.

Rook put his hand on Jacob's chest. 'What the fuck have you been doing, Marlowe?' he said.

'Experiments, Rook, experiments.' As Marlowe spoke he ran his finger – encased within surgical gloves – along the top of Karl's brow, in the slow manner of a possessive lover. 'Do you remember how I told you about all the special abilities the other species have? Could you imagine the improvements in medicine we could make if we understood Jacob's regenerative abilities? Imagine how that would aid our fight against outbreaks. Or how ghouls can eat almost anything without getting sick. And that includes most poisons. How vampires like Karl here' – he motioned towards Karl's cadaver on the bench – 'can be so fast and retain their strength? There's so much to learn from them. And that's what I'm doing,' Marlowe said, with the quiet fervour of a preacher describing the divine.

Rook remembered, early in his career, catching a man who had abused and then killed two kids: a six-year-old boy and his four-year-old sister. He'd kidnapped them from their mother, had his way with them over a weekend, then disposed of their bodies in a shallow grave in a nearby forest. When they'd first caught him, he'd denied everything. For hours, he had denied everything. But, once he realised his guilt was proven, the pervert couldn't stop talking about how and why he'd done it. As if he thought he could make everyone understand that mutilating those children was right and beautiful. Rook could hear that same tone in Marlowe's voice. A psychopath who believed that, deep down, everyone was as broken as he was and who revelled in showing off his work.

'That's bullshit. I'm no scientist, Marlowe, but there's no way you need to be cutting people into bits in the middle of the night to learn anything.'

'You're right. You're not a scientist,' Marlowe replied, chin wobbling as he spoke 'But I am. In any case, all your indignation is fruitless. All of this is approved. A deal has been made.'

'Approved? How is any of this shit approved?'

'You'll have to talk to the higher-ups about that,' Marlowe said with a conspiratorial waggle of his eyebrows, his fat lips curling into a grotesque smile.

The next sound Rook heard was a strangled cough. It took Rook a horrifying second to realise where the cough came from.

'Hey, Rook,' Karl said, the words hard to understand as they came out from his mangled mouth.

'Jesus, Marlowe, he's alive!' Rook was about to rush him, but Carver shook his head and made a point of straightening the arm pointing a gun.

'Only as long as he's got those tubes in him,' Marlowe said, his gloating voice grating on Rook's ears.

'Hey, Rook,' Karl spoke again, his words sounding like they were being wrenched out of his lungs with every ounce of strength he had. 'I need this to end.'

'Take them out, Marlowe,' Rook replied through his teeth.

'But I'm not done with him yet.'

'I'm not leaving until you've taken them out. And if you shoot me, I'm sure Jacob would be more than happy to finish up here.'

'Oh, I would,' Jacob said, stepping closer to Carver.

'If you must,' Marlowe said, casually walking over to Karl and yanking every tube out of Karl's body. Each tube made a tearing, squelching sound as it was pulled from the vampire's flesh. Within a minute, a final rattle had escaped Karl's throat. 'Now that you have finished interrupting my experiments, I think you can leave and take your orc with you.'

'This is not finished,' Jacob said.

'You take this up with Rowena and Steele and see what happens,' Marlowe said, his voice righteous as he stood over Karl's corpse.

Carver laughed his barbed laugh. 'No one has been murdered here, anyway. The worst thing that's happened is a bit of animal cruelty.'

Jacob moved a step towards Carver, and Carver turned his gun on the orc. Carver's face strained with panic as Jacob bore down on him.

'Not now, Jacob,' Rook said, against his best wishes. Carver was right. A firefight would likely lead to a bullet finding Rook. With Karl already dead, justice would have to wait until another day. They left the lab, walking half-backwards as Carver followed behind them with his gun trained on Rook. Rook wondered if Jacob would be willing to sacrifice him if it meant tearing into Carver. The anger on the orc's face suggested the thought had crossed his mind. Only once they had got back into the car did Carver turn back into the building.

As they drove away, Rook could feel his brain banging against his skull and his hands clenching against his will. He wanted nothing more than to go back into Marlowe's lab and tear them into pieces. But he had no doubt Carver would shoot to kill.

'So, we're expected to leave them alone?' Jacob asked, glaring out at the road ahead.

'For now. But I'll speak to Steele straightaway.'

'There needs to be justice, Rook.'

'There will be,' Rook said, wishing his mind shared the conviction of his words.

'You should have let me take Carver in his flat, Rook. We knew he was doing something. We should have at least taken him somewhere. I could have got him to talk.'

Rook looked out of the passenger window. They both knew what Jacob wasn't saying. If Rook had let Jacob have his way, Karl would still be alive, and not a mangled corpse in a cold lab.

'Jesus Christ!' Rook said after they'd been driving for a while.

'What?' Jacob asked, startled by Rook's outburst.

'He took me to Lab Two.'

'What?'

'When we went to his office to see Caleb's remains, Marlowe had him in Lab Two.'

'Why is that important?'

'If you had two identical labs, you would use Lab One first, right? Lab One. But we went into Lab Two. What if someone was in Lab One? That's where Karl was tonight. What if, while I was talking politely with that sick bastard about Caleb's corpse, someone else was in there... being vivisected?'

'You can't know that,' Jacob said, glancing at Rook.

But, as the distant lights of London came into view like a million dancing flames, Rook knew. This world was too cruel for it to be any other way.

CHAPTER THIRTY-NINE

'This can't be true,' Nicole said, voice shaking, brown eyes pleading, hands clutching the handbag in her lap as she sat in her chair. The office heating hadn't had the time to drive the chill out of the morning air so she hadn't taken off her winter coat. But Rook could still see her tremble as she tried to absorb the news.

'It is,' Rook replied.

'And they used the centre to find them?'

'They did.'

Nicole started to weep. Rook stood there, resting against the kitchen counter while he boiled the kettle for yet another cup of coffee. Rook couldn't say he'd broken the news to her gently. It wasn't like there was a good way to tell someone that they were indirectly enabling two serial killers. Especially since the smell of Karl's mutilated body still clogged up his mind, and Rebecca's curses rang in his ears.

Rebecca had raged when he'd told her the news, her mouth transforming into various angry shapes as she shouted at him. Rook didn't know if she blamed him for not stopping Marlowe and Carver or if he was a convenient target. In either case, he didn't correct her. He did share the blame. If he'd been more decisive, Karl would be alive. If he'd realised sooner that Karl was following Carver, he could have stopped the vampire from being caught at all. And maybe, if he'd checked the other lab when they were looking over Caleb's remains, he could have stopped Marlowe right then.

'And we didn't even notice them disappear.'

'Marlowe and Carver were careful. They picked people who were socially isolated. Few friends, little family. Once they had killed them, Carver would break back in and take their stuff. Make it look like they had cleared out. Carver's CV includes some breaking and entering. It wouldn't have been too difficult for him. Especially since he would have had their keys.'

'Why did they do it?' Nicole said, wiping tears from her eyes.

Rook poured himself a coffee, the boiling water splashing back onto his hand, causing him to flinch and swear.

'Because Marlowe and Carver wanted to. And because they could.'

'But... But he didn't seem like the type.'

'No one does. We like to tell ourselves we can tell when someone is evil. But we can't. People like that exist; they hide in plain sight. We don't see the truth until the mask is ripped from their faces.'

'How did they subdue them?' Nicole asked. She was trying to find a way in which it wasn't true, Rook realised. She'd enjoyed the thrill of the investigation when it was abstract, but the reality of learning that someone she worked with was a torturer and a murderer was too much for her sunny worldview to take.

'I don't know. Catching the ones they knew from the health centre off guard wouldn't have been difficult. They would say it was an appointment and drive them to Marlowe's. They would sit in the chair for him. Then he'd have to give them whatever drug it was he was using. I don't know how they got the drop on Karl. My guess is Karl didn't quite know what he was walking into, and he let Carver get too close.'

'Poor Karl. Poor all of them. Are we telling their loved ones yet?'

'Soon,' Rook replied. 'There's something else we need to discuss.'

'What do we need to discuss, Rook?' Nicole asked, her voice plaintive.

'Marlowe said there had been an arrangement.' He sat down in his chair with his coffee. He'd moved the chair around his desk to be closer to Nicole as he broached this subject. He wanted her to see his face, to see he didn't hold her accountable for any of this.

'An arrangement?'

'What he was doing had been signed off. By Steele and Rowena.'

'It can't have been.' Nicole squeezed her handbag tighter as she spoke.

'Maybe not. But we have to investigate. And either way we need to talk to Steele. See what he knows.'

'I can arrange that,' Nicole said, before exhaling a deep breath and adding, 'And then I need to resign.'

'You can't resign,' Rook replied, shaking his head.

'I set up a health centre that was used to find murder victims. How can I not?' she said.

'Okay, you absolutely can resign. Hell, maybe you should.' Rook took a drink of his coffee and allowed himself a sad smile. 'I'm sure you'd be much happier and very successful. But I hope you don't. You help the other species, and I'm not sure anyone else does. I thought I could help, but I'm here to clean up the mess. I don't know what Steele and Rowena's game is, but they're politicians, so I imagine it's about as straight as a corkscrew. You set up the health centre. It's not your fault someone perverted it. But you care, Nicole. And I'm sorry it's not working out for you in this shitty office. But if you go, will anyone else give a fuck about making these people's lives any better?'

'I'll arrange for us to meet Steele,' Nicole said, turning on her computer.

CHAPTER FORTY

'It's a bad business, Rook, a bad business,' Steele said, wringing his gloved hands. He'd agreed to meet in a back-alley close to Whitehall, where Rook presumed Steele had his actual office.

Steele was impeccably dressed in a smart suit and a perfectly pressed long winter coat, looking like the world's best-dressed funeral director. He stood bolt upright while Rook told him what had happened, taking the news of vivisections and serial killers like he was hearing about a bad day for the stock market.

'Did you let Marlowe kill those people?' Nicole asked. Her body vibrated with so much rage it was a wonder her bones didn't shatter.

'I was unaware of the torture,' Steele said.

'But you knew he was taking them?' she pressed.

'There wasn't funding available for the centre, Nicole. Or the will for it to happen. It was a good initiative, but I couldn't find the budget for it on its own merits,' Steele said, running his hand over his bald head.

'Then how did you find the budget?' Nicole said, her whole body focussed on Steele, not letting him squirm away from her questions.

He sighed, his eyes searching the back-alley for some reprieve.

'It was Marlowe's idea,' he said, with the air of a tired teacher imparting an unsavoury lesson on a naive child. 'Since the Coronavirus ravaged the world, we have been throwing everything at drug development and testing. Marlowe thought this was an excellent opportunity to use the other species' physiologies to find cures and vaccinations against new and novel diseases. A good idea, even if the execution was lacking.'

'Why the secrecy?' Rook cut in. 'There are drug trials all the time.'

'It was more than normal drug trials, Rook. Drug trials take time. There are various procedures and steps that must be taken. With the other species, we could circumvent these steps and test drugs at much earlier stages.'

'Why was I not told?' Nicole asked.

'Because we didn't deem it necessary. This is a secret operation,' he said with a wan smile.

Rook bit the corner of his mouth but couldn't stop his next outburst. 'Not necessary? It wasn't necessary because you didn't care how Marlowe got results. You didn't even try to put him on a leash.'

'There was... some scope for research. Into the genetics of the other species. But I gave no permission for anything like you described.'

'Did Rowena agree with this?' Rook said, watching Nicole's reaction to Steele's words. She'd stopped shaking with rage, her shoulders had sagged, and she was looking at the dirty pavement beneath their feet. Rook wasn't surprised. It was hard for a fundamentally good person to sustain anger like he could. At some point, their helplessness subsides into despondency. Nicole had been played, her altruistic ideas twisted from the beginning into something cruel. That had broken something in her. Rook wasn't sure it could be fixed.

'For this to go ahead, we also had to have Rowena's agreement,' Steele said, oblivious to the effect he was having on Nicole. 'She has a prominent position, after all.'

'What's going to happen to Marlowe and Carver?' Nicole said, looking down and moving a discarded crisp packet out of the way with her foot.

Steele took a deep breath, the air filling his pigeon chest like an inflating football. 'Jacob saw what was happening, yes?'

'He did,' Rook said.

'Then this cannot be contained. Which means we must act, and act swiftly.'

'What do you mean "act swiftly"?' Nicole asked.

'He means they need to die,' Rook said.

Steele gave a quick, tight nod. 'Regrettably, yes. If word gets out that humans are systematically killing other species without punishment, they may decide to make themselves known. After all, if they aren't safe in the margins of society, why bother hiding there?'

'Maybe they should be known,' Nicole whispered.

'Oh, Nicole, you must rid yourself of this naivety,' Steele said, his tone breaking from its civil-service serenity into something harsher. For a second, Rook saw the man behind the mask – a man sick of being surrounded by lesser intellects who didn't understand how the world works. 'Do you realise how many people are killed and tortured for being a different colour, sexuality, religion, or even sect of the same religion? I don't because it's not something we even bother to count. What would happen if people knew that orcs and vampires lived among them?'

'People would adjust,' Nicole said.

'No, they wouldn't,' Rook said, shaking his head. His thoughts filled with images of Karl's grotesque body, lying vivisected on that cold lab table. 'I'm sorry, Nicole, but they wouldn't. I thought that too until I saw what they did to Karl. Marlowe and Carver are not the only psychopaths in the world, and not all would be content to lurk in the shadows. If the other species were discovered, they would soon be destroyed one way or another.'

'Correct,' Steele replied. 'At first, there may be interest, even excitement. But soon it would turn to suspicion and then, inevitably and inexorably, violence. And no Government wants to deal with such a situation.'

'That's a bleak view of humanity you two have got,' Nicole said.

'It's one borne of experience and knowledge,' Steele said, looking to the skies and allowing a sigh to escape his lips. 'Assuming this discussion is over, we should focus on doing what needs to be done. And, to move forwards, I require your assistance. Both of you.'

Rook and Nicole avoided looking at each other, both contemplating the implications of what Steele was asking. For a moment all you could hear was the chatter from nearby streets, the noise of engines of cars stuck in London traffic, and the occasional whoops of tourists having fun.

'Nicole doesn't have to be involved. I'll do it,' Rook said, the sound of Karl's final breath still drilling into his ears.

CHAPTER FORTY-ONE

'He's dead, Rook. He came last night. Now he's dead,' the voice on the other end of the phone said, quiet and shaking.

'Who's dead, Abby?' Rook asked, although he had a pretty good idea who she was referring to.

'Nathan. He came to my place last night. Said he needed somewhere to crash.' The words struggled to be heard through her sobs.

'Okay, I know it's hard, but you've got to stay calm. Go into another room and wait.'

Twenty minutes later, he was on the street outside Abby's flat. Jacob was already there.

Jacob detached himself from the wall he'd been resting on and walked towards Rook with the certainty of a glacier, his coat pulled high against his chin.

'You been in yet?' Rook asked.

'It might upset her if I went in alone.'

'Well,' Rook said, 'looks like it's time to see another vampire corpse. Never would have guessed I'd need to get used to seeing dead vampires.'

Jacob shrugged and hit the buzzer. Within seconds, Abby rushed down the stairs in fast irregular footsteps, strands of untamed pink hair trailing behind her. Whatever she was going to say stuck in her throat as soon as she saw Jacob behind Rook. She threw her long-fingered hand up to her mouth, as if to stop the words from pouring out, then let them into her flat.

Nathan's corpse was by itself on the sofa, sitting among various colourful cushions and blankets. He looked like a puppet with its strings cut, his head lolling to one side, his brown eyes staring, his gaping mouth revealing his sharp vampire's teeth. There was no blood or signs of a struggle. He looked so weak, his slight frame barely managing to fill out his skinny jeans and a white T-shirt. Rook stayed standing. Jacob went up to the body to get a closer look.

'When did he arrive?' Rook asked.

Abby stood next to the wall, fretting with her hands. It was clear she had not heard Rook's question.

'I admit this is a strange question, given your friend is dead on your sofa, but is something else bothering you, Abby?'

She gave her head a short shake.

'I didn't kill him, Abby,' Jacob said, without turning around.

'I... I didn't think you did,' Abby said.

'Yes, you did. And it's not a stupid thought to have,' Jacob replied. 'It could have been me. Although, I wouldn't have left him on the sofa.'

Abby's shoulders relaxed and hands stilled, suggesting she believed Jacob.

'When did he get here, Abby?' Rook asked again.

'Last night sometime. He said he needed somewhere to stay, so I let him crash on the sofa.'

'Did he say why he needed somewhere to stay?'

'Said he'd been kicked out of his flat. It happens.'

'Did he say anything else?' Rook said.

'He said... he said you were going to pin what happened to Caleb on him,' Abby said, shifting on her feet like the floor was made of hot coals. Her eyes fixed on Jacob as the orc examined Nathan's corpse.

'We weren't going to pin anything on him, Abby. He killed Caleb,' Jacob replied.

Abby looked up at Rook, her eyes round, red, and searching for an answer she wasn't sure she wanted.

'I'm sorry, but he did it. He confessed before running,' Rook said.

Whatever had been holding Abby together snapped at that moment. Her body shook and tears broke through.

'Why?' she said through the sobs.

'He never said,' Rook lied, not seeing the point of burdening her with the truth or his suspicions. 'What happened this morning?'

'My flatmates had left for work. I asked him what he was doing, and he said he was working for someone in secret. He wouldn't say who. Said they were going to pick him up. I had to go out, and when I came back...' Her gaze drifted to the corpse.

'Thanks, Abby,' Rook said. 'Maybe you should go to your room.'

She shuffled away, making no noise as she closed the door behind her.

'You were telling the truth, right? You didn't kill him?' Rook asked.

Jacob gave Rook a sideways look.

'It's a fair question,' Rook said, walking over to where Nathan was lying.

'What do you think happened?' Jacob asked.

'I think he was an idiot. An idiot who thought he was important, when he was a sad man being used by someone more powerful. And when he stopped being useful, they broke his neck.'

CHAPTER FORTY-TWO

Twilight had given way to night-time as Jacob's car moved through the bare trees towards Rowena's office. The only sound had been Jacob's heavy drumming on the steering wheel, Rook's growling stomach, and the wheezing engine.

Almost as soon as they had parked in front of the decrepit country house, Alice opened the doors and skittered her way down the stone stairs on long, unsteady legs.

'I'll get in trouble for this,' she said as Rook got out of the car.

'I'm sorry, but I wanted to catch Rowena off guard.'

'It's okay. Not sure I wanted to work here anymore,' she replied, looking at the huge old building with its boarded-up windows – boards that had mould around the edges.

The moment they opened the door to the office, everybody stopped what they were doing and every head turned to Rook and Jacob. The silence punctured only when Rowena opened the door at the back of the room.

'I think you should come into my office,' she said, leaning on the door frame in a smart red suit that turned her shoulders into sharp angles. If Rowena was worried about Rook and Jacob appearing in her workplace, she didn't show it. She walked back into her office and motioned for Rook and Jacob to sit down, the door closing with a thud.

'If you don't mind, I'm going to make myself some tea,' Rowena said, performing the same tea-making ritual she'd used when Rook was last in her office: walking her fingers across the jars of leaves, pausing on a particular one, and selecting it. Finally, her tea made, she sat down. She looked at Rook and Jacob with those wide green eyes, which Rook noted had deep bags under them. 'What is it you're looking for today, gentlemen?'

'Did you know?' Jacob jumped in.

'About what, Jacob? So much has happened. It's getting hard to keep track,' Rowena said, taking a sip of her tea.

'About what Marlowe was doing with Carver. About vampires and orcs being cut up for fun,' Jacob said, leaning forwards and pressing his hands on the table.

'We know you had an agreement,' Rook said. 'Marlowe would run tests on the other species in return for the centre's funding. When did that turn into vivisection, Rowena?'

Rowena looked at her tea, paused, and took a deep drink. 'I knew he would take some of us, that they were taken to get Marlowe his results.'

'And you allowed that?' Jacob said, his body tense, his bald head bowed forwards slightly like he was about to charge.

'We needed healthcare, Jacob. Nicole had the idea to pilot a health centre, and we needed to get better healthcare. Disease crosses the species barrier. Orcs, like Jacob and me, can fight off most of them. For the rest of the other species, many are death sentences. We rely on old wives' tales mixed with over-the-counter drugs. We have twelfth-century healthcare in the twenty-first century, taking ibuprofen for cancer. Coronavirus ripped through our people. They can't go to hospitals, can't see doctors. We don't exist, and if you don't exist in this world you live a half-life and die in the dark. But being in need isn't enough to get aid in this world. You need to have value to prove you're worth the investment. And we couldn't prove our value. Until Marlowe came to me with a proposition. We could have our health centre, equipment, and facilities and he'd even help train some nurses. But Marlowe wanted more than just to use us for drug trials.' She kept her gaze on the depths of her tea, her head slightly bowed, showing the grey roots of her brown hair.

'What did he want?' Rook asked.

'He said to get what we needed, he needed to run more tests, more invasive tests. That way, he could get rapid results and gain greater insights into our genetics and physiology. And he'd green-lit the money for the health centre. He said just one person a year at most would be needed. But then more went missing, and he sent me more names. I didn't know... the extent... of what he was doing to them and...' Her voice cracked and then failed her, like an elderly person reliving a painful memory.

'You couldn't stop him without making your deal public,' Rook said.

'That's right,' Rowena said, her voice a quiet death-rattle rasp.

'Then Caleb started snooping around. Is that when you hired Nathan, or was he already on the payroll?' Rook asked.

'You think I keep idiots on staff permanently? Of course that's when I hired him. He was meant to feedback information on Caleb and his intrepid band of investigators. But he wasn't even good at that.' She allowed a mirthless laugh to come out of her mouth.

'I bet he was so happy to be useful. Made him feel important, like a spy,' Rook said.

'It was his need that made him useful, yes.' She ran a tired hand through her hair and dragged her attention to Rook. Her eyes seemed to struggle to focus, like they were fighting sleep. 'It's a powerful need. That *want* to feel useful. To have purpose beyond mere existence. A need that makes people easy to manipulate. It's how people get others to spend their lives toiling in offices, doing jobs they hate. It's how people are able to commit heinous acts and then go home to their happy families, a smile on their face. You give a lost person a purpose and they will do almost anything in its service. Even if it means twisting their morals into a knot.'

'So you ordered him to kill Caleb?' Rook pressed.

As Rowena took another drink of her tea, the powerful politician drained away, leaving the tired old woman behind. Rook had seen this before. The strain of concealing puts people under a lot of pressure, and when they come clean, the truth pours out of them like a dam bursting.

'Caleb called one of my people. It was clear he was close to putting it together. That's why I was forced to tell Nathan that Caleb needed to be stopped. For the good of all the other species. Nathan took care of it. More messily than I expected, perhaps.'

'I don't think your message was the only reason he killed Caleb, or even the main reason.'

'Did he tell you why he was so savage?' Rowena murmured.

'No. He wanted to believe he was the spy, assassin, or whatever stupid idea you had put in his head. It's a great justification, and as you say, it gave him a higher purpose. But it was a crime of passion. Too many frantic stab wounds for it to be a clinical assassination. He was jealous of Caleb's relationship with Abby. Maybe of Caleb in general. All you did was give a broken person an acceptable reason to kill. At least in his eyes.'

'I can see that,' Rowena said, face grim and straining, as if sitting still were causing her to expend a great deal of effort.

'Did you kill Nathan yourself?' Jacob cut in, leaning forwards.

'Does it matter?' Rowena said. 'After all, wouldn't you have killed him yourself if I gave you the order?'

'It matters to me,' Jacob said, his fists clenching so hard it looked like his knuckles might pop out.

'Then I owe you an answer. No, I didn't ask someone else. Wasn't the time. He called me, looking for rescue. I made sure he was alone and then I snapped his neck. Even an old orc with aching bones can snap a vampire's neck. I thought I could end your investigation if you found him dead.'

Rook looked across and saw Jacob grind his teeth. Rowena saw it too and said, 'I'm not proud of my decisions, Jacob. And it saddens me greatly that it has come to this. I have only ever done what is best for the other species. A few deaths were a compromise I needed to make.'

'You let our people get kidnapped, tortured, and killed and you call it a compromise?' Jacob growled.

'What do you think the endgame is, Jacob? Do you think there's a happy future for the other species? Our extinction is inevitable. We're not building anything here. We're only delaying our demise for as long as we can. The health centre bought us some more time. Soon there will be more across the country, our healthcare will improve, lives will be saved, and extinction delayed. I am willing to make sacrifices for that.'

'Sacrifices?' Jacob shouted, leaning forwards and slamming his hand on the table in front of them, hard enough that it caused Rowena's computer screen to jump. 'They were being gutted alive.'

Rowena held up a heavy hand to mollify his rage.

'Yes, Jacob, sacrifices. Sacrifices we must make if we are to survive.'

Jacob winced and ran his hands over his head. Rook stayed quiet.

Rowena was ignoring them, her efforts concentrated on saying what she needed to say. 'I'm revolted by what Marlowe has done to my people, Jacob. And I'm disgusted at my part in it. I know that is not a defence, and that now you will be figuring out what to do with me. Killing me could cause you some issues, even upheaval. No matter what has transpired.'

Jacob clenched his jaw but said nothing.

'It's okay, Jacob, I will make it easy for you. I think I owe you that. Nathan isn't the first person I've killed. I'm not sure I felt anything when I snapped his weak neck. I think I should have felt something, don't you?' Rowena said, with an ironic smile.

'Is now the time to confess to more murders?' Rook said.

'This is the only time, Detective Rook. And I think you will hear my confession. After all... you... policemen do like confessions. So yes, I've killed before. I've killed our people who have stepped out of line, and I've killed humans who have crossed the line. My methods... My methods weren't as violent as Jacob's, but they were effective. I've always been very good with herbs – I even grow my own. Green fingers, I guess.' She held out one of her hands and gave a faint smile at her own joke. 'Some herbs flavour tea, others work as poisons. I've even come up with my special mix to dispose of orcs. Some foxglove, some hemlock, and a pinch of ginger for flavour, and within twenty minutes you have a dead orc.' Her head lolled towards Jacob and she raised her teacup in a shaking hand. 'See, Jacob? I told you I'd make it easy for you.'

Jacob stormed around the table. 'What have you done?' he roared, knocking the teacup out of her hand and onto the soft carpet.

Drawing on her last reserves of strength, Rowena used the arms of her chair to push herself upright. 'Goodbye, Jacob. Now, let me die in peace.'

Chapter Forty-Three

Rook looked out the car window into the cold, dark night. As soon as they had pulled up outside Marlowe's house, Jacob was ready to go. Rook knew it was a good idea to get moving, even on a completely quiet suburban street at 11 p.m. They didn't want to risk attracting attention. But his legs seemed to weigh more than lead and he couldn't will his body to leave the car.

It had only been a few hours since they had left Rowena. She had been dead before they had left her office. Rook hadn't seen the point of lying to the people who worked for her. And, as it turned out, Alice wasn't the only one who'd been suspicious. Despite her actions, Rook had felt sorry for Rowena. Whatever her legacy would have been, it was now covering up Marlowe's atrocities.

'You shouldn't come in. There will be no mistakes,' Jacob said, looking at Rook with something approaching pity.

'No, I should be there,' Rook replied, in a voice he wasn't sure was his own.

'Why?'

'If I'm going to be damned anyway, I should see the consequences of my actions. That's why Steele wants me here, you know? To damn me' Rook said. 'So that, if this ever comes out, I'd be complicit. If the truth of other species came to light, we'd be painted as killers. One more incentive to keep up this whole masquerade, I guess.'

Jacob put his hand on the car door to open it, when he paused and sighed. 'Has anyone told you about the orc religion?'

'You're going Jehovah's Witness on me now?'

'We don't talk about it with outsiders much,' Jacob said, ignoring Rook's comment. 'But our afterlife starts with us on the great steppe, running from all our regrets. Our biggest regrets are the ones that chase us the longest.'

'So?' Rook said, irritated at this odd conversational segue.

'Executing Marlowe will not be one of the regrets that chases me, and it shouldn't be one that bothers you either.'

'Let's go,' Rook replied, hitting his legs and opening the car door.

Marlowe's residence was a detached house out in leafy suburbia, with huge hedges that hid its bottom floor from anyone standing outside. They passed through a gate under an arch cut into the hedge. The house inside stood three stories high and was probably around one-hundred years old. Ivy had crept over its cracked stone walls, and a thin light came from a solitary window on the second floor. Jacob picked the lock with precision and without noise.

It's strange entering a house that isn't yours, especially when the occupant is in. The air seems to sense your presence, moving around you like white blood cells sensing a virus that's entered the bloodstream. The house was dark, with wood-panelled walls. Only the light seeping out on the second floor gave Rook anything to navigate by. Jacob moved up the stairs first. Rook did his best not to make a sound as he followed behind, but each step was a battle with his legs to keep moving forwards.

The light was coming from a single desk lamp in Marlowe's study. It highlighted every line on the doctor's face but wasn't strong enough to reach the edges of the room, leaving the bookshelves on each wall in shadow.

Marlowe hadn't heard their approach. He was focussing on his computer, a glass of red wine in his hand and his tie loosened, allowing the flesh of his neck to spill out of the confines of his shirt.

'Hello Marlowe,' Jacob said.

Marlowe's body convulsed with a startled shiver when Jacob spoke, causing dark droplets of red wine to leap from his glass and hit his desk.

'You told me I was meeting you and Steele tonight,' Marlowe said, looking at Rook and trying to project composure. It might have worked but for the quiver of uncertainty in his voice and the tremor in his hand.

'I lied,' Rook said as they took a seat in front of the doctor's desk.

Marlowe looked nervous, like a frog who has found two snakes in his pond. 'Pity,' he said. 'I even had some superb wine prepared.' He motioned towards a side table where red wine sat in a decanter. 'I take it you have already visited Carver?'

Rook shook his head. 'He has gone to ground. He's cleaned out whatever he could from his flat and left. We'll find him.'

'I wouldn't be so sure. He is more intelligent than you might think.'

'He was smart enough to realise what was going to happen after we discovered your experiments. Yet you stayed around.'

'I thought Steele would see the bigger picture,' Marlowe said with a sigh.

'What bigger picture?' Rook said, his hands shaking and the beating of his heart hurting his chest.

'I've learnt more about the physiologies of the other species in the past year than anyone else has in the last five hundred. And I was making progress.'

'What did taking Karl apart like he was a damn cadaver teach you?' Rook asked, his voice full of sudden venom.

Marlowe's smile flickered. 'Sometimes you only learn by experimentation.'

'Bull. Shit.' Rook's rage caused his voice to shake in his throat. 'You did that because you could. Because you had power over them. You thought no one would even care.'

'I discovered—'

'Don't,' Rook said, holding up his hand. 'Don't justify yourself. Whatever intentions you had at the outset, you let your inner sadist out and now you have to pay.'

'Pay?' Marlowe said, glancing towards Jacob.

'You understand what that means,' Jacob replied.

Rook swallowed, his Adam's apple big in his throat.

Marlowe drained his glass in one gulp. 'Really, Rook?' he said, some red wine escaping his lips and dribbling down his chin. 'You're going to kill me because of a few orcs and vampires? They aren't even human. The law doesn't even extend to them – it isn't even murder.'

Rook was about to reply, but Jacob stepped forwards and said, 'That's enough. There's no need to hear you plead.'

The doctor's lips trembled and tears wet his cheeks. His body shook with tremendous sobs as he saw Jacob reach into his jacket and pull out a knife with a long, dangerous edge.

Marlowe's last words were lost among his sobs. In a couple of steps, Jacob was beside him. Marlowe raised his hands as if to ward off the orc as much as to stop his advance, but Jacob swept his hands aside and slit his throat in one quick slice. A slash of blood poured out of the doctor's throat. His cries became gurgles, then rasps, then silence as he slumped back onto his chair.

'Let's go. I'll let Steele know it's done,' Jacob said, wiping his knife on Marlowe's clothes.

Rook was stuck in his seat, vomit and bile clawing its way up his throat as he looked upon the result of his work: another bloodied corpse.

'Come now, Rook,' Jacob said, patting him on the shoulder. 'Time to go.'

CHAPTER FORTY-FOUR

The office was thick with silence. It pressed on Rook's skin and filled his lungs so that even the smallest utterance required the greatest effort. It had been two days since the execution, and Nicole had not asked about Marlowe. Rook could see the questions form in her mind, but then the words would stick in her mouth. Rook didn't blame her; he wouldn't know how to ask his partner about an execution they had been part of either.

They had spent the previous two days notifying the next of kin of those who had gone missing. Some had reacted with anger, others with grief. In either case, their outpouring of emotions felt like being drowned in a tidal wave. Rook knew it was worse for them, but he was still exhausted and drained of emotion by the end of the day. He called Caleb's father, who had taken the news stoically and then insisted on a face-to-face meeting today.

He spent the morning disassembling the crime boards, taking down each photo and placing it carefully in a file as Nicole watched, in between taking sips of coffee.

Too many cigarettes and not enough water had left Rook's mouth sore. The black coffee staining his mug wasn't making him feel any better, but he took another gulp as he willed the fatigue out of his body.

His phone vibrated with another message from his father, asking when they could meet up for another curry. They had intended to meet that night. But Rook knew his father would ask about his role, and Rook wasn't sure he could keep up the charade that this was a job he wanted. Not with the memory of Rowena's suicide and the blood gushing from Marlowe's neck still fresh in his mind.

His mood wasn't helped by the lack of leads they had on the whereabouts of Carver. Unlike his boss, who had thought his "status" or whatever deal he had would protect him, Carver had disappeared, his flat emptied, his car gone.

Under normal circumstances, an alert would have gone out and police officers all over the UK would have his description. But Carver knew too much to let him fall into the hands of the regular police force. So it left them relying on Rook's wits to figure out which rock that rat had crawled under, and Rook's wits weren't firing. All he'd been able to find was that Carver had also been a known member of some of the UK's more vicious fascist groups. A fact that gave Rook a lead but no hope.

Once the crime boards were back in the storeroom, Rook allowed himself to take off his winter coat. He placed it over the back of his chair, sat down, took another swig of now lukewarm coffee, looked at the ceiling, and said one word: 'Fuck.'

'You okay?' Nicole said nervously, like someone stepping on cracking ice over a frozen lake.

A twisted laugh escaped Rook's dry throat. 'Not even close.'

'I know... I know it must have been tough talking to those people yesterday. And worse, seeing what... happened to Marlowe. I don't like it either. But it's as close to justice as could be done.'

'It's not the justice – or whatever that was – that's bothering me.'

'It's not?'

'It's the futility. Carver is still out there, and he will be hard to find. Marlowe was punished. But not in a way that was close to civilised.'

'If you hadn't stopped them, more would have been taken.'

'If I'd have figured it out faster, Karl wouldn't have been ripped apart,' Rook replied, still looking up at the ceiling, where a water stain had spread itself outward from the light.

'You figured out who killed Caleb,' Nicole offered.

'I did, but he was killed by Rowena. Who killed herself. When you're solving a crime, you think you can find some purpose in doing this job. Some reason to keep the gears of your life moving forwards. But afterwards, all you are left with is other people's pain and some dead bodies.'

'You'll find Carver,' Nicole said, and Rook could hear her straining to sound confident. He appreciated the effort.

'Maybe, but it'll be like trying to find one rat out of the millions in London.' Rook stood up to go outside for a cigarette he needed but knew would make him feel worse.

A knock on the door prevented him from going outside. Caleb's father had arrived. He was short, with paper-white skin and soulful brown eyes under bushy eyebrows that were streaked with the same white that covered his hair. He was wearing a tweed suit, which had been carefully repaired in several places, along with a red tie and well-ironed white shirt. In one long-fingered hand, he clasped an old, wooden walking stick. He looked older and frailer than in the photos Rook had taken from Caleb's flat.

'Detective Rook?' he said in a sorrowful tremor.

'Yes. Caleb's father, I assume?' Rook said as he led him into the room and pulled around a chair. Caleb's father sat himself down, resting both of his tired, bony hands on the walking stick.

'Thank you for agreeing to meet me today, Detective, and apologies for being early. I am finding it harder to keep track of time these days.'

'It's quite all right, sir. Could I get you a drink?'

'No, thank you. But I'm hoping you can tell me about the murder of my son. And what led to someone taking my beautiful boy away from me?' His voice cracked and his fingers trembled on his walking stick.

'Of course,' Rook said. And then he began talking about what he'd learnt of Caleb. Of how his friends loved him, how they missed him, and how he had uncovered the kidnapping and torture of members of the other species. As he spoke, all the while looking into the sad eyes of Caleb's father, Rook warmed to his topic. He left out some bits (no father wants to be told of their son sleeping around or of indulging in petty crime) and embellished others, but overall what he said was true. When he had finished, Rook looked at Caleb's father, searching for a re-action on his tear-stained face. But the man was still resting his hands on his walking stick and gazing somewhere into the distance.

'Anything else I can do to help?' Rook asked, after wait-ing for half a minute.

'Help?' the old man said, a thin, sad smile splitting the lines of his face. 'I am afraid my wife and I are beyond help. But you have provided me with some solace. We cannot ask for more. For that, I thank you.'

'Solace?'

'Yes. Although my boy did not touch the world for long, he did not touch it lightly. People cared for him. Without his bravery, others would not know what happened to their loved ones. Vampires do not live long. Although I look like an old man, I am only fifty-five and will likely die in the next couple of years. A good age for a vampire. When you live such brief lives, you learn to appreciate that it is not the length of life that is important, but what impact you had on the world when you walked on it.' He sniffed back a few tears. 'My son had friends who were loyal to him. He brought evildoers to justice, and now other parents may have some modicum of closure. This world is better for him having lived. And what else can we ask for? And that gives me, and his mother, some comfort before we die.'

After that, there was nothing left to say. Rook gave him the photos he had taken from Caleb's flat, and the old man left after refusing another invitation of a drink. Rook went to the window to watch the vampire make his way home. He moved through the crowded streets on slow steps, using his walking stick like a mountaineer uses an ice pick to cling to the unforgiving cliffs.

'Well,' Nicole said from behind her computer screen, 'that was intense.'

'Parents are the toughest to talk to. After the death of a child, part of them will be dead forever. No point in pretending otherwise,' Rook said, taking out a cigarette and playing with it between his fingers. He watched the old vampire until he disappeared from view, taking the sadness he carried with him out into the world. Rook hoped that knowing whatever twisted justice they'd carried out had lessened the weight of that sadness. If he had provided Caleb's parents with some slight balm for a wound that would never heal, then perhaps his efforts had been worthwhile.

'What are you going to do now?' Nicole asked, breaking Rook's reverie.

'Now, Nicole,' he replied, putting the cigarette back in its packet. 'Now, I'm going to catch Carver.'

THANKS

I 'm Graham Sim, author of *'Screaming in the Shadows'*.

Thank you so much for reading my book! I appreciate it more than you can know.

As well as writing novels, I love to read them and recommend the good ones to anyone who will listen. If you want to receive these book recommendations, and other updates please join my newsletter hereor at my website www.grahamsimwrites.com

And remember, authors live off reviews, so if you are moved to leave a review please do.

With thanks,

Graham

ABOUT THE AUTHOR

Graham Sim hails from North East England, where he divides his time between his wife and kids, and his love of urban fantasy, noir mysteries, and science fiction.

When he's not weaving tales of gritty urban fantasy noir, Graham indulges his literary appetite by reviewing books on his website. If you're seeking engrossing reads, look no further than the recommendations on his website at https://grahamsimwrites.com/.

Graham promises he only refers to himself in the third person in his author bio. He's odd, but not that odd.

ISBN 978-1-7393965-1-0 (ebook)

ISBN 978-1-7393965-0-3 (print)

Published by Strange Angel Publications.

Printed in Great Britain
by Amazon